Chloe
and the
Kaishao
Boys

Chloe
and the
Kaishao
Boys

MAE COYIUTO

putnam

G. P. PUTNAM'S SONS

G. P. PUTNAM'S SONS
An imprint of Penguin Random House LLC, New York

First published in the United States of America by G. P. Putnam's Sons,
an imprint of Penguin Random House LLC, 2023

Visit us online at penguinrandomhouse.com.

Library of Congress Cataloging-in-Publication Data
Names: Coyiuto, Mae, 1994– author.
Title: Chloe and the Kaishao boys / Mae Coyiuto.
Description: New York: G. P. Putnam's Sons, 2023. | Summary: Seventeen-year-old
Chinese Filipina Chloe's father sets her up on a marathon of arranged dates in hopes
of convincing her to stay close to their Manila home for college.
Identifiers: LCCN 2022027457 (print) | LCCN 2022027458 (ebook) |
ISBN 9780593461631 (hardcover) | ISBN 9780593461648 (epub)
Subjects: CYAC: Dating—Fiction. | Family life—Fiction. |
Manila (Philippines)—Fiction. | Humorous stories. |
LCGFT: Romantic fiction. | Humorous fiction. | Novels.
Classification: LCC PZ7.1.C6936 Ch 2023 (print) |
LCC PZ7.1.C6936 (ebook) | DDC [Fic]—dc23
LC record available at https://lccn.loc.gov/2022027457
LC ebook record available at https://lccn.loc.gov/2022027458

Printed in the United States of America

ISBN 9780593461631 (hardcover)

ISBN 9780593619773 (international edition)

1st Printing

LSCH

Design by Suki Boynton | Text set in Iowan Old Style

To my brilliant mother, Elena.
When I was a kid, I dreamed of writing
a novel and dedicating it to my mom.
It happened, and it all started with you.

THE LIANG FAMILY lunch is far from the ideal setting to celebrate my dream coming true.

Unless you're abroad or on your deathbed, attendance at Sunday lunch is mandatory. When my cousin Peter got his wisdom teeth pulled out, Auntie Queenie still brought him to the same Chinese restaurant our family has been going to since the beginning of time. So when I tried asking Pa if I could sit this one out, he gave me his go-to answer: "If Peter can make it to the restaurant with cheeks as swollen as tennis balls, you can too."

Things would be more bearable if Pa hadn't already broken the news about USC to my aunties. I begged him not to post anything after I told him that I got off the wait list. He stayed silent on Instagram, but I'd completely forgotten about the Liang family groupchat.

His photo series went like this: a picture of my USC wait-list letter, me frowning, my acceptance letter, me smiling. All the photos had the accompanying hashtags **#FromWaitList-ToYesList #CantGoLowyWithChloe**.

Pa is weirdly obsessed with hashtags and adds them at the end of every message. He once spammed the groupchat with dozens of them, and I messaged him separately that they don't work that way. Auntie Queenie proceeded to reply with more hashtags and renamed the group **#LiangFamGang**.

In terms of USC, it's not that I want to keep secrets from my family. It's more that I already know what my aunties have to say.

"Chloe, I don't understand why you're considering going to America to study *cartoons*." Auntie Rita says "cartoons" like it's a dirty word. When my aunties first heard that I'd applied to a college in the US, they were shell-shocked. When they found out I wanted to study animation, they were downright offended. "How are you going to support yourself? You should choose a major that's practical. Something that you can build here." She turns to Pa. "Ahia, your daughter is getting too Americanized."

I bite my tongue and flash my polite smile, the one where I keep my mouth shut and lift the corners of my lips. It's the secret weapon I deploy when my relatives make me want to say what I actually think.

Americanized has become my aunties' favorite word around me. Just last week, Auntie Queenie shared an old picture of me wearing a crop top at the beach on our family groupchat with the message **Look at Chloe. She's so #Americanized!**

I shit you not, a crop top turned me American.

The thing is, I don't get why being Americanized is bad.

Just because I like some parts of American culture doesn't mean I'm rejecting who I am. And I'm still trying to figure out who I really am in the first place. What do you call a Chinese girl who grows up in the Philippines and whose mom lives in the US? I don't really know.

"You don't want to be a school's second choice, Chloe," Auntie Queenie chimes in. "Every woman who settles for being the second choice gets cheated on."

I can always count on Auntie Queenie for words of wisdom.

"No more hunting the Pokémon!" Auntie Rita scolds the kids' table. I peek at the smaller (and more fun) table behind us. Whenever my cousins' kids are on their iPads, Auntie Rita just assumes they're doing something Pokémon related. During my days at the kids' table, all I had to worry about was listening to my perfect cousin Peter enumerate his list of accomplishments. Once I moved to the adults' table, I had to put up with my aunties and more recently . . . Jobert.

"Ah, Chloe is still young," Jobert, of course, pitches in. "She'll move on from her cute little cartoons." Jobert winks at me like he's done me the favor of standing up for me in front of my family.

Ever since my cousin Claudia started dating Jobert, he's been a constant presence at Liang family gatherings. And from the first time I met him, he's treated me like a six-year-old. Don't get me wrong, I don't hate Jobert. The way I feel about him is the way I feel about flies.

Do I hate flies? No.

Do I get the urge to smack them whenever they come near me? Little bit.

Auntie Queenie clicks her tongue while we pass her our chopsticks so she can soak them in hot tea. She does this in every restaurant. The ramen place we go to automatically serves her a glass of hot water after she once lectured the staff on proper disinfecting practices. "It's all your festival talk," she tells Pa. "Their generation is obsessed with festivals."

While my dad did keep his promise to leave the USC news off social media, he still had his scheduled festival post. It's the same badly cropped screenshot of the Philippine Animation Festival website with the caption **Two months until baby girl's work is shown alongside the top animators in the country! #ProudDad #AnimationDomination**.

It wasn't supposed to be a big deal. When I first heard about the wait-list decision and thought USC was a lost cause, my best friend, Cia, convinced me to submit to this student showcase so I could still put my work out there. But Pa overheard our conversation and proceeded to report every single detail on Instagram. They haven't even started judging the applicants yet, and Pa's posts are building me up like I'm about to win an Oscar. I'm worried he might crash Instagram if I actually *do* make it.

"How were last week's numbers, Queenie?" Pa naturally segues the conversation to business talk when she hands him back his chopsticks.

If I were an outsider looking in, seeing a father post a photo collage of his daughter getting into her dream school and use hashtags like **#AnimationDomination** would make me think, *Wow, look at that proud dad.* But even though he could pass for my social media manager, Pa has hardly said a word to me about USC. With my art, he's always been proud on social media and indifferent in real life. Every time I try bringing up that I'm going abroad, he suddenly remembers some urgent Zip and Lock matter.

When my great-grandfather moved to the Philippines from China, he survived by selling buttons and zippers. My grandfather then turned it into a business, and the practice got passed down to my dad and his siblings. It's now evolved into the Liang Zip and Lock company. Pa even started a branch that manufactures denim cloth. I always wonder how he came up with the idea. Like, was he wearing jeans one day and suddenly thought, *These pants are so great! Why don't I sell the great material that makes these great pants?*

All my cousins have gladly accepted their fate and taken their seats in the empire.

Enter Chloe Liang. Instead of an obedient successor, Pa got a daughter who fantasized about becoming an animator.

When I first got the wait-list notice from USC months ago, I accepted that I was going to stay in Manila, study business management, and become a Liang dream daughter. But just as I had made peace with this vision of my future, USC popped out of nowhere and decided to accept me after all.

It's not like I *want* to be different. I would have no problem following Pa's path if I had a passion for selling zippers and jeans. I like wearing jeans, and I'm aware that zippers are very useful, but I never felt the calling to make a career out of that practical knowledge. When I think about choosing between studying business in the Philippines or going to USC for animation, I can practically hear my heartbeat pounding out *animation, animation, animation.* But the idea that I might be disappointing Pa gives me this feeling in my gut . . . It's like the guilt comes alive and slowly eats me piece by piece.

The best way to deal with guilt is to stuff myself with fried rice. The thought of tender, juicy sweet-and-sour pork mixed with Yang Chow fried rice makes sitting through my aunties' *Americanized* comments bearable. But instead of a beautiful, shimmering plate of pork, the waiter drops a bowl of tofu on the turntable. Unlike the usual spicy mapo tofu we order, this dish looks like it has zero seasoning. Right next to it, the waiter sets down equally bland-looking platters of bok choy, spinach, and eggplant.

WHERE IS THE RICE?

I turn to Auntie Queenie, who's seated beside me. "Is more food coming?"

Auntie Queenie tells me in Hokkien that those are all the orders.

"We didn't order fried rice?" I ask in English.

Auntie Queenie then looks at me sadly. "Di bwe-hiao kong lan-lang-ue ba?"

I don't get why she thinks asking me "Can't you speak Hokkien?" *in* Hokkien makes sense. First, a person who actually doesn't understand Hokkien would have no idea how to respond. Second, she *knows* I can understand Hokkien perfectly. I just don't speak it.

"I'm trying out a new diet," Auntie Queenie says, switching back to English. "No red meat, no sodium, no carbs, and plenty of wonderful leafy vegetables. It's supposed to be good for the heart."

"So not even plain rice?"

I sneak a glance at Pa, whose face looks like *his* heart is breaking. He and I both identify as carbohydrate enthusiasts.

"Here you go, Shobe." Jobert scoops up a giant serving of eggplant.

"It's okay, Ahia Jobert. I don't eat eggplant."

He ignores me and puts a bit of everything on my plate before facing Pa. "I was a picky eater when I was a kid too. She'll grow out of it."

Pa nods at Jobert, but he skips the eggplant dish when it reaches him. My father never grew out of his eggplant aversion.

"We can serve these dishes at your debut," Auntie Queenie says, "winking" at me. Auntie Queenie can't really wink, so she ends up closing both her eyes at the same time.

Aside from my Americanized crop tops, Auntie Queenie's favorite conversation topic is my eighteenth birthday party at the end of summer break.

"Debut planning was so easy with Auntie," Claudia adds.

Jobert nods. "Claudia had the perfect program for her debut."

You weren't even invited to that debut, Jobert.

Seriously. Claudia turned eighteen over a decade ago, and Jobert only met her last year.

I would most likely pass out from stage fright if I had the same debut as Claudia. For Claudia's Dazzling Eighteenth Birthday Bash (that's what Auntie Queenie called it on the invites), Auntie Queenie rented a hotel ballroom and decorated it like a winter wonderland. There was actual snow onstage. I still have no idea how Auntie Queenie found snow in the Philippines.

The standard debut includes the eighteen "roses," which are the closest guys in the celebrant's life, and eighteen "candles," the closest girls. The celebrant slow dances with each of the roses, and the candles take turns delivering prepared speeches.

As per Auntie Queenie's usual extra-ness, Claudia's program also included her eighteen roses serenading her one by one. That meant sitting through eighteen very bad renditions of Taylor Swift songs. I still can't listen to "You Belong with Me" without cringing.

Having a party that gathers all my friends and family together actually sounds like the perfect send-off before I leave for college. I just wish it weren't an Auntie Queenie grand production.

"Can we not make the debut a big deal?" I ask.

Auntie Queenie laughs like I just said the most preposterous thing she ever heard. "When do I make things a big deal?"

All the time.

"Oh!" Auntie Queenie whips her head to the restaurant entrance. "There's Peter and his *girlfriend!*"

Thank god for Perfect Peter. Hopefully my cousin can distract Auntie Queenie from further debut planning.

All my aunties crane their necks, hoping to catch an early glimpse of the famous girlfriend. Auntie Queenie won't stop talking about how her golden boy is dating a girl who's next in line to inherit her family's giant grocery business. To rub it in the other aunties' faces even more, Auntie Queenie sends pictures to the family groupchat whenever she's in one of the grocery stores. The last one was of her posing next to a shopping cart with the message **Supporting Peter's future in-laws? Hehe #MeantToBe**.

Auntie Queenie gets up and hugs the girl next to Peter. The Girlfriend is carrying a box that Auntie Queenie takes outside.

I watch Peter do the beso rounds—kissing all our aunties on the cheek. Through it all, he has the Girlfriend on his arm.

Everyone practically glows when they see Peter. Even Pa stands up and pats him on the back. Peter to my family is what Beyoncé is to everyone else.

Peter was his class valedictorian and part of this dance crew that competed around the world. A milk company even hired him for a commercial for a line of powdered milk that's supposed to boost brain power. The commercial showed a little boy struggling with his multiplication homework . . . until he starts drinking the vitamin-boosted milk. Cue a dance number where the multiplication kid grows up to be math whiz Perfect Peter. That final shot of Peter cradling a glass of milk has been Auntie Queenie's phone wallpaper for the last five years.

None of my angst about Perfect Peter has to do with Peter himself. Being around him just makes me feel like the multiplication kid, minus the magical milk. While I have to wonder what Pa thinks about my major, he has regular heart-to-hearts with Peter about Zip and Lock. While my aunties were all whispering about me being wait-listed at USC, they were gushing over Peter being an Oblation scholar at the University of the Philippines.

After the school released the list of scholarship recipients, Auntie Queenie posted Peter's graduation photo with the caption **#FreeTuition #BestOfTheBest #HeGotItFromHisMama**.

Lately I've been keeping a mental count of how many times he "mentions" that he's a scholar.

When Peter reaches me, I stand to greet him, and he pecks me on the cheek. "Sorry we're late. I picked up Pauline from the airport, then we had to make a detour to UP. Grabe! They make the scholars sign so many papers."

Scholar-mention tally: 1.

He pauses. "Oh! I don't think you've met my girlfriend. Chloe, Pauline. Pauline, Chloe."

The Girlfriend releases Peter's hand and leans in to beso. "It's so great to finally meet you!"

"Uh . . . you too."

No person should look this good coming off a flight. In normal non-airplane circumstances, I keep my hair tied up, since it lashes out at any sign of humidity. Her hair looks fresh from a straightener. She's like a Chinese Filipino Barbie doll. After a flight, I look like a pink troll.

I sit back down, and Peter pulls out a chair for Pauline. All my aunties' eyes are laser-focused on them.

"You know, this year, I'm celebrating fifteen years of marriage with my husband," Auntie Sandy shares. She gestures to Peter and Pauline. "How long have you two been dating?"

While Auntie Queenie is straightforward when prying

into our personal lives, Auntie Sandy prefers a more indirect (yet equally obvious) approach.

Peter says ten months and Pauline says five. They look at each other and erupt into giggles. In all my life, I never knew my cousin was capable of *giggling*.

"Sorry, Peter thinks our relationship started the day we met at the UPCAT," Pauline explains.

"That's because I knew my honey dumpling was the one the moment I laid eyes on her." Peter kisses Pauline's hand. "When I saw that we were *both* Oblation scholars . . . It felt like destiny."

Scholar-mention tally: 2.

Pauline giggles. "You're too sweet, honey dumpling."

"How cute," Auntie Rita gushes. She doesn't even mind when her grandson asks for more time on his iPad. Jobert puts his arm around Achi Claudia.

Who takes a college entrance exam and comes out with a girlfriend?

And what in the world is a honey dumpling?!

"Pauline!" I hear Auntie Queenie call out as she walks back to the table. She holds up a perfect pink fruit that looks exactly like the peach emoji. "Where did you get these peaches?"

"My uncle goes to Japan a lot to meet with buyers in stores there, Auntie. He always sends us peaches," Pauline says.

"Look at how big this peach is!" Auntie Queenie shoves the butt-looking fruit in my face. "Isn't Peter's girlfriend amazing? She brought the whole family a box of peaches! Imported peaches!"

Note to self: The key to Auntie Queenie's heart is imported fruit.

"It's the least I could do," Pauline replies. "I really appreciate you letting me join your family lunch." She smiles, and Peter kisses her for the millionth time.

"Ah, you're always welcome here. The more isko the merrier!" Auntie Queenie turns to me. "UP only awards the Oblation scholarship to the top fifty freshman applicants. Isn't it amazing that two of them are right here?"

"Amazing," I answer with my polite smile on.

"Toh-sia, Auntie," Pauline says, and Auntie Queenie looks like she's about to cry from happiness. The two of them proceed to have a full-blown conversation in Hokkien. It's like this girl was born to be the ultimate Chinese Filipino girlfriend.

My god. Perfect Peter found a Perfect Pauline.

SUNDAY LUNCH IS also the time we honor another sacred Liang family tradition: the staircase group photo. Auntie Sandy dedicates an entire table in her house to displaying the cousins' pictures over the years. Even in the age of smartphones, she still brings her digital camera and has her photos printed out. Pa, on the other hand, prefers his weekly Instagram post with the caption **Happy Sunday from my family to yours! #FamilyBonding #LiangFamGang #BloodThickerThan-Water.**

I take my usual spot on the fourth step next to Peter. All our aunts and uncles are ready with their phones when Auntie Queenie suggests, "Why don't the plus-ones join the picture?"

Oh no.

My cousins call out to their boyfriends, girlfriends, and partners. Peter yells out for his honey dumpling. I'm gasping for air because we're stuffing twice as many people onto this staircase as usual. Have my cousins been preparing for the second coming of Noah's ark?! Since when did everyone get paired up? I squeeze between Peter and Pauline.

"Chloe, we can't see you. Can you move down?" Auntie Sandy calls out.

The only space left is on the first step of the staircase.

In front of everyone.

I climb down, and Auntie Sandy coaches me toward the center. I might as well be carrying a big arrow with large block letters that scream THE WAIT-LISTED SINGLE ONE! I'm not even a third wheel; I'm a fifteenth wheel.

Auntie Queenie walks up to me and hands me my cousin Missy's baby—the one who always cries as soon as I start to hold him. The last time Missy's family visited our house, the baby saw my graduation photo and burst into tears.

"Hold the baby so you don't look so sad," Auntie Queenie says, and I can already hear him starting to whimper.

Seriously, I'd rather have the arrow.

We stay on that staircase for centuries as they take pictures. Missy finally puts an end to the photo shoot because her child is positively wailing for help. My ears are still ringing after I hand back her son, and I sense more than hear Auntie Queenie approaching.

"While I'm brainstorming for your debut program, is there anyone else you want to include in your eighteen roses?" she asks.

"Oh, the list I gave you was everyone, Auntie."

She looks at me skeptically. "Chloe, you sent me the names of your uncles."

"Uncle Nelson has good rhythm," I point out.

"Chloe, your eighteen roses can't be only relatives!" Auntie Queenie says. "You need to have some friends in there. Bo howe pa ba?" She gives me her double-wink.

"No boyfriend, Auntie." I activate my polite smile. "I'm trying to focus on my studies."

She shakes her head. "You shouldn't be too serious, Chloe. Look at Peter and Pauline. Your age is the time to date!"

I don't get her sudden interest in my love life. There's never been much action in that area.

The movies portray high school as the perfect backdrop to have a great love story. But there was certainly no epic love in *my* high school life. Even my prom night was way off. My best friend, Cia, forced her know-it-all brother, Jappy, into going with me, and I barely even spent time with him because I got in trouble for my animation clip that screened during the prom slideshow. A teacher deemed it "inappropriate."

All I did was draw a couple going to prom. It was like any other prom-themed cartoon, except when the girl kissed the guy good night, she also severed her own torso, sprouted bat wings, and sucked his blood before flying off into the night.

After getting reprimanded for an hour, I didn't even have time for a slow dance, which is a prom rite of passage, despite parent chaperones hovering and constantly reminding everyone to leave room for the Holy Spirit. Finally, Cia's brother drove me home and said goodbye with an awkward side-wave.

And that was the end of my epic high school love story.

"Even if I did include all your uncles and cousins," says Auntie Queenie, "you're still missing three roses."

"What about Jobert?" I suggest.

Dancing with my uncles, cousins, and Jobert sounds awkward, but I'm certain it's a whole lot less awkward than whatever Auntie Queenie has in mind. Her eyes suddenly light up, and she shouts for Pa. When he gets to us, Auntie Queenie is practically glowing. "I have someone perfect to kaishao with your daughter!"

Pa laughs. "Isn't she too young for that?"

YES. Extremely, very, waaaaaay too young.

Kaishao is Hokkien for "to introduce." It's when friends or family, mostly nosy relatives like Auntie Queenie, introduce single people to potential partners. You don't have to stick with the pairings like arranged marriages (thank god), but it still feels very *Mulan* matchmaker-esque to me.

I shake my head furiously. "I don't want to get set up."

Auntie Queenie laughs. "I just want to introduce you to a boy your age. He could add some spice to your eighteen roses."

"I don't think we need spice," I mutter.

"Chloe," Pa snaps at me. "Don't talk back to your auntie."

Auntie Queenie pats Pa on the shoulder. "It's okay, Ahia. That's what happens when you send kids off to America."

Ah, America. The root of all my evil thoughts.

"You should really rethink this whole college abroad idea," Auntie Queenie continues. "Chloe's so young and impressionable. Living there will brainwash her into staying. And girls in America are very . . . assertive. Do you know that girls there use the Tinder?"

I'm pretty sure Tinder is a universal thing.

"If it weren't for me, Claudia would've succumbed to the

Tinder." Auntie Queenie lowers her voice. "I was the one who kaishao-ed her with Jobert."

Pa and I try to act surprised, despite the fact that Auntie Queenie has told this to everyone. Multiple times.

"Rita was so worried about Claudia. Thank goodness I stepped in before Claudia reached her mid-thirties. Her future was up in the air before she met Jobert. Now he's asking if I can set up his little brother, Joberto."

Really hope they don't have a sister named Joberta.

I sidestep on the name. "Isn't Achi Claudia getting her MBA?"

Auntie Queenie waves that off like it's a minor detail. "Rita and I have been dropping hints to Jobert about proposing. Rita said they were in a bookstore the other day, and Jobert stopped to tie his shoe, right in front of the bridal magazine section!"

Like a sign from Jesus himself!

No matter how many promotions or awards Claudia has received over the years, my aunties have remained fixated on her single status.

"Does Achi Claudia *want* to get married?" I ask.

Auntie Queenie gives me the trademark Liang family tongue click of disappointment. "Of course she wants to get married. Sayang naman siya if she doesn't. Ahia, this is what I'm talking about. Chloe is still so impressionable! I don't understand how you can think of sending her to the US all by herself."

"I won't be alone, Auntie," I point out. "Ma is there."

She gives me the side-eye that all my aunties use when my mother comes up. "Your mother is from another world, Chloe. Americans have completely different values. Family doesn't matter to them. When their parents get old, they send them to a shelter!" Then she goes on to describe how she'll get back at Peter if he ever tries to send her to a senior home.

Ma is Chinese Filipino too, like all my relatives, but since she moved to the US when she was a teenager, she's always been the "American" to my aunties.

"That's one of the reasons I'm so happy Peter never considered going abroad." Then Auntie Queenie adds in a hushed tone, "I actually kaishao-ed Peter and Pauline. Pauline's mom is a great friend, and we planned for the two of them to ride to the UPCAT together. They hit it off instantly."

Then Pa out of nowhere asks, "Who did you want to introduce to Chloe?"

If you had asked me which would come first—my fortieth birthday or the time when my dad would be okay with me dating—I would've answered my fortieth birthday. Pa still covers my eyes when a kissing scene comes up in a movie. There was a time when we avoided movie theaters because they all had posters up for *Fifty Shades of Grey*.

And now he's open to setting me up?

I've never been on an official date, and my auntie is not setting me up for my first. I need to derail this conversation. Quickly.

"Uh . . . Auntie," I suddenly butt in. "You also mentioned something about a dress?"

Based on the joy visible in her face, Auntie Queenie's love

for debut planning is greater than her love for Japanese peaches, ambush matchmaking, and Pauline's ability to speak Hokkien. "I'm so glad to see you finally enthusiastic about your debut, Chloe. I know this excellent designer who also tailor-made my wedding dress. She said that she has the perfect vision for you!"

Wait. Why are we getting someone who makes wedding dresses?!

Pa clasps his hand on my shoulder and nods at me. "This is a nice thing you're doing for your auntie."

There have only been a few times in my life when Pa has given me his genuine nod: (1) When I was seven and he brought me to his office for a meeting. He thought I would fall head over heels for his work. (2) When I got the wait-list letter and told him that I'd consider studying business management here in Manila.

What actually happened: (1) Seven-year-old me spent the entire meeting doodling on office stationery. (2) Seventeen-year-old me couldn't stop thinking about animation.

This could be the one time that Pa's look of approval doesn't fade into one of crushing disappointment. And maybe, if I do this for Auntie Queenie, Pa might jump fully on board with me going to USC.

"Auntie, maybe we can tone things down just a little bit."

"Tone down?" she asks with her eyebrows knitted in confusion.

"We could make it more intimate?" I suggest. "No ballrooms, snow, or special effects."

Auntie Queenie gapes at me like I just slapped her in the

face. "You can't be serious. We might as well have your birthday right now in this restaurant!"

"Shobe." Pa pats her on the back. "Maybe more intimate is better. At least simple lang and within budget. You and Chloe can reach a compromise."

"Compromise? I'm trying to give your daughter a proper birthday, and you want to focus on the budget?"

"Well, someone has to!" Pa shoots back.

Then they start bickering about how Auntie Queenie overspent on the recent marketing campaign. I don't know how they went from debut planning to business talk, but at least they've forgotten about all the kaishao nonsense.

3

I WISH THERE could be a happy medium between my aunties' disapproval and my best friend's enthusiasm. Even when she's ordering french fries, Cia finds a way to insert the fact that I'm going abroad.

"Ate Sally." Cia leans against the counter of the Potato Corner stall. "Did you know that Chloe is going to the US for college?"

"Wow!" Ate Sally's eyes widen. "Harvard?"

"Close." Cia shushes me before I can say that I'm not going to be anywhere near Harvard.

"Harvard is a good reference point," she whispers to me. Then she goes on to explain to Ate Sally all the stats she has memorized about USC.

By the time she gets her fries, the whole of Wilson Plaza will have heard about some Chloe going to Harvard.

Wilson Plaza is where everyone from Mary Immaculate High School hangs out. There's a Starbucks, a milk tea stand, a Kumon learning center, and it's close enough to school that you can tell your parents you're doing homework when you're actually meeting some guy from the all-boys school.

During my many years of all-girls education, I've observed that there's a particular need for a space where young people can congregate with the opposite sex. Wilson Plaza is the venue for awkward seventh-grade flirting, elaborate promposals, and dramatic breakups. Set foot inside the space, and you'll cringe from the smell of teenage hormones.

But if you're like me and don't have a guy to meet up with, you come for an even more important reason: the food.

"Thanks, Ate Sally," Cia says when her ten orders of cheese-flavored fries are ready.

"Doesn't Jappy have a no-food-in-his-car rule?" I ask.

Cia waves me off. "It's fine. We'll get him milk tea."

Ever since Cia's brother got his license, their parents have been making him drive her everywhere. They asked if he could help pick up things for Cia's eighteenth birthday party tonight, and Jappy complained the whole fifteen-minute ride to Wilson Plaza. He really opened my eyes to the perks of walking.

After she places her milk tea order, Cia asks, "So what else happened with Peter's honey dumpling?"

"My family is already planning the wedding," I joke. "They're serving honey dumplings for the appetizers."

"Does that mean the dumplings are filled with honey or dipped in honey?"

"Only you would ask that question."

She laughs. "How did they meet, anyway?"

"Pauline said they met during the UPCAT. But Auntie Queenie said it was a kaishao."

"What's a kaishao?" Cia asks.

Although our high school has mostly Chinese Filipino students, Cia is actually full Filipino. But over the years, she's picked up a few Hokkien words from listening to Pa talk. I explain the term to Cia.

"*You* should get kaishao-ed," she says.

"You're really suggesting I get set up by Auntie Queenie?"

"All forms of vitamin D are good for your health." She wiggles her eyebrows. "If you know what I mean . . ."

"Gross." I groan at the innuendo.

"I'm just saying." She does an exaggerated hair flip. "It's why my skin is glowing."

To put it simply, my best friend is a total badass. I don't think I've ever met anyone who's as comfortable in her own skin. I mean, Cia is gorgeous, but people have always given her weird backhanded compliments like "You'd be even prettier if you weren't so maitim."

Whenever anyone brings up her darker complexion, though, Cia always has a speech ready about how the country's messed-up beauty standards are a product of the Philippines' history of colonialism. Auntie Queenie once gave her a papaya whitening soap for Christmas, and they had a full-blown discussion about why our society considers "whiter" more beautiful. I'm not sure if the message got through, since Auntie Queenie's takeaway was that everyone was becoming "too damn Americanized." Although she did stop buying whitening products after their conversation.

We pick up our orders and almost spill our drinks when we hear incessant honking coming from the parking lot.

Jappy rolls down his window and calls out, "How are you not done yet?"

"How have you not grown up yet?" Cia yells back, and shoots him her trademark disapproving look—lowered eyebrows and pursed lips. Then she grumbles to me, "He keeps complaining that I'm ruining his 'schedule' when all he does is shout at his computer monitor."

We get in Jappy's car, Cia taking the front passenger seat while I go in the back, and we try to balance all the cheese snacks between the two of us.

"If you get any cheese powder in my car—" Jappy starts, and I hand him his milk tea to pause his rant. "Wait, I said no pearls," he tells Cia.

"It was hard to check your order when you were rushing me."

"Do you know how much sugar there is in each tapioca ball?"

"Probably less than in the three slices of cake you had last night," Cia jabs.

I swear, watching the Torres siblings bicker is more entertaining than a tennis match.

When Jappy drives out of the Wilson Plaza parking lot, I notice he begrudgingly takes a sip of his milk tea. Cia reaches for the stereo, and we both start rapping along when a Saweetie song comes on. She's been a constant on our summer playlists ever since we found out she's half-Pinoy *and* a USC alumna.

"You cut off the best part!" I say when Jappy has the audacity to turn off the song before it hits the chorus.

Jappy peers at us through his glasses with his know-it-all judgy look. "I can't drive with all the noise."

When we were kids, I used to call Jappy "judgy Filipino Waldo" (as in *Where's Waldo?*). The only difference was, we were never *looking* for Jappy. He was always just there. Whenever Cia and I would play around the house, he'd peer at us through his glasses, judging us as if he weren't just one year older. He became more tolerable with age, but he still has this annoying habit of never letting anything go. Case in point: prom night. At the entrance there was a sign that said PLEASE QUEUE HERE. I had a mental slip and accidentally said "kwe-we" instead of "kew." A mature person would have let it go, but after that, Jappy found dozens of ways to insert "kwe-we" into sentences.

"Hopefully you have other songs in the *kwe-we*," Jappy says, and annoyingly smiles at me in the rearview mirror.

I grab Cia's phone and add Saweetie's whole mix to the queue because I'm (a) petty and (b) a fan of good music.

In the middle of flawlessly rapping both Saweetie's and Kehlani's verses, Cia says, "Chloe, you would kill this at karaoke."

"Yes, I would literally cause the death of this song," I deadpan. "There would be no survivors."

Instead of having a big debut celebration, Cia wanted her eighteenth to follow the tradition of her past parties—which means lots of karaoke. In the event invite, she requested that each of her friends perform a song that reminds us most of

"Maria Patricia Sotto Torres, aka your favorite person, Cia." She's been aware of my karaoke stage fright ever since we were in the second grade, but she keeps hoping that one day I'll perform.

"Don't tell me that Raph is singing," Jappy says with a groan. It would be an understatement to say that Cia's boyfriend, Raphael Siy, hasn't exactly won Jappy over.

Nobody could've predicted that Cia would end up with Raph, who had been crushing on her for years. I mean, girls in our grade do find him cute, since he's a head taller than most guys and has a baby face, but he's mostly known for his jokes. At one mass service, when the priest asked what people wanted to give up for Lent, Raph yelled out, "My virginity!"

Everyone, me included, thought whoever Cia ended up with would be the boss man to her boss lady. The Jay-Z to her Beyoncé. The Barack to her Michelle. So I was understandably skeptical when she and Raph started dating. But it was like two mismatched puzzle pieces finding some hidden jagged edge that made them fit. Cia works hard at pretty much everything in her life, and Raph puts the same effort into making her laugh.

Cia ignores Jappy's comment and tells me that she invited Miles Chua to her party.

"That is . . . very informational," I say, trying to hide the fact that my heartbeats suddenly feel really loud.

"Chlo, talking to a boy is like pooping. If you don't give it that first push, nothing will come out."

I don't know who gives weirder advice—Cia or Auntie Queenie.

Miles has always been the big crush ng bayan. As a basketball star, he's probably broken every single record in the country's history, and there were rumors that he was scouted by a team in Australia to play for them.

I was never really into basketball, since I always associated it with Pa and my uncles bickering in front of the television screen, but things changed when Pa signed us up for a gym membership. My first day there, I was scoping out the equipment and found Miles using the lat pulldown machine, his back and arms looking like they had been sculpted by gods.

Since he's basically a celebrity, I figured he would be the type to hog all the equipment. But when he noticed me waiting, he introduced himself—like I didn't already know who he was—and let me use the machine. From then on, whenever I'd run into him at the gym, he'd do the same greeting: raise his eyebrows, flash his perfect smile, and say in his ASMR voice, "'Sup, Chloe?"

One time, he paused mid pull-up to acknowledge my presence. That was the moment I understood what getting turned on meant.

Cia has been trying to convince me to extend our interactions beyond "'Sup, Chloe?" but I'm not the type of girl who can simply walk up to a guy and start talking. I didn't even have the guts to ask anyone to prom, hence my going with Jappy. Cia is the complete opposite. Back when they first started flirting, she was the one who straight up asked Raph if he liked her. When Cia wants something, she goes for it. When I want something, I pine for it from a safe distance.

Cia flicks Jappy's arm. "How do you get a guy's attention?"

"By not comparing talking with shitting."

She groans. "We're trying to improve your prom date's love life."

"Hello, still here." I wave my arm between the two of them. "Also, Jappy and I were prom *companions*, not dates."

Jappy grunts in agreement.

"Besides," I add, "dating sounds like too much effort for your brother."

After all, this is the same Jappy who eats instant noodles straight out of the pack because he thinks boiling water is too much of a hassle. He's one of those annoying people who coasts through life with minimal effort. Nothing ever fazes him. There was this one time his mom got upset about some chemistry test he failed, and Jappy just stood there completely silent until the sermon was done and then went back to his room as though nothing had even happened.

"Aren't you going abroad, anyway?" Jappy asks me.

"Love is like Friday-night traffic. It can go the distance," Cia says, spouting another metaphor. "And even if things aren't meant to be with Miles, at least Chloe would have experience flirting."

There's nothing more awkward than the mental image of me attempting to flirt. People react to getting kilig—that butterflies in your stomach, light-headed feeling when you're around your crush—in two different ways. There's me, honorary awkward turtle, and there's perfectly cool Cia. I wish I were like that too—the girl who leaves people in wonder instead of the girl wondering what the hell she's going to say next.

But didn't Auntie Queenie say that girls in America are assertive? If I'm going to college in the States, I have to be like them. Cool, confident, composed. The girl who acts completely chill around Miles and doesn't care that he's at the same party.

Chloe in America will be different, and I'm going to be her tonight.

Hopefully.

WHEN JAPPY DROPS us off at my house to pick up more food, the first thing we see is Pa and Peter hanging pictures on the wall.

"Patricia!" Pa greets Cia. He always calls her by her full name. "Nice to see you."

Cia kisses my dad on the cheek. "Hi, Tito."

"Peter and I just came from a company meeting." Pa faces me. "Everyone was raving about how mature he is for his age."

Activate polite smile. Even when he's not saying anything, Peter manages to make me feel bad.

"Uh . . . Tito," Cia chimes in, "I like your new pictures. They really . . . add to the décor."

Oh my god.

Pa actually printed his most-liked Instagram posts—with the captions—and had them framed. You know the Upside Down dimension in *Stranger Things*, where every place looks the same, only darker, creepier, and more disturbing? This Instagram Hall of Fame is the Upside Down version of my house.

"Thank you, Patricia. It's nice to have the house filled with memories."

There's a picture of me and Pa from my sixteenth birthday with the caption **My baby girl #Blessed #LifeGoals #Father-Daughter**. Right next to it is a quote that says **KEEP CALM AND DADDY ON** that got fifty-three likes.

I shoot Cia a look. *This is weird, right? Should I point out that this is weird?*

Cia shrugs. *I feel like it's very on-brand for your dad.*

When you've known someone as long as I've known Cia, you will also be blessed with the power of covert communication.

Before we decide what to say next about his Instagram wall, Pa asks, "Cia, how's the boy?"

"Uh, which boy, Tito?"

"Your . . . friend." Pa stumbles a bit when he says it. "The one Chloe talks about."

Cia glances at me. *Is your dad asking me about my boyfriend?*

Not once has Pa ever shown interest in my friends' love lives. When I told him that Cia was dating someone, he lectured me about focusing on my studies and avoiding "the disco" (his term for wild parties with copious amounts of alcohol). All of Auntie Queenie's kaishao talk must be going to his head.

"He's good, Tito," Cia says, averting her eyes.

"How did you two meet?"

"Uh . . ." Cia starts squirming like a jellyfish.

"Pa." I interrupt my father's random interrogation. "Cia and I are actually in a hurry. We have to get stuff ready for her birthday party."

"Oo nga pala. Wow. I can't believe you two are turning eighteen." Pa turns to Peter. "You're eighteen too, right?"

"Yes, Uncle."

"Why don't you join them?" Pa puts his hand on Peter's shoulder. "You've already spent the whole day with me. You should have fun with kids your age."

Cia and I look at each other. *Did my dad just invite Perfect Peter to your party?*

Pa checks his phone. "Sorry, I have to step in my study for a business call," he says. "Make sure to message your mom to tell her where you're going."

"You guys don't actually have to bring me," Peter says once Pa walks away. "I don't want to ruin your plans."

"No, it's okay!" Cia's using her girlboss negotiating voice. "We're doing karaoke, and we can always use one more person."

All I do is nod along with my polite smile on. One night with Peter can't be too bad. I might even get points from Pa for the impromptu cousin bonding.

"Karaoke?" Peter stands a little straighter. "UP hosted a karaoke night for all the scholars last month!"

My scholar-mention tally is going to shoot *way* up tonight.

4

CIA'S BIRTHDAY SPREAD is a crime against the lactose intolerant. Aside from the cheese fries we got from Wilson Plaza, her parents also prepared mac and cheese, cheese empanadas, and grilled cheese, and they stocked the fridge with cheese ice cream.

While we're following Cia's directions for where each dish should go on the living room table, Raph is filming another one of his "Day in the Life" videos. Raph runs a YouTube channel called *Laugh with Raph*. Every single video (all of which feature a thumbnail of him wearing a backward cap and throwing up a peace sign) has thousands of views. It turns out there's an audience for someone with an estimated one-out-of-ten joke success rate.

"Hey, guys!" He waves at his phone camera. "Currently vlogging from a birthday party. Check out this all-cheese buffet." Raph pans to the table, and I shield his phone with my hand when he points it in my direction.

"Chloe," he says with a groan. "I was trying to get a good shot."

"And I'm trying to avoid a sermon from your girlfriend."

Right on cue, Cia comes strutting back from the kitchen. "Whose idea was it to put the pizza next to the fries?"

"A highly stupid person's," I say, and she shoots me her disapproving look.

"Hey, babe." Raph does these little jumps whenever he comes up with a new joke. "Why did the clinic include cheese in their first aid kit?" Before Cia can even speak, he quickly blurts out the punch line: "In *keso* emergency."

I sigh. "Raph, you're supposed to wait for people to guess first."

"Do you get it?" He pokes my arm. "*In keso*, like *in case of*? It's funny because *keso* is Tagalog for 'cheese.'"

"You also don't need to explain the joke," I tell him.

Somehow Cia's icy stare melts, and she descends into a laughing attack. Raph starts chuckling too, because seeing Cia laugh always makes him laugh.

"Hot plate coming through!" Tita Gretchen carries a platter from the kitchen, and I'm greeted by the familiar smell of her turon. There's a huge stack of (mostly untouched) cookbooks on their kitchen counter, which Cia's dad gave Tita Gretchen after she once said she wanted to be a better cook. Both Cia and Jappy joke that their mom's go-to dish is her deep-fried banana rolls, because it was the first recipe she ever read and the only thing she ever had the patience to learn.

Tito Vince makes room for Tita's dish and kisses her on the cheek. "Smells great, mahal." No matter how many times

Tita serves her turon, Tito Vince still calls it her special dish and savors every piece like it's the world's finest delicacy.

The Torres house suddenly feels crowded with all the PDA.

"So, Chloe"—Tito Vince lowers his voice—"do you want to do a duet later? We can do 'Dancing Queen.'"

Cia wags her finger at him. "You only get one song."

"But how am I going to win karaoke?"

"I don't think any winning is going to happen if you're with me, Tito," I point out.

"And your song choice is so baduy." Tita Gretchen smooths Tito Vince's hair while he argues that "Dancing Queen" is an everlasting classic.

More people filter into Cia's place as we finish setting out the food and putting up the decorations. All the glee club girls show up, even some of the freshmen. Despite us graduating, Cia is still the legendary member who organized a mashup of "All I Want for Christmas Is You" and Lizzo's "Truth Hurts" during a schoolwide holiday concert. It was a shock to all the nuns and faculty in attendance.

In his defense, Peter has only made one scholar mention so far at this party. He's mostly been glued to his phone the entire time.

"Are you sending the fruit pictures to Pauline?" I ask when I catch him taking pictures of the metal mangoes displayed on the coffee table.

He leans back and clicks through the photos. "I'm sending these to my mom."

"You're joking."

"What's funny?" He looks at me as if I'm the weird one.

I shake my head. "Peter, you're the only person in the world who'd spend a party texting their mother."

He shrugs. "She likes art."

This is why the adults in my family have unrealistic standards for their children.

"My man!" Raph points at Peter with finger guns as he walks over to the couch we're sitting on.

Peter turns to me. "Why am I his man?"

I laugh. "That's just how Raph makes friends."

Raph squeezes between the two of us and holds up his LED light. "Do you wanna help me set stuff up for my video?"

Peter glances at me again, and I give him a reassuring smile.

"Sure?" Peter says. He follows Raph, and Raph flashes me a thumbs-up. The guy can't stand anyone not liking him.

A few minutes later, Raph is back, and everyone in the living room watches while he does pickup lines with Cia's school supplies. Peter plays a recorded laugh track after each joke.

"Are you a dictionary?" Raph says, lifting Cia's book. "Because you give meaning to my life."

Cue laugh track, intense laughing from Cia, and groans from everyone else.

Raph then picks up Cia's open laptop. "You must be a keyboard because . . . you're exactly my type."

Peter fumbles and plays the laugh track a moment late. "I don't get it," he says to me.

"What?" I ask.

"How is it a joke?"

"Oh! It's like computer typing."

I hunch my shoulders and mime typing on a keyboard to

get the point across. Peter stares at me like I'm a trigonometry problem.

"It's wordplay," I continue. "Like, you *type* on a laptop, and a person can be your *type*."

Jokes really do get *way* less funny the more you explain them.

"Ah," Peter says at last. "Clever."

Raph continues with his pickup lines, and I struggle to explain each of them to Peter. When he's finally finished with his video, Raph waves to the camera. "See you next time on *Laugh with Raph*. Don't forget to hit like and subscribe!"

After he stops filming, Cia calls me and Raph over to help her with the karaoke area. We pull down Tito Vince's huge projector screen, readying it for the random ocean-view video that plays with every karaoke number (which is always completely unrelated to the song).

Raph keeps stretching his mouth and practicing his "vocal exercises."

"No matter how much you flex your tongue muscles, you'll still never reach my top score," Cia teases him.

"I've been practicing." He wiggles his eyebrows at me. "Does Cia's eighteenth birthday mean we'll finally be graced with a performance by Chloe Liang?"

"Nope, nope, nope," I say, shaking my head.

"I've tried for a decade," Cia adds.

This might get my Filipino card revoked, but I dread karaoke. Whenever someone asks me to join in, I lip-sync and then quickly pass the mic. I love watching everyone else sing, but I get too self-conscious to let anyone hear my voice.

I'm attempting to turn on the karaoke machine, but the screen keeps showing me an old basketball game. "Uh. Cia? How do you work this?"

Cia groans and takes the remote. "Jappy is the only one who knows how to fix it."

"Where is he, anyway?"

She shrugs. "Avoiding human interaction." As Raph tries to help her figure out the machine, the doorbell rings. "Chlo, can you get that?"

I swerve to my plate and stuff some popcorn in my mouth as I head over to answer the door.

Oh god.

"'Sup, Chloe?" Miles asks while flashing the kind of smile I only see in toothpaste commercials.

I think of saying "hi" and "hello" at the same time, so I end up saying a muffled "hi-lo."

Jesus, Chloe. You can get kilig and still function like a normal human being!

Of course, Miles's response to my disastrous greeting is another killer smile. "Nice seeing you outside the gym."

"Yeah!" I blurt out in perhaps the squeakiest and highest-pitched voice I've ever heard come out of my mouth. "I'm the birthday Cia . . . I mean, I'm friends with the birthday girl."

"Bro!" another guy calls out to him from the kitchen. Miles waves at him and says we should catch up later before scooting around me to join his actual friends.

Cia glances at me as I walk away from the scene of my humiliation. *I saw that moment you guys had.*

A moment I want to take back, I telepathically answer.

I flop back on the couch next to Peter, who's holding a plate of ensaymada. The way he's staring at the kitchen, I don't think he'd notice if I grabbed one of his cheese-covered pastries. "What's up with you?" I ask.

"You're friends with *him*?" He points (very obviously) at Miles, who's casually leaning against the counter with a horde of people surrounding him. The glow from the fridge illuminates him like sunbeams shining on a Greek god.

"*Friends* is a very strong word," I say, and quickly push down his finger. "You know Miles?"

Peter's eyes drift back to his plate. "I've seen him in basketball games. He's Uncle Jeffrey's favorite player."

Right. Pa and Peter have regular dates to the interschool basketball tournaments too.

"Chlo." Cia sits next to me on my other side. "Fixing the karaoke machine is really stressing Raph out. Can you help me get him some ice cream?"

Ice cream? Like from the fridge next to the Greek god?

"Ask him which team he's playing for in Australia," I hear Peter whisper.

Cia raises her eyebrows. *You can do it! Talk to him!*

That whole I-need-to-shit-my-pants feeling is suddenly rushing over me.

"You know what's a better idea?" I say, clapping my hands. "Why don't I grab Jappy so we can get this karaoke thing going?" I stand and rush upstairs before Cia says another word.

5

GREAT. THE THOUGHT of talking to a guy has me hiding out in my best friend's bathroom. I thump my head against the cabinet above the sink. What happens if I go to USC and find someone cute there? I can't plan my entire college life around the proximity of restrooms.

I sigh and grab the jar of Vicks from the top shelf.

Vicks VapoRub is Pa's medicine for everything. If I get a fever, he'll rub the menthol goo on my forehead. When I sprained my ankle, he rubbed it on my foot. Cough? Vicks on the chest! On the night before the SATs, he even rubbed some Vicks on me for good luck.

I take a dab of the ointment and massage it onto my forehead. Ooh. This is actually making me feel better.

Okay, Chloe. You can go downstairs. The power of Vicks is within you. You can face Miles and form some words that actually exist, maybe even entire sentences.

As I step out, I hear yelling coming from behind the door

across from the bathroom. It's a symphony of every curse word I know in both English and Tagalog.

"GAGO! GET BACK, GET BACK! WHAT THE FUCK ARE YOU DOING?"

The whiteboard hanging on Jappy's door always has what I call his anti-inspirational quotes. Today's quote is another one from *The Good Place*:

> "I'm too young to die and too old to eat off the kids'
> menu. What a stupid age I am."
>
> —*Jason Mendoza*

I knock on the door and hear Jappy yell, "I'M BUSY!"

Ugh. Typical.

When I barge into his man cave, Jappy is at his usual station—sitting at his desk, headset on, and shouting at his computer.

"GO, GO, ATTACK!" Jappy cries out.

I hop across the piles of clothes and junk on his floor. Ugh. I don't want to know how long that empty milk tea cup has been lying there.

"Hey," I say, "Cia needs your help with the karaoke machine."

Jappy adjusts his glasses and keeps furiously clicking his mouse, ignoring me.

"Cia. Your sister. The one who's celebrating her birthday."

Nothing.

"You just missed Cia announcing her pregnancy. She and

Raph are running away to Palawan together. They're dropping out of college and raising their family at the beach."

Still nothing.

"She wants everyone to wear a bikini to the wedding. I helped her pick yours. We thought the hot-pink lace thong would suit your personality."

His eyes are still firmly glued to the screen. He moves his mouse across the desk and yells, "GO RIGHT, GO RIGHT!!!"

I lean over his shoulder and shout, "LEFT, LEFT!"

Jappy tries to wave me away and repeatedly taps the space bar. I know I'm getting to him when he runs a hand through his hair and it sticks straight out, making him look like a human pineapple.

"GO BACK, GO BACK!" he cries.

"GO FORWARD! GO FORWARD!"

I hear frantic screaming from his headphones as he slides them down in a huff. "You're messing up my game."

"You're ignoring your pregnant college-dropout sister."

"I was focused on the beach wedding," he says, completely deadpan. "I think purple is more my color. Besides, me in a hot-pink thong might distract everyone from the bride."

When he moves to put his headset back on, I snatch it from his head. "Karaoke machine," I remind him.

Jappy grunts and pauses his game. "I thought Cia wanted her eighteenth to be low-key."

"Your definition of low-key is inviting no one."

"Sounds fun." He finally gets up and begins rummaging through the clutter on the floor. "Is there anything without cheese downstairs?" he asks while digging through a pile of clothes.

"You know all-cheese spreads are a tradition on Cia's birthday." I dodge the cap he tosses in my direction. "By the time we get downstairs, Cia will be thirty."

"Found it!" He pulls his phone out of the jeans lying on the aircon. "Aren't you guys sick of doing the same routines for a decade?"

"Routines are what keep people healthy and pretty."

"You should read up on how much saturated fat there is in cheese." He pauses and scrunches up his nose. "Why do you smell like medicine?"

"Why does your hair always look like you just rolled out of bed?" I start pushing him out of his room. "Yay. Jappy Torres is joining the outside world. The air quality is worse, but that'll make you stronger when climate change comes for us all."

He stops me when we get to the stairs. "Once I fix the machine, I'm going right back to my game."

While Jappy tinkers with the remote, Raph showers him with compliments. "Fixing this should be easy for you, Kuya Jappy. I bet you could even build your own machine if you wanted."

While Cia has a disapproving look, Jappy has a disapproving grunt. Whenever Raph tries to talk to him, he huffs like an angry pig.

I escape the awkward energy surrounding the karaoke machine and grab my cup to get more ice.

When I was a kid, I used to list Cia's place as my address

on school forms because I practically lived here. The closet by the front door is where Tita Gretchen stashes her old DVDs and photo albums. The carpet stain next to the foot of the stairs is from when Cia and I tried making "art" with tissues dipped in paint. (Eventually we decided art would be more fun if we threw them at Jappy.)

I step into the kitchen and straighten the postcards on the fridge. Cia and I used to write on them, pretending we were sending messages to each other from all over the world.

As I'm looking at the Greece postcard, the Greek god enters the kitchen. "Hey, friend of the birthday girl, right?"

I startle and almost knock over the small TV by the fridge.

"You okay?" he asks as I move it back into place and salvage what's left of my dignity.

"Great!" I answer, casually resting my hand on the fridge door.

He slides next to me and gazes at all the postcards. "I've always wanted to go to Greece."

"Um." I clear my throat and try to channel the soothing feeling of Vicks. "Cia does too."

"Yeah?"

I nod. "She's always had this plan to go on a big trip before starting med school. When that day comes, she says she'll put her postcard collection in a can and blindly pick a destination."

"Are you also going for med?"

"No, I'm—" I pause and realize I can actually say I'm going to USC for real now. "I'm going for animation."

"Oh, cool, like Hayao Miyazaki?"

I say *animation*, and the first person he thinks of is the guy behind *Spirited Away*? This is hotter than watching him do pull-ups.

"Sort of?" I end up answering.

"Solid."

Solid. He thinks *I'm* solid.

"Do you . . . draw too?" I ask.

"No." He shakes his head. "I wish. I'm still figuring out what I'm good at."

"Didn't CNN call you the basketball Jesus?"

He laughs. "I think they used the term 'basketball messiah.'"

"Either way, getting nicknamed after the son of God means you're pretty good."

Miles then gives me this sexy lopsided smirk that I've only seen actors pull off. "Is this you?" he asks, pointing to the greeting on the back of the postcard, which says *To Chloe Elaine Ang Liang.*

"Oh yeah, Cia thought addressing each other by our full names would make the postcards more legit."

And Miles says in his perfectly smooth ASMR voice, "Chloe Elaine. I like that."

"Um." My brain feels like that endlessly spinning wheel that appears when a computer is having a hard time loading information.

Someone from the living room calls out his name, and Miles yells back that he'll be right there. "Can you tell Cia I had to go, but thanks for the invite?"

"You betcha!"

You betcha? God damn it, Chloe, that's cringier than kwe-we.

He gives me a beso and smiles. "See you around, Chloe Elaine."

Miles takes off, and I stand there, stunned.

After I finally regain feeling in my legs, I return to the living room and hear what sounds like the wailing of a tortured rooster.

Raph is jumping around, singing into the mic, "Dun dun dun dun errrrr dun dun dun errrr dun dun dun skweeeeee!"

Of course, Raph chose a DJ Tofu song. It's mostly bass and trap music beats, so Raph is basically just mimicking noises for a solid three minutes. It should be a Karaoke Commandment that thou shalt not pick an EDM song that has "Let's get sizzled" as its only lyric.

I slide next to Cia by the snack table. "So does this turn you on?"

"Love makes you see what others don't, Chlo," she says, sipping her drink.

Raph sounds like screeching tires. I wonder if love also makes you hear what others don't.

"It's a miracle that my brother is still here," Cia adds.

I take a peek and see Jappy alone by the staircase, looking very, very confused. "It's hard to ignore DJ Tofu performing live in your living room."

Raph calls out for people in the room to sing along, and one of the glee club girls actually joins in before the next beat drop.

Cia bumps me on the shoulder. "So did you get to continue your conversation with Miles?"

"Oh." I pause. "Um, kinda? He wanted to say thanks for inviting him."

She turns to me and freaks out. *You talked?*

I bite my lip to stop myself from smiling.

"Did he make a move on you?" Cia teases.

That conversation was full of moves, right? I held my ground and spoke multiple sentences. We even have inside jokes now about messiahs and being solid.

Not only is a guy like Miles making a move on me, I'm making moves too. Maybe I do have what it takes to be Chloe in America.

Raph does a fist pump when the TV flashes his score of 85. "Who dares challenge the karaoke king?" he bellows, and raises the mic.

Cia spits out some of her drink when she sees me raise my hand.

6

THE SECOND KARAOKE Commandment should be: If thou shalt do karaoke to Beyoncé, thou must fully believe that thou *art* Beyoncé.

Riding my sudden burst of confidence, I want my karaoke number for Cia to be epic, so I punch in the numbers for "Love on Top"—a song with a thousand different key changes.

But once I step in front of the machine and face the people crowded around Cia's living room, I suddenly notice . . . the people. I see Jappy staring at me like he's evaluating a slideshow presentation. Peter's on his phone, probably documenting this whole party for Auntie Queenie. Cia flashes me a thumbs-up while her eyes are screaming, *Oh god, I hope she knows what she's doing.* The glee club girls, who I barely know, are watching and . . . Why the hell did I think singing in front of people who could *actually* sing was a good idea?

The intro to "Love on Top" starts to play, and it sounds

like the beginning of my funeral march. Beyoncé tells me to bring the beat in, but I feel incapable of bringing anything.

Lyrics start flashing on the screen.

C'mon, Chloe. Sing! Rap! Mumble! Jesus Christ, at least hum?!?!

My god. Has the song always been this long?

But then the screen unexpectedly flips back to the basketball game rerun.

"Hang on." Jappy, still holding the remote, walks up to the machine and snatches the mic from me. "The machine needs to reset to stop glitching."

I take that as my cue to sneak away from this karaoke tragedy.

After hiding out in Cia's bathroom long enough for people to forget my existence, I return to the party and spy Jappy hovering by the staircase.

Of all people, why do I have to run into the guy who's going to rub the karaoke disaster in my face?

"Welcome back," Jappy huffs while biting into a chicken nugget.

"Where'd you get that?"

"Delivery. Had to get something nondairy to eat around here." He offers me his plate, and I reluctantly take a piece.

Just when I think he might be capable of letting things go, he adds, "Impressive choking."

"I would've done it if you'd fixed the machine properly."

"Sorry," he says, to my surprise. "You should sign up for another song. Heard the *kwe-we* for karaoke is getting pretty long."

I roll my eyes. "You should really think of new material, Jappy. Your jokes are getting older than you."

Before he answers, I see Tito Vince step up to the front and pause the karaoke beach background video.

"Hello, hello," Tito says. He clinks his glass of calamansi juice with a spoon. "Sorry for the short intermission, but I wanted to say a few words about the birthday girl." For as long as I've known Cia, Tito Vince has always made the same speech on her birthday.

"You're not staying?" I ask Jappy when he says he's going back to his game.

"Not really in the mood for the story of my sister's conception."

I grab another nugget from his plate. "Killjoy," I tease, before joining Cia by the couch.

"*Mahal*. As an adjective, it means 'expensive.' As a noun, it means 'love.' Gretchen, my mahal, is my priceless love." Tito Vince does an exaggerated sweeping gesture toward Tita, who urges him to just finish his speech.

He goes on to tell the story of how he and Tita Gretchen first met. They were in college, both architecture students, except Tito Vince was a year older. Tito Vince spent his first year being hailed as the course's most promising architect, who wowed every professor with his designs . . . that is, until Tita Gretchen arrived. With Tita Gretchen, Tito Vince felt things he had never felt before: challenged, annoyed, and completely in awe.

"I was about to ask her on a date—ready na ako with

flowers and my best cologne." Tito reenacts fixing the collar of his shirt. "But before I could say anything, she suddenly told me that she had to transfer schools so she could be closer to her relatives in the province."

Tito Vince pauses for dramatic effect like he always does.

"So I thought, that's it. I lost my shot with this amazing girl. Four years went by, and I never heard from her or saw her again, until I had my first architecture job. I was so proud pa that I was the only fresh grad who got hired by this prestigious company. Then in walks Gretchen Sotto, stealing my spotlight . . . *again*."

Even Tita Gretchen lets out a short chuckle at that part.

"We were given the same new-hire orientation, and I introduced myself, since I didn't want to assume she'd remember me. Then she gave me this terrifying poker face and asked, 'So when are we going on our date?'" Tito smiles and shakes his head. "Buti nalang I wasn't taken pa."

Cia groans next to me. "Every single year."

Okay, I know Tito shares his love story with Tita Gretchen every opportunity he gets, but I've always found it really sweet. Having never witnessed any semblance of a love story between my own parents, I guess it's nice to know it could be different.

"Mahal." Tita Gretchen cuts Tito off before he segues into chronicling Jappy and Cia's childhood. "I think we should let the kids go on with the party."

"Right. I heard our daughter was just about to take down Mr. Siy over here." Tito crosses his arms at Raph.

"Ohhhh." Tita turns to Cia, beaming. "You're saying you need help with your karaoke number?"

Cia takes three mics and hands two to her parents. "Let's go, parentals."

The family performance is another staple of Cia's birthday.

Tito Vince's solo preference might be "Dancing Queen," but for their group number, it's always "Total Eclipse of the Heart."

Cia, Tito, and Tita stand in the front with their backs to the rest of us. When the piano notes hit, they simultaneously spin and take turns singing, "Turn arooooooound." The rest of us in the humble audience sing along and laugh when Tito drops down on his knees and gets really into it. After the three of them belt out the final "turn around," we give them a standing ovation.

"What an excellent singer!" the TV screen announces and flashes a big "100!"

GOT 2 BELIEVE is Cia's all-time favorite Filipino romance movie. It has all the classic rom-com tropes—enemies to lovers, a bet, a love triangle—not to mention very attractive actors.

Cia always loves capping off her birthday with a *Got 2 Believe* screening. She's seen the film so many times that she knows all the lines by heart. I mean, she's reciting the exact dialogue right now as the characters enumerate the signs that someone's falling in love.

"Ang final proof na na-in love siya ay . . . sinok," Cia says, even hiccuping in time with the actor.

I grab a handful of leftover cheese popcorn from the party. "Do you think people actually hiccup when they're in love?"

"We don't look to love stories for realism, Chlo."

"Think about it. Wouldn't that be convenient?" I ask. "If the universe offered you a clear sign like that?"

She pauses, looking deep in thought. "Hiccups might get in the way of making out, though."

"Having a boyfriend has really corrupted you."

We hear a knock on the door, and Tita Gretchen peeks in. "Is that *Got 2 Believe?*" She slides next to Cia on the bed and watches with us. Tita lets out a squeal when the couple share a kiss.

"Tita, how do you still get kilig with this movie?" I ask, laughing.

She motions to the guy on the computer screen. "How can you not get kilig with Rico Yan's face?"

Cia always jokes that her mom has two great loves—Tito Vince and the late actor Rico Yan.

"Did Raphael not want to watch the movie?" Tita asks.

"He had some family thing," Cia explains.

"Speaking of . . ." Tita Gretchen looks at her watch and turns to me. "What time does Jeffrey want you home?"

I groan. "Midnight."

Cia pauses the movie. "He hasn't lifted the rule yet?"

I'm basically an adult, and my dad still won't let me go on sleepovers. When I tried asking him if I could stay over for Cia's birthday, he gave me one of his favorite lines: "Why would you want to stay in someone else's house when you have a bed here?" I hope he understands that studying abroad means I'll be sleeping in another bedroom.

"I think we can push it a little bit," Tita Gretchen says. "Say that I took forever to clean up and the traffic was really bad . . ."

I hug Tita Gretchen. "Thank you, thank you!"

"Thank the traffic." She winks at me and puts her arm around Cia. "I should go check on your brother and make sure he didn't get swallowed by his computer. Happy birthday, 'nak." She kisses Cia on the cheek and leaves the room.

"Hey, before we finish the movie . . ." I take the stack of coupons I made out of my bag.

Another sacred tradition of the Chloe-Cia friendship: birthday coupons. We started giving them to each other as kids, and every year, we add new ones.

Cia gasps when she sees the coupon that I drew a dog and a hand on. "You're giving me a puppy?"

"Yes," I answer, completely deadpan. "Shake that five times, and your stuffed animal will come to life."

"How cool would it be if that were really true, though?"

I toss her stuffed corgi at her while she laughs. "That coupon actually grants you a one-time bitch slap," I explain.

"Not once in our eleven-year friendship have we slapped each other."

I shrug. "I would've if I'd had a coupon."

She throws her pillow at me. "Wait. I also have something for you."

"Cia, the birthday celebrant is supposed to *receive* gifts."

She shoots me her disapproving look and hands me the index cards from her desk. Cia hates having to draw, so her coupons are always plain index cards with all-caps writing on them. The first few read "1 FREE HUG," "SERENADE FROM CIA," "YOUR PICK FOR MOVIE NIGHT."

"Oh my god." I beam and flash her a card. It says "SNOW CONES" and has a picture of the emoji that's smiling with a single tear. "Really?"

"I really don't get your obsession. It's flavored ice."

"It's tasty snow, sculpted into an artistic shape."

Cia rolls her eyes. "Right. Well, I'll get snow cones with you during the summer fair."

"What in the world is a summer fair?"

"Since it's Mary Immaculate's seventy-fifth anniversary, the school wanted to have another fair over the summer," she explains. "The glee club invited me to come back for their variety show performance."

"And you're of course doing it."

"Maybe," she says, leaning back on the bed, but her face tells me that she already has a whole set list planned out.

Thinking about school fairs and movie nights makes my insides feel all jumbled. I've been so preoccupied with my aunties and getting off the wait list that I haven't even thought about the idea of life without Cia. She, Raph, and all our other friends are going to college in Manila, moving on together. While I'm missing everyone from the other side of the world, will they get used to living their lives without me?

I bite my lip and swallow the lump rising in my throat. I have this thing where it's hard for me to cry in front of people, especially if I'm the only one crying. It's like my tear ducts get shy when they're on their own.

"What's this one?" I show Cia the card that has "SOS" written on it.

"Oh, uh . . . that's one of the serious ones I made." Cia pauses and takes a deep breath. "It's for when you need someone to be there for you. I know that I'm going to be far away, but just send me a picture of the coupon, and I'll drop everything."

The thought of missing Cia washes over me, and I try to push it far, far away.

"Or I could also make a printout of a crying emoji and frame it like your dad does," she continues. "We can include it in his Instagram Hall of Fame."

I try to chuckle with her, but my eyes start to water.

"Wait. Chlo, what's wrong?" She holds on to my shoulder, and my lips quiver more.

"We weren't supposed to think about me leaving yet."

She passes me the tissue box and apologizes, which further activates my tear ducts.

"Who will I get milk tea with or get drunk with at bars?" I ask.

"The only alcohol you've ever had is from when the priest soaks the Communion bread in wine."

"College is the time for change." I pluck out more tissues, blow my nose, and groan. "God, I hate crying."

"Wait." Cia closes the *Got 2 Believe* window and pulls up another video. From the music, I immediately recognize the beginning of the movie *Up*. It's the montage of the couple growing old together, which ends with the wife getting sick and the husband mourning her death alone. The scene always makes her bawl her eyes out.

And then it hits me. She's making herself cry so we can cry together. My tears start flowing even more because that is the sweetest damn thing in the entire world.

As the movie plays, we cry for the cartoon couple and about being so far away from each other for the next four years. We eat leftover cheese fries, and we don't even mind that they're spotted with tears. The video ends, and we hug each other because we're still crying.

"Love you, Cia."

"Love you, Chlo."

Is it possible to feel homesick before I've even left home?

7

THE DAY I got my USC acceptance letter, I couldn't sleep from all the thoughts circling in my head.

Don't get me wrong. If someone made a video of the highlights of Chloe Liang's life, reading "Congratulations" on the USC letterhead would be up there. Knowing that I'll actually walk through the iron gates I've been fantasizing about since I was a kid still feels unreal.

If I had gotten into USC back in March, I'd have said yes in a heartbeat. I'd have screamed to the heavens and animated an obnoxious "Chloe got into her dream school!" video. Hell, I'd have even considered flooding the Liang family groupchat with hashtags. But when I got the offer from the wait list, the first thought I had was *I only got in because someone else said no.*

I'm usually great at tuning out Auntie Queenie, but what she said about being USC's second choice feels true. What if I go to USC and everyone realizes I'm the school's consolation prize because they couldn't get anyone better?

And if I'm really meant to go to USC, shouldn't I be itching to go right now? Are all these nerves about leaving home some kind of bad omen?

I check my phone and see that it's five in the morning. Stress insomnia again. I push open the window next to my bed and listen to the clicking noises of the geckos outside.

That's when I smell it.

There's nothing I love more than the scent of incoming rain. Whether it's going to be a drizzle or a typhoon, my nose has a gift for anticipating precipitation. Cia once said that I was prouder of my rain-smelling talent than I was of my drawing ability. I mean, between the two, psychic rain-sensing is closer to a superpower.

I kick off my covers and prop my arms on the windowsill. I breathe in and feel the humid air stick to my skin.

Wait for it. Wait for it.

Minutes later, I hear the slow pattering of rain on the roof.

A sudden gust of wind blows some papers and files off my desk. When I go to pick them up, I see the flyer for the Philippine Animation Festival sticking out of a folder. I was so preoccupied with working on my video entry that I didn't see the testimonial section on the back.

There's one past showcase winner who wrote, "I wouldn't have made it so far in my career if not for the wonderful colleagues and mentors I met at the USC School of Cinematic Arts."

That has to mean something, right? The rain bringing the flyer to my attention, the in-my-face tribute to USC. The couple in *Got 2 Believe* looked to hiccups as a sign. Maybe if I do well in the showcase, it'll be a sign that I'm meant to go.

My phone pings with a message from Ma. With the fifteen-hour time difference, it's two in the afternoon in LA. We usually have our weekly video calls on Saturday mornings, but not *this* early in the morning.

Can't wait for our call! Have lots to show you!

I text her back, **I'm up now!** with the raised hand emoji.

Ma calls, and when I pick up, I see that she's in Target.

"Why are you awake so early?" she asks.

"Couldn't sleep," I say, rubbing my eyes.

"Anything wrong?"

I shake my head. She moves on and starts showing me stuff she thinks will go great in my dorm room.

Talking to Ma is so much lighter than when I try to have conversations with Pa. She actually tries to listen and hear me out. When I tell her I'm okay, she believes me and gives me space. With Pa, everything is blown out of proportion.

But in terms of interior decorating, I think Pa might have the upper hand.

"I think your roommates would love this!" She flips her phone to show me a rug with a panda pooping on a toilet.

"Ma." I laugh. "I actually want to make friends in college."

"It can be a conversation starter. You can bond with your roommates over how funny the rug is!"

She then suggests that I get towels shaped like eggs and bacon. After she somehow manages to find every quirky thing in the store, I agree to getting a pillow that's shaped like a mango.

The screen switches back to her face. "Hey, you know what I realized? That showcase you entered is the same weekend as your debut. Can you have an extra person cheering you on?"

"Oh . . . wow!" I slap on my polite smile and try my best to sound excited. I've been looking forward to Ma flying here for months, but her attending the showcase just adds a thousand times more pressure. "But, Ma, I'm not so sure if I'll make the cut—"

"Chloe Elaine Ang Liang." Ma's version of the tongue click of disappointment is saying my whole name. It's way less fun than when Miles called me Chloe Elaine. "How can you convince other people to believe in you if you don't believe in yourself?" she lectures. "Do you think Beyoncé would've made it as a solo artist if she thought she wouldn't make the cut?" She always knows which words will speak to my soul.

"No, Ma," I say.

"Good," she says with finality, as if all my doubts were suddenly vanquished. "How's the debut planning going?"

"Auntie Queenie messaged me yesterday asking how comfortable I am with performing aerial stunts."

Ma groans. It's the special groan that she saves for my aunt.

Auntie Queenie's nickname for Ma: "the entitled American."

Ma's nickname for Auntie Queenie: "Meanie Queenie."

Yeah, Ma's maturity goes out the window when it comes to Auntie Queenie.

"Do you need me to talk to her?" she asks.

"It's fine." I put on my most convincing smile to keep her from stirring something up between the two of them. "I'm sure she was joking about the aerial stunts."

And hopefully about whether I'd be comfortable delivering spoken-word poetry.

"We can continue your birthday celebration when you get here too. I found this new campsite that we can check out before your orientation. Wait. I forgot to tell you!" She pauses, and her whole face lights up. "I ran into this woman on my camping trip who works at an indie animation studio. I told her about you, and she said she would *love* to look at your portfolio."

"Oh, wow . . . Sounds great," I say, but the dread of Ma seeing my work swirls in my gut.

"I'm so excited for you, babes!" she says as she grabs another panda-themed item from the shelf. "You're finally going to see the world."

"Yeah," I mutter, activating my polite smile again. "So exciting."

I hear a voice in the background directing Ma to the cashier. "I have to go," she tells me. "Love you, babes."

"Love you, Ma."

She blows me a kiss, and the screen blinks off.

Nobody in my family ever talks about my parents' situation. The Philippines is still the only country in the world where divorce isn't legal yet, so my relatives are allergic to any mention of them being separated.

Pa started dating my mom when he went to California for

a postgrad program. Even though Ma's family had migrated to the States a decade prior, Pa recognized her since they went to the same preschool.

My relatives use their story as a cautionary tale, because Ma's pregnancy was unplanned. But even without my grandparents' interference, I'm pretty sure Pa would've married Ma without hesitation. A strict commandment practiced by Catholic Chinese Filipino families is "When thou hast a baby, thou must marry," and my father is definitely a devout follower.

After I was born, we lived in the US a few years, but then my grandfather got sick and asked Pa to come home to help run the family business. Ma came and tried to stay for a while, but her life was rooted abroad. Eventually, they decided things weren't going to work out. Ma went back to the US, and Pa and I stayed here.

Ma came to visit a few times when I was younger, but now I mostly see her when I go to the States. My mom never seems relaxed in Manila, and she's been dropping hints about me moving in with her since I was in grade school. I don't blame her. How can you feel at home in a place that never felt like yours?

When my aunties judge me for being "Americanized," they always say, "You get that from your mother."

I wish I was like my mother. Ma leaps for every single opportunity that comes her way. She works in journalism, and when a new position opens, she goes for it without hesitation. If my mother were an animator, she wouldn't be afraid of showing *anyone* her videos.

Even though I go on and on about becoming an animator, I start hyperventilating when I think about Ma seeing any of my recent work. Ma was the first person who'd get to see any of my drawings when I was a kid. After I got my braces, I made my first animation of a sloth dentist. Ma played the video on repeat while Pa kept asking why a sloth would be interested in teeth. These past few years, though, ever since I started taking this whole animation route more seriously, my heart quickens whenever Ma asks to see my work. I never even showed her the portfolio I made for my college apps.

Since I got wait-listed, I've been overcompensating by pretending that I'm still 110 percent confident in my dream. With my aunties and Pa, I'm used to the animation-bashing and indifference. But if Ma actually watches my videos and sees that the rest of the family's criticisms were valid . . . I'm not sure I could handle that.

If strangers hate my work, at least they're only criticizing what I put out there. If my own mom, my biggest supporter, hated it, it would feel like she hated *me*.

What happens if the person who's supposed to know me best doesn't like how I express myself?

But . . . what if *really* credible strangers like my work?

The headline on the showcase flyer feels like it's popping out at me in 3-D. If I get picked as one of the top young animators in the country, that could be enough to prove I'm not just a second choice.

I hold my breath as I hear footsteps outside my door. I glance out the window and see the rain has stopped, and the slight glow of the sunrise is looming on the horizon. Pa usually wakes me up to join him for his six o'clock runs, which doesn't sound too appealing after staying up all night.

Then I think about how many more mornings I have left to run with Pa. I quickly get out of bed and grab my running shoes. Maybe if I run fast enough, I can stop worrying about leaving.

8

PA ALWAYS RUNS the same five-kilometer loop around our gated community, and he always wears his Golden State Warriors jersey. The one thing I never figured out is why he insists on wearing the jersey with a T-shirt underneath. Manila is so hot that you *never* need to layer, but my father is the ultimate creature of habit.

We wave to the security guard who mans the subdivision entrance. In here, there are only trees and houses lined up along the streets. Outside the gate is where all the action is. That's where you see the bustling city with its highways and tall buildings. This place is like a little neighborhood bubble.

Christmas is still months away, but one of our neighbors has already started putting up their belen and Christmas lights. Pa spends weeks complaining that the lights are a safety hazard and an unnecessary expense. But every year, he gives in, decorates the house, and posts a hundred pictures to his album "Christmas House [insert year here]."

It sinks in that this might be the first year I'm not going to be home to help decorate.

I let my guard down as I reminisce, and just then Pa zooms right past me.

"Should've named you Slowy instead of Chloe!" he yells out.

Oh, it is *so* on.

I consider myself a pretty chill person, but the stakes are different when I'm running. I always get a thrill when I run past a random person I've never met. I've even gotten excited from overtaking a group of elderly power walkers. Some guy at a fun run once called me "overcompetitive," but I like to think I have an admirable inclination for winning.

I pump up the volume on my phone and sprint down the damp roads.

We're on the last street of our loop, and it's neck and neck. My legs and arms are coated with beads of sweat. Pa lets out a loud "Ha!" every time he exhales, which used to throw me off but doesn't bother me anymore. I push harder, and I reach the street sign that serves as our unofficial finish line first.

I bend one elbow and straighten my other arm to the sky. I am the freaking Usain Bolt of the Liang family.

It's too late when I notice that Pa has taken his phone out.

I shield my face. "Pa, no! No photos!"

He ignores me. "Look! I have four likes already!"

Who checks Instagram at six in the morning?! My hair is gross, and you can see my armpit sweat. Thank god no one my age follows him.

We start our trek back without saying a word. The sun is now fully up, and Pa pulls me to the inner side of the sidewalk as more cars stream down the street. He's always paranoid that a car will somehow swerve and jump the curb.

Morning runs with Pa are always drama-free, and it's the one thing we both like doing.

Or at least they used to be drama-free.

"Queenie asked when you can go in for a dress fitting," Pa suddenly says.

Oh god. If it were up to Auntie Queenie, she'd make me wear a *Bridgerton*-level ball gown to my debut.

"Can't I wear something I already have?"

Pa takes two steps in front of me and swings his arms to the left. He always looks like he's karate chopping the air when he gives directions, and he always points out every turn we're going to make, as if I don't know the way to my own house.

"Your auntie is doing something really nice for you," he says. "She's sad that you're going to be so far away."

Is this his way of saying that *he's* sad I'm leaving?

"Hey, Pa," I say after a moment. "I talked to Ma. She went camping last weekend—"

"Camping?" Pa shoots me a look as if I just said Ma went skinny-dipping.

"Yeah. Ma likes camping."

Pa continues to stare at me weirdly.

"Y'know, sleeping in a tent under the stars. Appreciating the beauty of nature . . . She said that we could go camping before I start classes."

He clicks his tongue. "Why would anyone want to sleep in the dirt?"

I sometimes wonder how my parents were ever a couple.

"Maybe we could do something together before I leave."

Pa points out our next turn to the right. "Aren't we already doing something now?"

"I mean, something we've never tried before. Like bonding activities."

He turns to me. "I work hard to have a bed and a roof over my head, Chloe. I don't want to sleep in the dirt."

And the award for best father-daughter communication goes to . . . not us.

I sigh. "We don't have to go camping. We can go somewhere with lots of Instagrammable spots," I add, trying to tempt him.

"I'm really bogged down at the office. You don't get summer vacations anymore when you're working."

Now I feel guilty for even suggesting a trip in the first place.

"Right. Sorry," I say, and we continue walking to our house. I guess he really doesn't mind that I'm leaving in August.

Once we get to our gate, Pa pulls out his key. But before we step inside, he clears his throat. "I saw that there's a fun run going on in a few weeks. Maybe the two of us can register?"

"You're not busy?"

"I can push back meetings." He shrugs.

I actually feel a tiny bit of my heart melt.

"Sure," I say. "Sign me up."

It's not a trip to the beach, but I'll take it.

9

OUR SUNDAY ROUTINE was ingrained in my veins before I was even born. Pa wakes up, puts on his church polo shirt, and we leave at 9:00 on the dot for the 10:00 mass. Yes, he likes getting to the church thirty minutes early so we can get "the best seats in the house." After the service is over, he makes small talk with some of the other 10:00 mass regulars, then we head to family lunch.

It's already 9:05 by the time I get downstairs, and I brace myself for a "time with the Lord is sacred" lecture. But Pa is lying on the couch, still in his home polo shirt and watching another Warriors highlights video on YouTube. I have to raise my voice because no matter where we go, his phone's volume is always set to the highest level.

"Was mass canceled?" I ask.

He looks up. "Let's leave at ten."

"But mass is at ten."

"We're going to the eleven o'clock service today."

Pa is a 10:00 mass person. Not 9:00, not 11:00.

"Why aren't we going to the ten o'clock one?"

"Queenie's joining us."

"But you hate going to mass with Auntie Queenie."

During the mass at Peter's graduation, Pa put me in between him and Auntie Queenie because she kept scolding him for not singing along to the hymns.

He clicks his tongue. "Chloe, it doesn't matter what time we go. It's the same service." He then turns back to his phone, and the noises from the NBA game fill the living room.

Things get even stranger when we pass by to pick up Auntie Queenie. I don't think I've ever seen anyone more excited about going to church.

"Mary the Queen is such a nice parish. Remember when Missy had her wedding here?" Auntie Queenie looks back at me from the front passenger seat. "Don't you think Mary the Queen is really couple-friendly?"

"I guess if you're Catholic?"

"You know, that's a good way to weed out suitors. Bad boys don't hang out in churches."

More of Auntie Queenie's words of wisdom.

She then eyes me from top to bottom. "You should put your hair down, Chloe. You never know who you might run into," she says with her double-wink.

I keep waiting for Pa to interrupt the conversation, but he just keeps grumbling about how someone else took his parking space. When he finally finds a spot, I linger in the car and wait for Auntie Queenie to go out first since she keeps mentioning that she wants to fix my hair.

That's when someone comes up the window and knocks on the door.

I jump and yelp, then hear the familiar laughing attack.

"Not funny." I slap Cia's arm when I climb out the car.

"Hi, Patricia," Pa says, and Cia greets him and Auntie Queenie with a beso.

"Are you guys on your way out?" Cia asks.

"We're going to the eleven A.M. service today," Pa replies.

Cia shoots me a look. *What happened to ten o'clock?*

I have no idea, I silently reply.

Auntie Queenie has her neck craned, and her eyes keep skittering to the people gathered around the steps of the church entryway. "Is your mother here?" she asks Cia.

"Oh, I think she'll be here soon. I came early for choir duties."

"Great!" Auntie Queenie exclaims, and clasps her hands. "I'm so excited to see Gretchen."

I lightly nudge Cia. *Has Auntie Queenie ever met your mom?*

Don't think so. Cia shrugs.

"I have to get ready for the next service, but nice seeing you, Tito. Tita." Cia heads back to the church and wishes me luck with her eyes.

When I spot Tita Gretchen's car pulling into the parking lot, Auntie Queenie waves at them like the pope has just arrived.

Jappy gets out of the passenger seat, and it's the first time I've seen all his hair swooping in the same direction. Did he actually comb and style it? The rest of him also looks generally good. His orange collared shirt paired with khaki pants looks like what someone would wear for an "outfit of the day" picture.

I remember thinking he looked kinda cute during prom, but I wrote that off as rose-colored prom glasses. All guys have the potential to be cute if they wear a suit. I guess Jappy Torres has cuteness potential in church too.

When he sees me, he does his usual hip-to-shoulder side-wave.

"Gretchen!" Auntie Queenie cries, and the two of them beso like they're closer than me and Cia. "How are you? It's been too long."

"Chloe is always in the house. We should all get together more often!"

I hope she's just being polite, because I'd rather keep my second home separate from my first home.

Pa then slaps Jappy on the back. "Jappy! You've gotten so tall. What are you, six one, six two?"

"Uh . . . five eight, Tito."

"So *tall*!" Pa beams at him even though he missed by a good five-inch margin. "And I hear you're taking up engineering?"

"Computer science, Tito."

"Jappy and Chloe have always been good friends. Right, Chloe?" Tita Gretchen smiles.

I assume that's a rhetorical question until I notice that Pa, Auntie Queenie, and Tita are still staring at me, waiting for an answer. "Sure. I've known Jappy for forever."

More creepy smiling from the three of them. Have Pa's teeth always been this white? I try to catch Jappy's eye to see if he thinks our parents are acting weird too, but he seems to be more focused on the ground.

When the church bell rings, Auntie Queenie steers us all inside. I grab a program and genuflect by the entrance before looking for a place to sit. This is the first time I'm not here ridiculously early, so our usual spot is already taken. The five of us walk up and down the red carpeted aisle that stretches to the altar until I finally find one empty pew at the back.

After Jappy and I slide in, Pa says, "I think we should sit closer to the front."

"This is the only empty row, Pa."

"There might be something there." Tita Gretchen points to the section beside the altar.

Just as I'm about to move, Auntie Queenie holds up her hand to stop me. "You two stay here. That side is the . . . adult section."

"I don't think churches have adult sections." I look at Jappy to get some reinforcement, and just then, I become fully aware that he is a boy.

I remember what Auntie Queenie said in the car: "Bad boys don't hang out in churches."

Shit.

Are they trying to kaishao me? In church?!?

Tita Gretchen gives my shoulder a traitorous squeeze before the three of them leave me and Jappy. When the choir begins the opening hymn and everyone rises to their feet, all I want is to dig a hole in the ground and hide out there forever. Cia waves at us from the choir stands by the altar, and I pretend nothing's wrong so she doesn't find out I'm being set up with her brother.

It doesn't help that I have to scooch closer to Jappy because the woman next to me is wearing what is probably the strongest perfume ever concocted.

"In the name of the Father, and of the Son, and of the Holy kaishao."

"The Lord be with you. And with your kaishao."

"A reading from the book of kaishao."

Am I really hearing the word *kaishao*, or am I getting drugged by the woman's perfume?

I try to hold in my feelings, and then I catch Pa sneaking a peek at me and Jappy. Part of me is pretty impressed that Auntie Queenie actually talked my dad into matching me with a guy. Why in the world did it have to be Jappy, though?

When we take our seats for the offertory, Jappy whispers, "Is it me or are they watching us?"

I glance over and find the kaishao-scheming trifecta staring at us even more obviously.

"Okay." I cross my arms. "Promise you won't make fun of me for this."

Jappy narrows his eyes and pulls out his judgy eyebrow. "For what?" He's definitely going to give me shit for this for the rest of my life.

"There might be a small . . . slight chance that we're getting set up." I sigh. "But I didn't ask for this," I quickly clarify. "Auntie Queenie was weirded out that I didn't have guy friends for the roses in my debut, and she brought up wanting to kaishao me with someone. So you're, like, the kaishao boy."

His judgy eyebrow is on full blast. "Kaishao boy?"

"They basically used church as an excuse for ambush matchmaking."

"And they did this without telling you?"

"Obviously." I flail my arms between me and Jappy. "Why would I want to get set up at Mary the Queen?"

"Yeah, Christ the King has a way more romantic ambiance," he deadpans.

I groan. "Jappy, I'm dealing with a crisis here."

We stand when the priest prays over the Eucharist.

"You can't blame your dad." He lowers his voice. "I'm very in demand for dating daughters."

"Yeah, you're exactly my father's type."

The priest starts reciting the Lord's Prayer, and everyone around us joins hands. Right when I place my hand over Jappy's, I catch Auntie Queenie very indiscreetly smiling in our direction.

Spiritually holding hands is very different from romantically holding hands!

I carefully lift my hand so there's a pocket of air separating me and Jappy. He doesn't seem to notice and keeps reciting the lines of the prayer.

Once the prayer finishes, the priest calls for us to offer the sign of peace. I bow and mutter "Peace be with you" to the people around me and get a strong dose of perfume when the lady beside me brings me in for a beso.

Jappy faces me, and I'm not sure whether I should bow or beso him. There's nothing in the Bible that advises on the least flirty way of offering peace. I settle on throwing up a peace sign, and he answers with a judgy peace sign back.

Then he kicks down the cushion in front of the pew, and I carefully kneel next to him.

I flinch when I feel his elbow graze mine. "You're too close," I whisper.

"Should I leave space for the Holy Spirit?"

I groan when I hear him chuckle under his breath. "Weirdo."

He pauses and asks, "So what's the game plan?"

"We should try to act super platonically."

"What does that even mean?"

"Just, like, really formal," I say. "If they act this weird when they're trying to set us up, imagine what would happen if they thought there was a thing between us."

"So act like I hate you."

"No." I shake my head. "That would make them suspicious. Just . . . emphasize that you only see me as your little sister's friend."

He lets out a deep breath. "This is really getting in the way of my spiritual celebration."

Once mass ends and the priest dismisses us, Jappy and I wait for our parents at the back of the church. Pa walks up to us with his creepy smile again. He faces Jappy and asks, "What did you think of the service?"

"Me and my *sister's* friend"—he side-eyes me, practically yelling the word *sister*—"found it very enlightening."

I hold in my laugh when Pa takes this seriously and Jappy gets stuck hearing Pa's dissection of all the readings.

"Ahia." Auntie Queenie interrupts Pa. "This is a fascinating discussion, but maybe the kids would rather talk about something else." She shoves Jappy toward me, and he trips over my foot. "You seem very light on your feet," Auntie Queenie says after he almost knocks me over. "Do you dance?"

"Um." Jappy's hair starts returning to its panicked pineapple state.

I butt in and say, "I don't think he's much of a dancer."

"Ah." Auntie Queenie turns pensive. Her expression reminds me of the lions in those nature videos, looking all elegant and poised while secretly plotting an antelope assassination. "I'm not sure if Chloe mentioned it, but she has her debut coming up soon. And we still have some spots open for her eighteen roses . . ."

Tita Gretchen quickly goes along with it. "Jappy would love to be in Chloe's roses!"

"Sure," Jappy says with a shrug.

Sure?!

"Isn't that great, Chloe?" Auntie Queenie beams, and the rest of the adults are looking at me with terrifying levels of enthusiasm.

If my auntie and my dad would set me up at church, who knows where they'll stage the next kaishao. Oh god. What if they bring someone to family lunch? Then I'd have to deal with some random guy, plus all my aunties.

I guess if Auntie Queenie is insistent on bringing in a

guy for my roses, Jappy might be the slightly less awkward option.

"Great . . ." I squeak out.

Auntie Queenie double-winks at me. "Why don't you two exchange numbers so you can coordinate?"

"Um. I can just ask Cia."

"No, no." Auntie Queenie scoots Jappy and me closer together. "Numbers are much more intimate. So much better than Instagram or the TikTok."

The adults take a few steps away from us and pretend they're inspecting the church. Pa is even running his hand across a white column, which signals incredible dedication, because he's a known germaphobe.

This is all way too much for me to process.

Jappy clears his throat and says loudly, "I can add my number to your phone."

"What are you doing?" I mouth at him.

His fingers go to his phone, and he shows me the screen.

Your aunt is monitoring.

I don't even need to look to feel Auntie Queenie's eyes on me. "Sure!" I follow along, making sure my voice reaches the eavesdropping relatives. "Here you go!"

When I hand my phone over, it looks like he's actually typing something.

"Don't go through my messages," I warn him.

"There's not much to see," Jappy whispers, and gives me back my phone. "Got your number!" he calls out.

Pa swivels around like he wasn't listening the entire time. "This church really has the most beautiful architecture."

"Aren't we going to be late for lunch?" I ask. I usually delay family lunch as much as possible, but anything seems better than prolonging this bizarre church matchmaking.

Pa and I say goodbye to Tita Gretchen, who pats me on the cheek after I beso her.

"I'll be in touch with the debut color scheme." Auntie Queenie points at Jappy and walks to our parking spot with an extra bounce in her step.

Moments later, I feel my phone buzz in my pocket and open the new message.

Jappy entered his name in my phone as **Kaishao Boy**.

See you around church, Chloe!

I groan and shoot back a reply. **Weirdo.** 😶

AUNTIE QUEENIE STILL hasn't budged on her bland, flavorless diet, so Pa immediately orders delivery when we get home.

While Auntie Queenie spent the entire lunch interrogating me about my guest list and cake options, Pa has been watching me with even more hyperfocus than usual. As we're digging into the fried chicken, he keeps sneaking glances at me, obviously having something to say.

Should I be the one to bring up what happened in church? Should I even mention it? If I act like it wasn't a big deal, maybe Pa will tell Auntie Queenie that kaishaos don't work on me. But what if my silence signals to them that I was totally fine with it?

Sigh. These are the situations that fried chicken was made for.

I moan when the slab of juicy chicken thigh slobbered in sweet gravy melts in my mouth. Nothing in this world is better than Jollibee's Chickenjoy and white rice. It literally has joy in its name.

From the looks of it, Pa is on the same page. At the other end of the table, he's biting into a chicken leg dripping with gravy. No matter our differences, good fried chicken has the magic to pull us together.

After he puts down his piece, he finally speaks. "Father Jed wore new shoes today."

"Oh, I didn't notice."

He nods. "They were a darker brown."

Pa might also be the only person in the world who pays attention to priests' footwear.

After a beat, he clears his throat. "The Jappy boy . . . Is he nice?"

Is this his way of talking about what happened?

"Um. Yeah, I guess."

"Good." He starts peeling off the skin from his chicken. "Don't go inside his bedroom. It doesn't look good for a girl to travel bedrooms."

Where in the world did he get the concept of bedroom traveling from? Okay, maybe I *should* drop hints that there's no church-related flirting going on between me and Jappy.

"We don't really talk much," I say.

"Don't you see him at their house?"

I shrug. "I'm mostly there to see Cia."

"Oh."

"Jappy and I are just friends," I emphasize, to drive the point home even more.

"Right, right. It's good to have friends."

Then silence stretches out between us.

"Oh, I got you something while I was in the mall." He wipes his hands and pulls out a paper bag.

I try to act excited when I see the familiar National Bookstore logo on the bag. When Pa buys a book, he always makes sure to give me a copy too. I love reading, but Pa's reading list is always filled with dense textbooks on finance, entrepreneurship, and business.

I take out the book, and it weighs more than my whole bookshelf. *Business Studies: Fifth Edition*. The first four editions are still gathering dust in the back of my closet.

"The bookseller says this version is more relevant to today's business landscape," Pa says. "I'm making people in the office read it too."

Polite smile is fully activated. "Thanks, Pa."

"There's one more book in there."

I reach in the bag and feel another thick book spine. Don't tell me they already published the sixth edition.

"I told the bookseller you liked cartoons," Pa says, "and she told me that's the book to get."

I stare at the copy of *The Animator's Survival Kit* in my hands. The bookseller was right. Every single blog on animation says that this is the must-read for anyone who wants to go into the field. I already have a copy in my room, but I don't care. Pa actually went to the bookstore, told the bookseller that he has a daughter who wants to be an animator, and found a gift for said aspiring animator daughter. This is his blessing for me to study animation!!!

The smile I have on my face is so big that I don't think I can call it polite.

I want to hug him, but that's not something Pa and I do. So I say thank you with all my heart and hope that it's enough to show Pa how much the gift means to me.

He nods and I'm about to start attacking a drumstick when he drops a bombshell.

"Chloe, I was thinking. What if you stay here for college?"

What?

"Colleges here offer quality education," he continues. "Even Peter is staying here instead of going abroad. It also makes sense businesswise for you to network with people in your community. When I came back from abroad, I had to adjust because being far away didn't grant me those connections. It's better that you get your feet wet sooner so you can familiarize yourself with the denim business. I can mentor you, and we can go on site visits and check the factory in the province together."

I have to hold on to the table to steady myself. How did giving me an animation book spiral into this? "What about USC?"

Pa brushes this off. "It's still early. We can reach out to the admissions office and explain that some extenuating circumstances happened and you decided to stay closer to home. I'm sure they'll understand."

I raise the bookstore bag for evidence. "But you gave me an animation book."

"Yes, you can go to college here, help out with the business, then learn cartoons with this book."

I don't even know how to respond. My father thinks that four years at one of the best animation schools in the world is the same as reading *one* book.

"And you still have that festival to look forward to!" he says as he reaches for more gravy. "Lots of ways to continue your hobby here."

Is this why he's been posting so much about the festival? So that I'd change my mind about USC?

"But, Pa . . ." I brace myself when his focus returns to me. "I still want to study abroad."

He's quiet for a moment, then asks, "Is this about the Tinder?"

I mean, *HUH?*

"Queenie explained it to me," he continues. "Did you meet someone from the States on the Tinder? I don't like the idea of random strangers from who knows where looking at your pictures. You can't trust people you meet on the internet, and you know how different Americans are," he warns. "Queenie also mentioned there was a lot of swiping involved, and that doesn't sound safe."

"Tinder is not the reason I want to go abroad," I snap, completely exasperated. "I've always wanted to go there since I was a kid, and I still do now. I—"

"All right." Pa doesn't even let me finish.

"We also already gave the deposit, so it might be hard to get back."

He slides his chair back and picks up his plate. "Tama na. Let's discuss this another time." He clears the boxes of chicken and walks away like our conversation never happened.

"Pa," I call out, and follow him. "Are you sure—"

I'm cut off by Pa's ringtone.

"I need to take this." He swerves past me and goes to the living room to answer the call.

The gnawing, chomping guilt is burrowing through my insides again. Maybe I am asking too much. How can I ask him to support me doing something he doesn't want me to do?

Or . . . is he so against my art because he doesn't think I can make it? But I really want this. More than anything in the world.

I wish we were like those fathers and daughters on TV who can open up to each other and hug after they fight. I watch Pa on the phone and wonder how someone who's so great at negotiating and selling can be so bad at communicating with his own daughter.

11

ONE GREAT THING about having a second home is that I have somewhere to retreat when I'm avoiding my dad. When Pa gets home at the end of the day, I hide out in my room and draw. If I need to go downstairs, I check to make sure he's in his study. Even when I asked permission to go to Cia's, I did it through text so I could avoid actual physical interaction.

I guess it's a blessing in disguise that I have baking to distract me.

"How do I know when the flour is ready?" I ask from the stove.

"When it's golden brown!" Cia answers while wrapping polvoron in cellophane at an alarming rate on the kitchen counter. Beside her, Raph's on cookie-shaping duty, but he's still struggling to keep his first piece from crumbling.

Before Cia barks at me to look up the recipe again, smoke starts wafting from the stove. She hurries over while I frantically flap my hands at the pan. Cia coughs and opens a window.

"Sorry," I say. "I don't know how it started burning."

She purses her lips at my baking fail. "The only thing in the pan was flour. It's supposed to be as simple as boiling water."

I hunch my shoulders. "I find that hard too."

She prods the pan, still completely bewildered. "I gave you the simplest task."

"I told you I'm more useful as a spectator."

Cia had asked Raph and me if we wanted polvoron for our movie night. I thought that meant eating the tasty shortbread, not making it.

"This is really concerning." She crosses her arms, turning completely serious. "It makes me worried that you're not ready to join the family, sis." She's been calling me "sis" ever since I told her what happened at Mary the Queen.

"You could've brought homemade polvoron to your next church date with Jappy," Raph adds.

I flick flour at the two of them when they crack up at my expense. "Sige lang. If you keep on going, I'm throwing that pan in your faces." I've been dreading Jappy giving me shit about the whole kaishao incident when I should've been worried about Raph and Cia.

"You two would make a great couple." Raph holds up Jappy's high school graduation picture, which is displayed in the living room. "Doesn't Chloe fit in perfectly next to Jappy's scowl here?" I don't get why some guys think pouting at the camera looks better than wearing an actual smile.

Cia snorts. "To be honest, I imagined someone more . . . *exciting* for Chloe."

"Oh, right." Raph strokes his chin. "Like the basketball guy."

I groan. "Can we *please* change topics?"

"I'm just saying"—Cia gets back to work, stirring the butter into the batter—"if you're looking for a pre-going-abroad summer fling, it would be more fun if it were with a guy who didn't spend all his time gaming in his room."

"I'm not looking for a fling," I emphasize.

"But hey," Raph pipes in, "Jappy might be an expert at finding fun things to do in his room."

"Gross," Cia and I say in unison.

"I was thinking video games or watching anime." Raph puts up his hands defensively. "You two went there."

Cia gives her disapproving look when I munch on a polvoron piece from the reject pile. "It's weird that they did that whole kaishao thing without telling you, though."

"The lengths Auntie Queenie will go to for debut planning."

Cia turns to Raph. "Does this happen in your family too?"

Raph's hands linger over the polvoron mold. "My family?"

"Yeah, the kaishao stuff. Is it a common Chinese Filipino thing?"

"Maybe for other people?" he says with a shrug. "It doesn't really happen in mine."

I scoff. "Lucky you."

His smile falters when his phone screen lights up.

"Nemesis posted again?" Cia asks.

Raph's "nemesis" is this other vlogger who, according to

Raph, has been "stealing" his audience. He wipes his hands with a dish towel and passes his phone to Cia. "Every single time she and her boyfriend go to the beach, they get thousands of views. There isn't even creative content in these videos! All they're doing is hugging each other and showing off their six-packs. I could do that too."

"Babe, you don't have a six-pack." Cia pats his tummy. "You have one big pack."

I snicker, and Raph frowns. "I don't see you laughing like that at my jokes, Chloe."

"Hey, I was one of *Laugh with Raph*'s first subscribers." I crane my neck to get a glimpse of the infamous nemesis.

Wow. They really do have six-packs. The guy's stomach looks like it was carved with a knife. And the girl's silky hair looks like the kind actresses flip and brush in shampoo commercials.

Wait. That's Perfect Pauline.

"Your nemesis is Peter's girlfriend?" I ask.

"Peter's girlfriend?" Cia repeats.

"That's her." I motion to Pauline's Pantene hair. "That's *the* honey dumpling."

Raph winces. "Looks like she's been sharing her honey with someone else."

"Poor Peter," Cia says, shaking her head.

No matter how I feel about Perfect Peter, no one deserves to get cheated on and traded in for a guy with hazardously pointy abs.

Cia faces me. "I think you should tell him."

"*Me?* We're not even close."

"How would you feel if you found out your boyfriend had been cheating on you and your cousin knew all about it and didn't say anything?"

"I would understand where my cousin was coming from, because we're not close," I answer, and Cia shoots me another disapproving look.

"I'm siding with Cia on this one," Raph says, and gives Cia a high five. "When I talked to your cousin at the party, I could sense his heart was yearning."

"How can you even sense that?"

"It's always better to be honest," Cia points out. "Breaking up with someone who's wrong for you is like peeing when you have a UTI. It burns while you're doing it, but it's healthier in the long run."

"We really need to update your metaphors," I tell her. She stares me down until I concede. "Fine, I'll *maybe* bring it up when I see him next."

Before they push me further, I take the plateful of finished polvoron to the area by the projector. I turn on the screen, and it keeps flashing a notice that it has no signal.

"Cia!" I call out. "How do you change the projector's settings?"

She glances from the kitchen. "Sorry, Jappy's the expert there."

"Why don't you ask him, sis?" Raph offers, and I hear the two of them have a laughing attack.

Whenever I do go on a real date, I'm not telling my friends *anything*.

12

TODAY'S ANTI-INSPIRATIONAL QUOTE is from *The Office*:

> "I am running away from my responsibilities. And it feels good."
>
> —*Michael Scott*

The way my insides feel all tangled makes me want to retreat to Cia's bathroom and grab the Vicks. Why am I so nervous?! Sure, Jappy and I got kaishao-ed, but he's still *Jappy*. Literally nothing has changed between the two of us. There isn't even an *us*—we're just two discrete individuals that occasionally interact.

"Shit." Jappy almost falls off his chair when I walk into his room. He grabs a shirt from the floor and throws it over his computer. "How did you get in here?"

"I opened the door," I answer, navigating around the sea of Jappy's clutter.

He kicks his feet to roll his chair in front of his desk. "But I locked it."

I narrow my eyes at him. "What are you hiding?"

"Nothing," he says, glancing back at his computer.

I've probably hovered around his monitor while he played *League* or *Dota* a million times. He wasn't even this jumpy when I once caught him playing some My Little Pony game.

Maybe he's not hiding a video game . . .

"Oh my god," I exclaim. "Were you watching porn?"

"What?"

His room suddenly feels a whole lot dirtier. I get that he's a guy, but Jappy is my best friend's older brother. A guy I've known since he was eight. It's like finding out the snowman from *Frozen* watches porn.

"Did you make sure the actors in the video were, like . . . treated properly?"

"Treated properly?" Jappy gives me a weird look, and I realize what I said could be interpreted as dirty.

"I mean, because a lot of porn actors, especially women, are underage and victims of human trafficking—"

"Chlo." He cuts me off and ruffles his hair so he looks like an even more disgruntled human pineapple than usual. "I was not. Watching. Porn."

"Don't worry. It's normal . . . I mean, it's not a big deal. I know that a lot of guys . . . girls too . . . all genders and identities . . . enjoy it." I ramble on, then I add, "You should enjoy yourself."

Ugh. That sounded dirty too.

He looks at me from his chair like I'm the one who was caught watching porn. "You know what? I'm just going to show you."

"Jappy, no! I don't need to see it."

Before I can shield my eyes, he unveils his computer, and the monitor shows me . . . a 3-D model of a building?

"See?" Jappy spreads his arms out. "Nothing sexy here."

He moves his mouse around, and a block with a face and legs stumbles through the model, which has row after row of houses. Except I've never seen any actual houses that were designed like this. They all look like different versions of grand modern nipa huts.

It's like a little world on the screen.

"Did you make this?" I ask, crouching lower to get a better look. There are so many details and patterns on every building. I can practically feel the bamboo screens beneath my fingertips and the narra floors beneath my feet.

"Just a side project," he says, pulling up another chair for me.

I sit and scoot closer to his desk while he moves the block man inside one of the houses. When Jappy clicks on a window, the block pushes the screens and exits onto a beautiful balcony. It's just like how I imagine the setting looks in those old love stories when a girl walks out to a suitor serenading her.

"Wait." I take the mouse from him and explore more parts myself. "Go deeper."

"Funny. That's what they said in the porn video I was just watching," he deadpans.

I elbow him. "Weirdo. I didn't know you were into architecture too."

"This doesn't classify as architecture." He grunts when the block climbs up the stairs. "He looks like a walking cardboard box."

"A cardboard box with character," I point out at the same time the block bumps into a wall.

After Jappy drags the block back onto the right path, he circles the cursor around the screen. "I, um . . . started working on this my senior year." Then he pauses, like he's choosing what words to say next. "Just fooling around when I had free time . . ."

While he's still struggling to get the words out, I interject, "Okay, *that* sounds like the description of a porn video."

The edges of his mouth tug up. When Jappy was little, Tita Gretchen used to always pinch his cheeks because he has these dimples that pop up when he smiles. I haven't really noticed them in a while. He usually doesn't smile long enough for anyone to catch them.

"So these are your designs?" I ask.

"Sort of. I used to copy my parents' sketches a lot, then I started improvising my own." His face lights up more and more as he talks. "I found a way to sketch through code. I made some calculations based on what parameters would work, like the number of windows per room or which way the sun would be facing—" He cuts himself off, then fidgets in his seat. "Sorry, all of this is super boring."

It's weird seeing him second-guess himself. I'm only used

to smug Jappy who lords over everyone with his "superior" knowledge.

"Those were the most interesting things to ever come out of your mouth," I say.

"Your aunt and dad find me very interesting," he counters.

"Yeah, about that . . ." I wince. "I don't think I ever said sorry that you were ambushed in that whole setup thing too." I lightly bump him on the shoulder. "So, um . . . Sorry."

Jappy gives me an amused grunt and returns the awkward bump. "We were going to mass either way. Plus, seeing you squirm was entertaining."

"I don't squirm," I insist.

He laughs and goes back to tweaking his model. "Is your aunt still on the hunt for potential roses?"

"God, I hope not."

"Yeah, about the dancing . . ." Jappy starts.

"If you want to back out of that, I can talk to Auntie Queenie," I offer.

I guess Jobert could still be a replacement.

He pauses and assesses me. "Do you want me in your roses?"

"Well, yeah." My cheeks feel warm when I realize how that sounded. He keeps a straight face, but I can already feel the relentless teasing building in his throat. "Not that I want to dance with you." I make myself clear. "It's strictly precautionary because I'm terrified of Auntie Queenie's alternatives."

"You might be missing out on her getting a Jabbawockeez member."

"I'll take my chances."

He smiles and shakes his head. "Yeah, I'll do it."

I whip my face toward him to make sure he isn't joking. He's weirdly not.

"I just wanted to make sure there wasn't, like . . ." He does this thing with his hands that makes him look like he's milking an imaginary cow.

"What *is* that?"

"Choreography," he says, like it's supposed to be obvious.

I laugh. "No, I'm pretty sure it's going to be awkward slow-dance swaying."

"Got it." He nods. "So like 'Let It Go' dancing?"

After I was finally done being reprimanded over the animation video, our whole prom table was ready to take off. I almost asked Jappy if he wanted to squeeze in a dance, but then the DJ switched the song to "Let It Go." Yes, the Elsa-building-an-ice-castle "Let It Go." If the constant reminder to make room for the Holy Spirit didn't douse any sparks, playing the *Frozen* soundtrack sure did.

"You're going to owe me after this, though," Jappy says.

I sigh. "Does it entail playing video games?"

Jappy pushes the monitor toward me. "So many worlds are just waiting to be unlocked."

I let him ramble on about the mechanics and rules of his latest gaming addiction. It's the least I can do after sucking him into my whole debut drama.

13

I SPIRAL DOWN a full-on YouTube wormhole once I get home.

Seeing Jappy's model sparked something inside me that I haven't felt in a long time.

After watching behind-the-scenes clips of Pixar animators working in studios, I click on the video of the animators behind *Coco* winning an Academy Award.

The part of the speeches that always makes me tear up is when the winners thank their families and the camera pans to their loved ones. It's cliché and embarrassing, but I've always dreamed about winning an Oscar. I've practiced my speech many times, using my pencil case, my shampoo bottle, or my hairbrush as a mic. In my fantasy, Beyoncé (who shocks the world with her presence at the Oscars) announces my win, then I get handed the statue from a reunited Destiny's Child. While "Independent Women, Part 1" plays, I raise my award and point to my parents, who are in the audience, beaming with pride.

I'm watching Domee Shi, the animator behind *Bao*, giving a shout-out to the nerdy girls who hide behind their sketchbooks when there's a single knock on my door, immediately followed by Pa entering my room.

I quickly sit up and wipe my eyes. To my father, a knock is not a gesture requesting approval for entrance. It's a signal that means *Surprise! Walking in without giving you a chance to deny entry.*

"We're getting hot pot for lunch tomorrow." It's the most words he's said to me since the animation-book fiasco.

"Um. What did I do?"

Pa hates hot pot. We only ever go when it's my birthday and that one time I actually got better grades than Peter. He always asks, *Why would I pay to go to a restaurant and end up doing all the cooking?*

"Queenie invited us," he replies.

"But we just saw her."

"She wants to have lunch again."

Is this another kaishao?

"Is Peter going?" I ask. If my cousin is going to be there, maybe that could be a matchmaking buffer.

Pa shakes his head. "Queenie said she wanted quality time with you."

Good lord. It *is* another kaishao.

"I, uh . . . already made plans," I say.

Pa's eyebrows hike up. "What plans?"

"Big plans."

Wow. A+ excuse, Chloe.

Pa clicks his tongue. "What's more important than time with your family?"

Avoiding matchmaking by my family.

I'm about to make another excuse when I realize I don't have much proof. What if Auntie Queenie really wants to have lunch? She has been going on and on about how I need to be taking debut planning more seriously. If Pa misinterprets this as me avoiding family, it might spiral into him forbidding me from going abroad.

"I'll be ready at eleven," I say.

He gives me a curt nod and leaves my bedroom.

I sigh and stow away my laptop. I can't possibly stay in bed with the dread of another awkward setup swirling in my gut.

When I kick off my covers, the animation festival flyer pinned up on my wall stares straight at me. I grab my tablet and take a seat at my desk.

The theme for the showcase is all about gunita, or "memory." When I first started drafting my entry, I imagined a corgi dancing to a K-pop song that Cia performed when we were kids. But then this memory popped in my head. Back in the first grade, our teacher told us to draw our families for an art project. All the kids called mine weird because I drew myself split in half between Pa and Ma. Our teacher said to show the portraits to our parents, and I was bracing myself for Pa to call it weird too. But instead, he asked me to sign my name on the back and taped the drawing on the wall in his study. It's still the sweetest thing anyone has ever done for me.

Then, for the first time ever, I started drawing *actual*

scenes from my life. Instead of making Cia a corgi, I sketched the day we became friends. I was in the school clinic with a cotton ball stuffed in my nostril since I had a nosebleed, when this random girl sat next to me. I faced the wall because I was understandably embarrassed by my bloody mess. Her reaction? She grabbed two cotton balls, shoved them up both nostrils, and introduced herself.

After that, I started drawing more and more vignettes from my memories. Moments I had with Cia, times I spent with my parents.

When I turned in the entry on the festival website, it felt even scarier than usual.

I let my hand wander as I add more frames to the video. For some reason, I keep feeling like working on the project even after submitting it.

The outside world fades into the background when I draw. I can forget about things like Pa's disappointment, and even Ma being so far away.

I think about how so many characters and stories started from one person's idea. I think about how mind-blowing it is that something from inside you can inspire another person in a potentially life-changing way. How wonderful it is that there are platforms in our world for ideas to be heard. People actually shut up and listen when they're in a cinema. Where else can you find people sitting for two hours and paying attention to what somebody else has to say?

Getting lost during these late-night doodling moments is when I believe I might make something that matters one day.

14

"**KEMBOT PA MORE,** titas! Move those sexy hips!" The Zumba instructor's voice fills the dance studio. "Pretend you're Shawn Mendes's señorita!"

Naturally, Auntie Queenie is front and center, staring more at her reflection in the mirror than at the very peppy instructor teaching the dance moves. Actually, half the class isn't looking at Peppy Girl, but rather at Peter, who's outdancing them all.

Before our lunch, Auntie Queenie called Pa to say that we should meet her at the mall for debut planning. From the look of total horror on his face, I don't think he expected debut planning to mean joining Auntie's Zumba class either.

Both of us are standing in the back, far away from my auntie's body rolling. Pa startles when the Zumba music cuts to sirens and the room gets drowned in red light.

"Ladies and gentlemen!" Peppy Girl announces. "Are you ready for our one-minute booty sprint?"

The room erupts into squeals and cheers.

What in the world is a booty sprint?

"You two!" Peppy Girl beckons to me and Pa in the corner of the studio. "Why don't you join us?"

"Sige na, Uncle!" Peter calls.

Pa clears his throat and waves her away. "No, thank you."

Wow, I've never seen his cheeks turn this shade of red before.

"Ahia!" Auntie Queenie yells from her spot. "You and Chloe are wasting your sexy hips!"

A remix of J.Lo's "Booty" starts blasting, and Peppy Girl leads everyone as they put their hands on their knees and (attempt to) twerk.

I'd rather my hips stay unsexy, thank you very much.

"Remember to power through your core!" Peppy Girl coaches. "Let your core pull those sexy hips! Imagine you're warming up for some bedroom action!"

All the ladies hoot and squeal, and I can feel the heat from Pa's face as he glues his eyes to his phone. We could have gone our whole lives without imagining Auntie Queenie or Peter warming up for bedroom action.

After what feels like the longest minute in history, my auntie and her friends finally stop twerking and follow Peppy Girl as she cools down with some stretching. The only time Pa looks up from his phone is when the instructor officially ends the class and people start exiting the dance studio.

"You two should've joined!" Auntie Queenie says when she and Peter approach us.

Peter wipes his forehead with a towel and adds, "It really is a great workout."

"Queenie," Pa says with a sigh. "What are we doing here?"

Auntie Queenie clicks her tongue and changes into her usual flats. "You know, Ahia, a little dancing would make you less grumpy." She takes out a piece of paper from her purse. "I was going to introduce you to the best instructor, Martina. She's a dancer for the *stars* and usually choreographs for celebrities, but she said she's willing to work on Chloe's debut. She was nice enough to give me a quote—"

"This is for one person?" Pa's eyes widen as he stares at the paper.

"Ahia, this is a once-in-a-lifetime event for your only daughter," Auntie Queenie scolds. "Naturally you're going to have to shell out some money."

"Auntie?" I chime in with the obvious question. "Why do we need a dance instructor?"

Auntie Queenie beams. "When I was watching the *ASAP* variety show last Sunday, I came up with a brilliant idea for your debut." She pulls out her phone and shows my dad a video of a girl singing a J.Lo song while a horde of topless men lift her up on their shoulders. "What if, in between the regular eighteen roses and candles program, we add a choreographed dance number? I already asked Martina, and she said she could do something similar for Chloe!"

No. Nonononono. There is absolutely no way that I am going to be carried by random naked men in front of my family.

"You want to hire backup dancers?" Pa exclaims, looking flabbergasted.

"Uh, Auntie," I interject before Pa passes out, "maybe a performance this . . . *extravagant* doesn't fit with my specific debut."

"Of course it does! You have to put on a show for people to remember, Chloe." Auntie Queenie double-winks at me.

Why would I want anyone to remember this?

"All of Peter's dance performances are ingrained in my memory. People are still talking about the last show they performed for the *World of Dance* championships." Auntie Queenie pauses and shows us a screenshot of an article she's sent to our family chat a million times. "His high school did a feature on him as their dance *phenom*."

"Someone from UP messaged me about tryouts for their street dance club," Peter adds.

Counting that for my scholar-mention tally.

Pa clicks his tongue. "Can't Peter do the dance, then? Since he's obviously qualified."

For the first time, Auntie Queenie looks like she's agreeing with Pa. "The article did say his choreography is masterful work."

But working with Peter means hanging out with Peter. And I still don't know whether to tell him about Pauline and the pointy-abs guy.

"I'm sure Peter has a lot on his plate," I say. "He's a UP Oblation scholar after all."

"Peter is used to multitasking." Pa faces Peter. "Making the dance isn't too much trouble for you, is it?"

"No, Uncle," Peter answers, standing up even straighter. He always did have annoyingly perfect posture.

"See what happens when you use your resources?" Pa returns Auntie Queenie's budget, his eyes brimming with smugness.

Auntie Queenie puts her hands on her hips. "We still have to settle on the studio rental."

Pa's eyes bulge once he sees the second part of the quote. "They're charging you *this* much?"

"It's their peak hours, Ahia," Auntie Queenie tries to explain, but Pa is already heading out the door. "Where are you going?"

"To talk to someone who actually has their head on their shoulders," he huffs.

"Ahia!" Auntie Queenie calls out. When he doesn't come back, she yells, "Don't you dare ignore me." Her flats hammer on the hardwood floor as she chases after Pa.

Which leaves me with Perfect Peter.

I break the silence hovering between us and ask, "Are you sure you're okay with doing this?"

"Yeah." He nods. "I actually just helped Pauline choreograph something."

Oh god. He brought up Pauline.

"Peter—" I start to say when he asks, "What's your go-to dancing style?"

"Uh . . . the good kind?"

He stares at me blankly. "Is that more contemporary or hip-hop?"

I sigh. "Peter, the only dancing experience I have is watching Beyoncé videos."

"Maybe there are some mixes here . . ." Peter goes to the

studio's sound system and tinkers with some of the cords. Suddenly, the speakers are blasting some trap song that sounds like a "Baby Shark" remix. I wince when Peter turns a knob that makes the kid singing "Baby Shark" sound like they're having a seizure.

"How're things with Pauline?" I ask over the music.

"Good," he says, focused on whatever he's doing with the sound system.

God. What's the best way for me to approach this? "You're still seeing her, right?"

"Now?" His eyes scan the room. "Is she here?"

Mental note: Remember that Peter takes everything *very* literally.

"No, she's not here," I say. "I wanted to ask because my friend follows Pauline's account and saw some . . . weird videos."

Peter looks up at me. "What was weird about them?"

"Um." Oh no. I can't say this out loud.

But my conscience is screaming at me that I can't hide this from Peter. No matter how I feel about him, I don't want him getting strung along. Cia's right. Breaking this to him is like peeing with a UTI. Painful, but necessary.

I carefully show him Pauline's page and let the couple videos do the talking.

Peter's jaw tenses, and he starts fiddling with the cords again. I brace myself for my cousin's heartbreak, but he just says, "Oh, that's Chris. Nice guy."

Out of all the reactions I imagined, this was definitely not one of them.

"Peter," I sputter. "I think this guy's been dating Pauline."

He nods. "For almost two years now."

The "Baby Shark" song fades and ends while I struggle to comprehend what Peter's telling me.

"Are you in a threesome?" I ask.

All he does is stare at me, and I panic, worried that I offended him.

"Sorry," I hurriedly add. "I meant to say throuple, or do you call it a three-way relationship? A *three*-lationship?"

Peter saves me from my rambling. "I'm not dating Pauline."

I wait for him to expound, but Peter doesn't offer anything else.

"But you brought her to family lunch," I point out. "And called her your honey dumpling."

He averts his eyes and keeps wringing the cords in his hands. "Pauline was doing me a favor," he finally says. "Ma kaishao-ed us without knowing Pauline already had a boyfriend, and we've been playing along. She went to the family lunch, and I've been helping her with some dance videos."

"Why didn't you tell Auntie Queenie that she was taken?"

He shrugs. "She was so excited and kept saying we were perfect for each other. I didn't want to let her down."

I should change his nickname from Perfect Peter to Saint Peter.

"What if you start liking some other girl?" I ask. "I know being the perfect son is your thing, but you can't keep lying about Pauline forever."

I stop talking when I notice Peter staring at me again. Oh

god. Is he going to start lecturing me about being so Americanized too?

"Boy," he suddenly says.

"Huh?"

"You said what if I like another girl." His eyes drift to the sound system again. "I've only liked guys."

"Oh."

OH.

"Is—is that okay with you?" Peter asks me, his voice turning quiet.

"Peter, of course." I look him in the eye to make sure he knows I mean it. "This is . . . *your* thing. Who you like isn't something you need to ask permission for."

"A lot of people aren't okay with it," he says. "I don't know what would happen if Ma found out . . ." Peter stops himself from saying anything else, and I notice the face he used to make when we were little kids.

He used to cry a lot when we were younger, and Auntie Queenie kept telling him to hold it in. "What would people say if they saw a boy cry this much?" she'd say. Ever since then, Peter would always suck his lips and bite the side of his cheek whenever his eyes misted over.

Our family has never been the exemplar for physical affection. The one time I hugged Peter was when we posed for a photo for Pa, but in this moment, the only thing that feels right is to reach for Peter's hand and hold it with my whole heart.

Before I let go, he gives my hand a squeeze back.

Another silence lapses between us until he says, "Can I ask you something?"

"Sure."

"Do you really think I'm perfect?"

Usually, Peter isn't a person I'd pinpoint as someone who needs an ego boost, but I'll give him one today. "Peter, I drank milk from a carton that called you the perfect child."

"That milk tasted like spit." He winces. "Maybe Jobert would like it."

My ears immediately pick up the grumbling undertone in his voice when he says Jobert's name. "*You* don't like Jobert?"

"He's the one who recommended that weird diet to Ma," Peter says with a groan. "I haven't tasted anything with flavor in weeks."

I can't help but laugh. It's unbelievable that it's Jobert who's bringing me and Peter together.

Peter then looks over to the studio door and lowers his voice. "Giving you a heads-up. Ma has a kaishao planned for your lunch."

Oh my god. I knew it.

"I'll tell you more later," he says when the stupid "Baby Shark" remix restarts. "Why is this playing again?"

I pull the plug, and the room turns silent. "Peter, tell me more *now*."

"Okay, okay." He quickly glances at the door again, then focuses back on me. "She was on the phone this morning and building you up to some friend. I didn't get any names, though."

I sigh. "What is wrong with your mother?"

"She has high blood pressure, and I think she's dealing with repressed childhood trauma caused by not being her parents' favorite."

I actually feel something snap in my head as I try to figure out how to even respond to Peter.

Before I can press him for more details, the studio door flies open.

"Great news! I got an amazing discount!" Auntie Queenie announces to the beat of her ballet flats. "Your father was terrifying the poor receptionist at the front desk, but I managed to smooth things over."

Pa clicks his tongue. "I was negotiating."

Auntie Queenie takes out her phone and begins typing. Is she texting the next kaishao boy now?

As I crane my neck to get a better look, she glances at the studio's wall clock. "Ooh, we should head over to Eight Seasons, or we'll miss our reservation."

I flash them my polite smile.

I am so, so screwed.

15

IF I WERE in charge of designing heaven, it would look something like Eight Seasons Hot Pot. As we get closer to the restaurant, I can practically taste the beef and fish balls melting in my mouth.

I don't care what Pa says—hot pot is the equalizer of dining experiences. Even if you have zero cooking skills, hot pot grants you the experience of being a chef. I mean, that's downright magical.

It's a shame that it'll forever be tainted by another ambush kaishao.

The restaurant host greets Auntie Queenie as soon as we enter. "We have your usual table available, Ma'am Queenie." He grabs some menus and motions to the dining area.

I try to peek around the front for signs of any boy who's close to my age. If I were a boy about to be set up, where would I hide?

Pa catches me while I'm checking behind the host stand. "What are you doing?"

I straighten and take one last look around. "Just checking to see if we're waiting on anyone."

Auntie Queenie clicks her tongue. "Ah, Chloe, our table is waiting."

Don't you mean a boy is waiting? I almost say.

The host leads us to the middle of the restaurant, where a large group sits at three joined tables. It reminds me of our family lunches. There are the parents, the kids, and . . . Raph?

I'm about to say hi when the man at the head of the table stands and calls out, "Jeffrey! Queenie!"

Pa waves at him and bumps me on my shoulder. "Greet your uncle Dennis."

I move to beso him. It's like God copy-pasted Raph's face on a man's body. I don't think I've ever met a dad with a baby face before.

"Ah, this is your daughter. I've heard so much about you!" He beckons Raph to stand up. "This is my son Raphael."

"Oh, we've met," I say. "He's my friend's—"

"Tutor," Raph cuts me off. "I used to help Chloe's friend with science."

Um. *What?*

Also, Raph used to ask *me* for chemistry help.

Before I can ask Raph what the hell he's talking about, Auntie Queenie and Pa are flashing me their freakishly huge smiles again. Seeing Pa smile like this is like seeing a flying cockroach—it just doesn't look natural.

"What a small world!" Auntie Queenie exclaims. "You two have friends in common *and* are both incoming college freshmen."

"Chloe likes drawing cartoons," Pa randomly points out, then turns to Raph. "Do you like watching cartoons?"

"Sure?" Raph says.

"Lots in common!" Uncle Dennis exclaims.

Yes, we're *basically* the same person.

"Do you have room for three more?" Pa asks.

I look at Pa. Did he just ask if we could join this giant family gathering?

"Of course!" Uncle Dennis says.

I look at him. Did he just agree to let three outsiders join their family gathering?

Ho-ly shit.

Is this . . . the kaishao?

They're setting me up with Raph?!

But . . . how can Raph's dad agree to a setup when his son already has a girlfriend?

"Chloe"—Uncle Dennis snaps me out of my thoughts—"your dad was telling me that you're studying in the US." I nod, and he asks, "Do you know what's beside the USA?"

"Um." I pause, trying to recall whatever geography I've learned. "Canada?"

"USB!" His shoulders and belly bounce as he laughs.

So this is where Raph inherited his sense of humor from.

But instead of laughing along with his dad, Raph has this weird grimace on his face.

"Come, come!" Uncle Dennis makes me trail him as he

introduces us to Raph's family. "This is my eldest, Dennison. We're here to celebrate his engagement."

When Dennison gets up, he extends his hand and gives me the world's most severe handshake. "Nice to meet you," he says.

"Um," I say, feeling like I'm doing a business transaction. "You too."

"I named him after me!" Uncle Dennis chuckles. "*Denni-son*. Like *son* of *Dennis*. Clever, right?"

Thank god Pa wasn't that clever. I would hate to be named Jeffreydaughter.

"That's his fiancée, Grace." Uncle Dennis gestures to the girl Dennison is pouring soup for. She waves at me, and I give her a wave back. Auntie Queenie swoops in and asks the couple about their wedding venue.

Uncle Dennis continues the introductions with Raph's mom, Auntie Cherry. I beso her, and she beams at Pa. "Jeffrey, you didn't tell me your daughter was so pretty!" she exclaims, then turns to face me. "You must tell me what skin care you use."

When she keeps inspecting my face, I realize she's actually waiting for an answer. "Usually . . . soap?"

"And this is my one and only mother." Uncle Dennis motions to the lady sitting in the seat across from Auntie Cherry. "Amah, this is Chloe. Her family manages the Zip and Lock company."

The woman scans me from head to toe. Even though she's a tiny lady, she *feels* tall. While I'm debating whether to beso her, her whole face lights up. "Is that Queenie?" she asks with her arms open.

Auntie Queenie goes for a hug. "Amah! You haven't aged a day."

Amah's face instantly softens when Auntie Queenie introduces me as her niece.

Once I'm done making the rounds, Uncle Dennis tells me to take the seat between him and Amah. Raph is sitting right across from me, next to my father, who's still smiling like he's about to go through a dental exam.

What's going on???? I send him a quick text under the table.

Raph just sits there and watches the soup in the pot boil, his expression annoyingly unreadable.

"Dennis, how's the dental business?" Pa asks.

"Ah, Jeffrey, it's the weekend!" He chuckles. "Let's not talk about work at a nice gathering like this. What do young people do for fun nowadays?" he asks, directing the question my way.

I take a sip of my water. All the attention is suddenly on me. This is the one time I'd rather talk about jeans and denim. "I watch movies and go jogging."

Auntie Cherry nods. "I'm always telling Raphael that it's important to find a girl who prioritizes fitness."

"Yeah, Cia is—"

Raph coughs violently like his lungs are going to heave out of his chest. "Sorry, got something in my throat."

Is he acting weird because he's sick?

"Chloe," Uncle Dennis says, "your dad mentioned he was so proud when you got into USC."

He did?

"I loved the photo collage!" Uncle Dennis continues. "It's very impressive."

Meanwhile, Pa is stirring the garlic and sesame paste in his sauce bowl, completely unimpressed. I don't know why I was expecting some change in enthusiasm. I keep gulping my water, pretending none of this gets to me.

"Chloe actually has her debut right before going abroad," Auntie Queenie adds, sneaking in a double-wink.

"Ah, to be eighteen again." Auntie Cherry smiles wistfully. "The planning must be so exciting."

"She's actually having a bit of trouble with her roses . . ."

This must be how Auntie Queenie closes deals at Zip and Lock.

"If you need another rose"—Uncle Dennis smacks his palm on Raph's shoulder—"Raphael is your man. The Siy family are regulars at debuts." He turns to Raph's grandmother. "Ma, remember when Dennison attended five debuts in one month?"

Zero amusement crosses Amah's face. "Yes, that's when he was dating the huan-a."

Uncle Dennis chuckles, but I don't find anything funny. *Huan-a* is Hokkien for "foreigner," and I hate it when my relatives refer to non-Chinese people as huan-a. I find it messed up that they'd call someone a foreigner just for being different.

Auntie Queenie sidetracks the conversation. "You must be so excited about Dennison and Grace."

Auntie Cherry nods. "It's hard to believe our baby is getting married."

Uncle Dennis elbows Raph. "Been trying to teach our bunso some moves to get him ready for his first girlfriend."

Wait. Did Raph not tell them about Cia? But they've been dating for more than a year . . .

Amah tilts her head at me and tells me in Hokkien that I have big ears.

I don't know if that's an insult or a compliment.

"She has bigger lobes than the other girls you introduced to Raf-Raf." Amah grins at Auntie Queenie. "We should've asked for help from the kaishao queen a long time ago."

Auntie Queenie pats Amah's hand, feigning embarrassment. "Just because I've had a couple successes doesn't make me the queen."

I quickly flag the waiter for a water refill. I'm going to need to down a whole pitcher to process the fact that I'm getting set up with my best friend's boyfriend.

This would be the perfect time to start drinking alcohol.

The waiter interrupts this bizarre living nightmare when he places plates of food in front of us. Pa is in the middle of dropping corn in the boiling pot when Auntie Queenie calls for his attention and points her lips toward the entrance. "Jeffrey, isn't that a colleague?"

"Oh, yes!" Pa abruptly drops his utensils. "That *is* a very important colleague." He rises to his feet and nudges Raph's dad. "You and Cherry should join. You might have some business matters to discuss."

Business matters? Our family sells the material that makes

jeans, and Raph's family cleans teeth. What business could they possibly have in common?

For some reason, Raph's parents are also ridiculously excited about this unnamed colleague and insist that the whole family join them. But when Raph and I move to stand, Amah tells us to stay put in Hokkien.

"Not a conversation for children," she tuts. "You two talk."

This is Mary the Queen all over again.

Everybody else makes their way out of the restaurant with Auntie Queenie constantly repeating that they'll just be a minute.

Many, many minutes pass. Raph and I sit among the multiple plates of uncooked fish balls and beef strips.

"They really just left us," I mutter in disbelief.

"I'm pretty sure my dad already paid for the meal."

I quickly kick Raph under the table.

"Ow!" he yelps, and glares at me.

"I can't believe I trusted you." I would pour the soup on his head if I weren't so scared his amah would kill me for murdering her grandson.

"Hey, hold on," Raph says, shielding himself with his chopsticks when I fling a fish ball in his direction.

"I actually thought you were going to be nice since you weren't her usual fuckboy type. Do you think you can find someone prettier or smarter than Cia?" I snap. "Just because you're a wannabe influencer, you think you can cheat and go on kaishao dates behind her back?! You know I only subscribed to your channel as a courtesy to my best friend, but now . . ." I pull out my phone and pound in the *Laugh with Raph* username.

"Chloe, please, I can—"

"I'm busy." I flash him my phone as I unfollow every one of his pages. Even the Instagram account he has for his dog.

Raph lets out a heavy sigh. "I—I don't know what to do." A bit of my rage melts away when I hear the crack in his voice. "I've tried to tell them, but I'm scared of what would happen if they found out she wasn't . . . *Chinese*."

Ah, shit.

"You have a Great Wall," I say.

He nods.

Okay, to explain the Great Wall, I think there needs to be some more clarification on who is a Fil-Chi—or a Chinese Filipino—in our world. In my case, Chinese is my ethnicity, and Filipino is my nationality. By blood, I'm probably something like 99 percent Chinese. But I call myself Filipino too, because I grew up here and it's what feels right to me.

This minutia matters when it comes to dating. To keep the community and culture intact, most Chinese Filipinos prefer that their children date and marry other Chinese Filipinos. I've broken down the two types of Chinese Filipino parents:

1. *The Great Wall parents:* These parents prohibit their children from dating people of other ethnicities. They build an invisible but powerful force field in front of their children that only makes way for Filipinos of Chinese descent.

2. *The Great Fence parents:* These parents have a *preference* for other Chinese Filipinos, but they'll give in if you push hard enough. You'll get quicker

access through the force field if you have Chinese heritage, but others could be allowed entry.

I'm lucky my parents have a Great Fence. But I have friends whose parents are more traditional and fall strictly under the Great Wall category.

"My brother's ex was Filipino, and my relatives made their lives miserable," Raph explains. "They'd talk about her like she wasn't there or act like they didn't even see her. My grandparents gave Dennison an ultimatum and said that he couldn't work for them if he married her." He exhales and shakes his head. "Fuck, you know how much I love Cia. And I don't want her to ever experience what Dennison's ex went through, so I didn't tell my family. But they've been introducing me to these random Chinese girls since I graduated, like whatever this lunch is." He gestures toward the empty tables. "I guess they're hoping to keep my Great Wall intact."

I was fully prepared to start hating Raph with every fiber of my being. But I can kind of see where he's coming from. "It's messed up that they ban you from dating Filipinos when you're living in the Philippines."

He raises and drops his shoulders. "They told Dennison that it's harder to date someone from another culture."

"Sounds like rationalizing for being racist."

Raph goes quiet and switches off the boiling pot at his side.

"Cia needs to know," I tell him.

After a beat, he sighs. "I just—I hate that it'll hurt her."

Me too.

16

MOVIE MAKEOVER SCENES are among my favorite things to watch. Some of them really haven't aged well, but watching Andy from *The Devil Wears Prada* strut and flip her hair with the glow from her new wardrobe still feels so satisfying.

Well, if these dresses were the movie wardrobe, I think the devil would wear *nada*.

Auntie Queenie called me up this morning saying that she had asked for a favor from Lara Capulong, the designer who did her wedding gown. "She just made some wonderful dresses that I think would be perfect for you!"

Now I'm in a fitting room, and it's like a reverse makeover scene, where every outfit just keeps getting worse and more . . . yellow. I put on one that makes me look like a giant human highlighter. Was Auntie Queenie *really* thinking about this dress when she said that? If I stood by the school supply section at the bookstore, people would mistake me for a Stabilo mascot.

"It's not bad." Cia holds in her laugh as I stare in horror at my reflection. She slides next to me in front of the full-length mirror. "It's like that time you were a banana for Halloween."

"And I was worried this shade was more mango."

While we wait for Auntie Queenie to come in with another dress suggestion, I ask how she feels about Raph's Great Wall and the whole hot pot incident.

"You've asked me that a billion times."

"So this is a billion and one."

"I am *O-K-A-Y*," she says, emphasizing every single letter. "I'm *fine*."

Raph messaged me a couple days ago to say that he'd had a heart-to-heart with Cia and told her everything: what happened with his brother, how his parents have been setting him up, even about the lunch where we were abandoned with seven boiling pots at Eight Seasons. He said he'd promised he would come clean to his family soon and that Cia took everything well.

Well, I know Cia better than anybody—and I'm not buying that she's fine.

When I grill her some more, she starts turning the conversation on me. "And when are *you* going to confront your auntie and tell her that she set you up with my boyfriend?"

"It hasn't really come up . . ."

More like I refuse to bring it up.

After that lunch at Eight Seasons, I was on a mission. I was going to message my auntie and tell her that I am completely capable of finding my own roses without her trapping me into these dates. It was all drafted in my Notes app, with perfect grammar and a couple carefully placed emojis to communicate that I was serious but also still respectful.

Just as I was about to press send, I suddenly . . . couldn't do it. It was like my finger choked. The thought of confronting Auntie Queenie feels empowering. Actually confronting her in real life is plain terrifying.

"Can't Tito Jeffrey talk to her?" Cia asks.

"You want me to ask for communication help from my dad?"

"You said you've been talking more," she points out.

"Yeah, about the fun run."

He's been messaging me all day to remind me that the fun run is this weekend. The scheduled start time is at five A.M., so naturally Pa keeps telling me that we have to get there at four.

Auntie Queenie pulls back the curtain of the fitting room. "Wow! Ang ganda!" she squeals. "Parang artista!"

"She really does look like a celebrity!" Cia adds, and I shoot her my stink eye. "We should take *lots* of pictures."

Auntie Queenie eyes me up and down. "You do look like someone I've seen on TV."

"Big Bird?" I offer.

"Who?" The joke goes completely over Auntie Queenie's head.

I lie and explain that Big Bird is some new rapper while Cia is on the brink of a laughing attack.

The longer I'm in this dress, the more I feel like it's squeezing my stomach. "Auntie, I don't think this is the right fit."

"Ah." She clicks her tongue. "The zipper didn't go all the way up." She grabs ahold of my back and quickly zips up the dress. The squeezing in my stomach has now extended to my rib cage.

"It's a little tight," I squeak.

"Chloe, that's fashion." Auntie Queenie double-winks at me. "Clothes are supposed to make you feel beautiful, not comfortable."

This dress is doing neither of those things.

Even though the dress is cutting off my oxygen supply, Auntie Queenie tells me to pose for pictures. She squints and frowns at her phone. "Chloe, you look like you're in pain."

"I show what I feel," I mutter.

"Um, Tita." Cia taps Auntie's arm. "I already got a lot on my phone."

Auntie Queenie clicks her tongue again and relents. "Okay. Chloe, you can put the dress back. I'll tell Lara we're done."

Cia glances at me. *You're welcome.*

I smile at her. *I've never loved you more than in this moment.*

When Auntie Queenie returns, I'm thankfully back in clothes that I can actually breathe in.

"Guess who's here!" she whispers, her eyes wide. "Cherry and Dennis!"

I turn to Cia, and I can tell she immediately recognizes the names.

"Cherry's having some dresses fitted for Dennison's wedding," Auntie Queenie says. "We should go say hi." She pulls down my hair and grimaces at the Beyoncé T-shirt I have on. "Maybe you can change back?"

While Auntie Queenie quizzes me about all of Raph's family members, I get a sudden light bulb moment that's as bright as a yellow highlighter.

"Auntie," I interrupt her telling me about how Auntie Cherry complimented her cavity-less teeth. "Why don't you go ahead while I fix up here?"

"Cherry and Dennis are waiting."

"I know, I know." I slap on my polite smile. "I just want to fix my hair first."

She considers me and slowly nods. "All right. But be quick."

Once Auntie Queenie is out of sight, I whip toward Cia. "I can introduce you!"

"*What?*"

"To Raph's parents!" I point toward the curtain. "You always kill at first impressions, and I can hype you up. They love Auntie Queenie too, so you'll get automatic plus points."

"Chlo—"

"And they'll *love* you. Uncle Dennis makes jokes that are as corny as Raph's, and Auntie Cherry loves girls with smooth skin—so with you, that's a jackpot."

"Chloe, stop!"

I shut up on the spot.

She crosses her arms, and her voice turns quiet. "I don't want to meet them."

"Oh. Okay." I ball my hands into my jean pockets, since I'm not sure what else to do. Should I be trying harder or apologizing?

My phone on the fitting room bench starts buzzing with a call from Auntie Queenie.

"She's probably looking for you." Cia hands me my phone, and I see the pleading in her eyes.

"I'll be really quick."

She scoffs and lets out a short chuckle. "I think I'll survive."

I force a smile and grab the gowns left in the fitting room. Once I step outside, I keep glancing back at Cia, trying to silently communicate that I'm sorry.

But she never looks my way.

17

NOT EVEN BEA Alonzo's monologue can crack Cia.

I picked *Four Sisters and a Wedding* for movie night since this film always triggers me and Cia to let out our feelings. When all the sisters start confessing to their mom that they know she has her favorites, I always feel like sharing my own childhood drama.

We're already halfway through the movie, and I keep waiting for Cia to open up about what happened with Raph's parents. My mind was so messed up this afternoon that I even got plain popcorn instead of cheese. I don't know how Cia can focus and mouth along with the movie lines.

Then Cia pauses the movie and sits up on her bed. "I just thought of something."

"That the two younger sisters should've gotten more screen time?" She lightly swats my shoulder, and I cross my legs to face her. "What's up?"

"You know how your aunt set you and Raph up?" she says. "What if you told your families that you're dating?"

I wait for Cia to say she's joking, but the punch line never comes. So I very eloquently ask her, "Huh?"

"Well, don't you want to stop your aunt from doing all this kaishao stuff?" she asks. "If you two are dating, Tita Queenie and Raph's parents would have to stop all the matchmaking! If Peter managed to pull it off with Pauline . . ."

"I don't think Peter and Pauline are the couple we should be aspiring to."

She keeps staring at me expectantly.

"Wait." I rub my temples. "You're seriously suggesting I date Raph?"

"Not *actually* date," Cia says. "But he can be the alibi you need."

"Are you high? Because I really wouldn't judge you if you are."

"I am not high on drugs, Chloe. I am high on this idea."

I give her my own version of the disapproving look.

"I mean, isn't love like a . . . Netflix account?" she says. "It's meant to be shared." She offers me the bowl of popcorn in the wake of this very questionable metaphor.

"Cia," I say, feeling my head start to hurt. "Your boyfriend is not your Netflix account. I don't want to *share* Raph."

"Come on, Chlo. It makes sense." She leans forward. "You need a fake boyfriend to get your family off your back. If Raph's parents think you two are dating, that will get them off *his* back. It's a win-win situation."

"And how are *you* winning in all of this?"

"Well, I wouldn't have to worry about his parents introducing him to more girls. If his family thinks he's dating you, everything would be so much easier."

"Wouldn't it be easier if he told his family about you?"

"Yeah, but he has that Great Wall." Her voice trails off as she glances at her phone. The wallpaper is a photo from when Raph took Cia out of town to visit her favorite museum. That date was the first time he said he loved her.

"But it's messed up," I say. "The fact that you're Filipino shouldn't even matter. I mean, I feel more Filipino than Chinese. I've never even been to China."

"But when people look at you," she says, "they think you're Chinese. It still matters."

There were times, especially when we were little kids, when I'd hear my aunties call Cia my "Filipino" friend. I realize I never asked her how she felt about that.

"You're right." She laughs and shakes her head. "It was dumb."

"It wasn't *so* dumb."

"You're just saying that because you feel sorry for me."

"Partially true," I admit. "I don't think I can fake-date your boyfriend, but any other thing you need from me . . ." I give her a salute. "First volunteer."

A smile crawls across her lips. "Even if I want to use a friendship coupon?"

I pause. "Are you going to bitch-slap me?"

She hops off her bed and takes the stack of index cards I

gave her from her desk drawer. Her smile gets even bigger when she flashes me the one that says "Anti-Self-Deprecating Makeover."

I groan. "Can we do the bitch-slap one instead?"

"You don't want to be wearing fruit-inspired dresses forever," she says, waving her hands around. "Finding the perfect dress is like getting your first period—"

I grab her stuffed corgi and hold it to her face. "Please spare me and your innocent stuffed animal the rest of that menstruation metaphor."

There's no use in trying to talk Cia out of this. She's already throwing half her wardrobe at my face.

"Cia, I look like Minnie Mouse," I say after reluctantly slipping something on. This red polka-dot dress is cute on Cia, but it makes me look like I should be gathering sheep.

"Piso," she says, holding out her travel jar.

"Hey, that wasn't an insult," I complain. "I aspire to be more like Minnie. That mouse has kept the same guy chasing after her for decades."

On the friendship coupon, I stupidly added that I had to donate to Cia's travel fund if I said anything self-deprecating during the makeover. I wrote it as a joke, but Cia seems determined to milk me until I finance her whole trip to Greece.

She shakes the jar, and I drop in a coin.

"That dress really doesn't fit you, though," she says, going back to her closet.

"Wait. You can't make me pay for insulting myself, then go ahead and insult me. That's like extortion."

"That's called doing business." She taps her temple. "Your

dad would be proud of this transaction." Then Cia lets out an excited gasp. She smiles at me and pulls out *the* red dress, the one with a long slit up the right leg.

Raph almost had a heart attack when Cia showed up to his graduation ball wearing that dress. It was hosted by Raph's school, so our teachers from Mary Immaculate couldn't do anything, but there was some super-uptight parent who thought Cia should've been suspended on the grounds of that leg slit.

"You're joking," I say.

"You don't have to wear it to your debut." She pushes the dress at me. "I just want to see it on you."

My hands stay firmly at my sides. "That dress would be an even worse fit on me."

"Why? Because it would actually show that you have a body?"

"Having a body is not the same as having a good body."

She gives me a disapproving look, and I drop another coin in the jar.

I finally relent and grab the dress. "We're ending the makeover once I put this on." After I shimmy the dress past my hips and hold in my stomach so Cia can zip it up, I turn around and throw my hands in the air. "Happy?"

The edges of Cia's mouth tug up like she's trying to hold in a laugh.

"Okay, I told you this would look ridiculous." I reach back for the zipper, but Cia stops me.

"Chlo, wait. You look *amazing*." She spins me to face the mirror.

I would never in a million years show off this much skin, but I do look kind of . . . not bad? I hate it when Pa forces me to wear red whenever a relative has a birthday, because red comes off as a hey-look-at-me sort of color, but the girl in the mirror seems like someone people *would* look at.

I startle when Cia's speakers start playing Beyoncé's "Naughty Girl." Cia plops on her bed and sings along while Beyoncé croons, "I'm feeling seeeeeeexxxxxxxy."

"Imagine the parents' reaction if the glee club performed this at the variety show," I say, sliding next to her. We both laugh when Cia's voice cracks as she tries to reach the song's falsetto. When the song finishes, I ask, "Are you sure you're okay?"

Instead of the usual brush-off, Cia takes a deep breath. "Raph said he's not ready to introduce me to his family."

"I'm sure he'll change his mind if you say you want to meet them."

"I don't want to meet them," she says quietly. "What if . . . Raph hasn't introduced me for a reason?" Cia shakes her head, and I feel the bed shudder with her breaths. "Maybe he knows his family wouldn't like me, or that they'd think I'm not good enough." She whimpers and says softly, "Maybe he knows there's something wrong with me."

"Hey." I immediately cut her off. "This is not on you. It's their loss that they've never met you. Do you know how many people would be announcing to the whole world that they were dating *the* Maria Patricia Sotto Torres?" I reach over to give her a hug, but she waves me off.

"I'm fine. I'm fine!" She changes the music to an upbeat

Saweetie song. "Don't give me that concerned look." She points at me.

"I'm not!" I totally am. Only someone numb to emotions wouldn't be concerned right now. "Letting out your feelings is good for the soul, Cia."

"Says the person who's allergic to crying."

How did this turn into me getting called out?

She stops and beams at me. "You know what'll really take my mind off things?"

"Healthy emotional coping?"

"Ice cream," she says. "We still have tons of leftovers from the party."

I sigh. "If I feed you, will you promise to think about what I said?"

"Sure!"

The love hiccups in *Got 2 Believe* are a hundred times more convincing than her "sure."

I get up, and the clothes I left on the chair are gone. "Didn't I put my stuff here?"

Cia hunches her shoulders. "Guess you have to stay in the sexy red dress a little longer. Maybe it's a sign you should try on some sexy shoes."

"We're seriously never doing another makeover after this." I give her a warning look and head downstairs.

Before I make a beeline for the kitchen, I spot Tita Gretchen's heels by the front door.

One of my core beliefs: High heels are a product of a sexist society that forces women to suffer for the sake of their appearance.

On the other hand, they really do make your legs look amazing.

I make sure the coast is clear and slip on the black heels. Wow. I always thought I'd be a disaster in heels, but. Check. Me. Out. I could totally pass for a Beyoncé backup dancer in these stilettos. I step out and prepare to strut when I feel my leg start to wobble. I grab on to the wall so I don't crash to the ground.

"Whoa." I suddenly hear a voice from behind me.

I'm going to forever look back at this memory as one of my life's most embarrassing moments, aren't I?

Heat rushes through my cheeks as I cling to the wall for dear life. "Do you mind removing the right shoe?" I ask Jappy. "I'm going to roll my ankle if I move."

Jappy doesn't say anything as he helps me. Once I'm free from the shoes of death, I quickly wrap my arms around myself in an attempt to cover up the dress.

"What?" I ask when he gives me this strange look through his glasses.

"Nothing." He clears his throat. "Just rethinking the lies from my childhood. When I watched *Cinderella*, I got the impression that Prince Charming was supposed to put *on* the shoes, not take them off."

I roll my eyes. "I'm only down here to get ice cream."

"See, *Cinderella* didn't prepare me for that either. What else did these movies get wrong?"

"Maybe making all those little boys believe they were Prince Charming?"

He answers with a grunt and leads the way to the kitchen.

"Going somewhere?" I ask when I notice his laptop bag.

"Hanging out at Sean's."

"Oh, right. Your friend with the PlayStation?"

"Xbox. Completely different," he says, and I laugh when he looks offended. "Got another hot church date?"

"I'm not sure if you've heard, but my dad doesn't let me go on dates if I know they're dates in advance." I open the freezer and grab the tub of cheese ice cream. "Want some?"

Jappy gives me his judgy eyebrow and reaches for the tub of vanilla. "The superior flavor."

"It's bland like your personality," I tease.

"And your flavor is cheesy like yours," he shoots back. Jappy opens the cupboard and hands me bowls and spoons.

"Auntie Queenie had a new location for my last kaishao, though," I tell him.

"Christ the King?"

"Even better." I smirk. "Hot pot."

"Wow. I could've gotten food on our date?" He laughs when I shove him. "So who was kaishao boy number two?"

"Just . . ." Maybe spilling Raph's secret to the guy who already hates him isn't the best idea. "Some random family friend," I say. "It was all an awkward mess."

He leans on the counter and scoops some ice cream into his bowl. "Maybe you'll like the next guy they set you up with," he points out.

"No way."

He faces me. "So you're giving up on the whole male species, then."

"To be honest, your kind hasn't really impressed me."

Jappy grunts and rolls his eyes at my joke.

"Would you actually go out with someone you got set up with?" I ask.

He shrugs. "At least you don't have to go through the whole hassle of *finding* someone. It's a convenient shortcut."

"Some things shouldn't get shortcuts."

"If you click, you click."

"You make it sound like some computer thing."

Jappy holds up his bag. "These devices can make magic happen, Chlo."

I groan, and he taps my bowl with his spoon. "How about you?"

"Oh, I have many kaishao boys in line. We're thinking of bringing even more family members to our next date."

He smiles at that. "Your dad can document your kaishao adventures on his Instagram."

"My claim to fame," I say, laughing. "Isn't dating supposed to be special, though? Like, finding your person should be as monumental as . . . climbing Mount Everest. This whole kaishao thing is like taking a shortcut to your destiny. I feel like it takes the magic out of it."

My cheeks feel warm when I realize how long I've been rambling.

He narrows his eyes. "So instead of taking a leisurely stroll with a kaishao, *you* want to torture yourself by scaling the planet's highest mountain?"

"Yes, exactly," I deadpan.

It's not that I've sworn off guys. My heart palpitating at the sight of Miles is proof that I appreciate the male form. But whenever I hear Tito Vince and Tita Gretchen's love story, it always seems like the universe laid out all these signs that they should be together. No one writes songs about love when it's arranged by people's relatives.

"Oh, I almost forgot." I go to my Vimeo page on my phone and click on the folder with the block prototypes. "I drew up some characters for your model."

I show him the little block corgi, the square-headed people, and the robot that looks like it was built with Legos that I animated. Jappy moves closer and scrolls through my videos.

When he doesn't say anything, I add, "You don't have to use any of them. I still think the block man in your model was cool—"

"Is this me?" He points to the sketch at the bottom.

"Yeah, kinda? I thought it would be cool if a cartoon you was walking through the model."

He keeps staring at the screen, and I'm suddenly worried that he hates it all.

"I can't believe you drew me," he finally says.

"It's a rough draft."

He cracks a smile. "Yeah, I don't think you nailed the hair yet."

"Well, it's hard to capture this *mess*," I say, ruffling his hair.

He looks at me for a weirdly long time.

"What?"

"This is all really . . ." He bumps me on the shoulder with his fist. "Thanks."

I bump him back with my bowl. "Weirdo."

"You're telling me this drawing doesn't look like a brown Prince Charming?"

"No."

"You're a really harsh kaishao date."

"Hey." I swing toward him. "Do you want Auntie Queenie to set you up?"

He narrows his eyes. "Is this a joke?"

"I mean, if you're looking, she loves matchmaking." I nudge him. "And that would take her mind off me."

"I'll pass." He reaches out and steals a spoonful of my cheese ice cream, and his face cracks into that dimpled smile of his.

18

SOME DAYS, I find my six o'clock runs with Pa relaxing. There are even days that I look forward to them. But waking up at four o'clock in the morning is something I will never be fond of.

The sun isn't even close to rising when Pa barges into my room. At first, I think I must still be dreaming because he's wearing a Spider-Man tank top. Pa is not a tank-top person. I don't know if I've ever seen this much of his arms before.

I didn't realize the fun run we signed up for had a super-hero theme. Good thing I have an oversized Scarlet Witch T-shirt in my closet.

The run is near Mall of Asia, which usually takes at least an hour to get to. If there isn't any traffic yet on EDSA, that's a sign that it's way too early.

When we arrive, the huge speakers are blaring the "Baby Shark" remix I heard at the dance studio, and a very peppy girl is onstage with a microphone headset like she's a pop star.

Wait. That looks like Auntie Queenie's Zumba instructor. I don't find it at all surprising that she hosts five o'clock fun runs.

I sit on the curb while Pa and the other runners warm up. One guy is wearing a full-on Batman costume. He has everything from the cape to the mask to the utility belt. He's even wearing his underwear over his pants.

"GOOD MORNING, RUNNERS!" the Peppy Girl's voice booms through the speakers. "ARE WE READY TO RUN?"

No one answers because it's freaking five in the morning.

"Doo doo doo doo doo doo!" she sings along as she dances. The song finally ends, but Peppy Girl is still screaming her head off. "TWENTY MINUTES UNTIL WE BEGIN, RUNNERS! WOO-HOO!"

I slap my face a couple times to wake up and stand. I guess I should stretch a little. I don't want to end the day with no sleep *and* a pulled hamstring.

I'm bending over with my butt sticking out when I notice a lady behind me in a short all-white dress and visor. She looks like she's on her way to a tennis club, not a fun run.

She lifts up her visor, and it's . . . Auntie Queenie.

I automatically spring back up.

"Ready for some running?" she asks, jogging in place next to me.

Maybe I'm still asleep and stuck in some very realistic, very bizarre nightmare.

When Pa joins us, Auntie Queenie asks him if he wants to borrow one of her Nike wristbands.

"This is so fun!" She bends her hips and surveys the area. "It's a good thing I found a costume in time."

"Which superhero are you supposed to be?" Pa verbalizes the question in my head.

She puts her hand on her hip and poses—which leaves us even more clueless.

"Naomi Osaka!" she says after Pa and I have zero guesses. "A modern-day superhero with really cute outfits."

"I didn't know you were into running, Auntie," I say.

Or that you were joining.

"It's a great combo with my Zumba." She bops me with her elbow. "My friend's son is also coming to this same run."

Oh god.

Not this shit again.

No. More. SONS.

If I don't say anything now, she's really going to keep setting me up wherever I go.

"Auntie," I start, feeling low on sleep and patience. "I appreciate you thinking of guys for my eighteen roses program, but can we please . . . stop? I'm really fine with Pa, Uncle Nelson . . . Peter can dance for two people," I point out. "We don't even have to fill the whole eighteen roses. I can have a debut that has sixteen."

Auntie Queenie clicks her tongue. "Hay, Chloe. The trick to meeting boys is to collect and select. You're supposed to collect as many potential suitors as possible before you select the best one. You can't stop after two!"

Before she can continue, Pa places his hand on Auntie

Queenie's shoulder. "If Chloe isn't comfortable with this, then maybe we should cancel."

Are Pa and I actually on the same wavelength?

My vision of a modern-day superhero: Jeffrey Liang in a Spider-Man tank top.

"But Miles is already on the way," Auntie Queenie says.

Did she just say *Miles*?

C'mon, Chloe. Of course it's a different Miles. There must be a hundred different guys named Miles my age.

"He's usually at the gym this early anyway," Pa says.

Wait. I was going to get set up with Miles Chua? ASMR-voice, basketball superstar Miles? I'm not a fan of this whole kaishao craze we have going on, but when it's *Miles Chua*?

While Auntie Queenie complains to Pa about how improper it is to cancel at the last minute, I interject. "I mean, if he's already on the way . . ."

Joy immediately floods Auntie Queenie's face. "See, Chloe? Collect and select!" Her phone starts ringing, and she scurries away a little too excitedly.

"You don't mind?" Pa asks when we're left all alone.

"I know how much it means to Auntie Queenie," I lie. I feel slightly guilty when Pa gives me a nod of approval.

Okay, I have ample time to prepare for when Miles gets here. I can be a good conversationalist. I have very proficient language skills. Let's not forget that I was the Mary Immaculate third-grade spelling bee champion. I was the only eight-year-old who knew how to spell *mustache*.

I see Auntie Queenie waving at us and ushering Miles in our direction.

Let's go, Chloe. You are ready to converse, to dazzle him with your eloquence.

Then he attacks me with that damn smirk again. "'Sup, Chloe?"

And . . . I got nothing. I've completely forgotten how humans say hello. I can't even remember if there's an *e* at the end of *mustache*.

God. The only restroom nearby is the porta-potty, and it would be *way* harder to have an emergency freak-out session in those close quarters than in Cia's bathroom.

Auntie Queenie thankfully picks up the conversation. "Did you know Miles is going to play basketball for the De La Salle Green Archers?"

"He's going to be the Philippines's Steph Curry!" Pa mimics shooting a basketball, which looks more like him doing jazz hands in the air.

Auntie Queenie glances at Miles. "Where's your race bib?"

"All the spots were taken when I tried to sign up, Auntie," Miles says. "I was thinking I could run nearby and catch up with you later."

"Nonsense!" Auntie Queenie brushes this off. "How can it be a fun run without the run?"

And then I have to avert my eyes because Pa starts taking his shirt off.

WHAT IS MY FATHER DOING?

Pa hands his tank top and bib to Miles. "Here! You can run with my number."

Miles stares at Pa's shirt, while trying to shield his eyes

from my father's nakedness. "Uncle, are you sure? I don't want to take your place."

"Of course! We're here for you to have fun," he says, slapping Miles on the back.

"We'll go around the mall down there and wait for you two," Auntie Queenie says, and Pa tells me to text him when we're done.

Wait. I didn't want to be *alone* with Miles.

I look at Pa, hoping he'll understand my telepathic message—*Please don't leave me alone with this perfectly crafted human being*—but he doesn't hear me.

So it's just me and Miles.

Who then takes off *his* shirt and slips on Pa's tank top.

Of course, the guy would have abs.

The tank top also highlights his *really* nice arms. Everyone should take up basketball if it means they'll get arms like those.

My awkwardness with Miles is about to reach an all-time high. I snap out of staring at his arms and start searching my brain for things to talk about.

Relax and build from the momentum you had at Cia's party. Remember Greece? Being solid? All your moves!

Ugh. He's the buff one. *He* should be the one carrying the weight of this conversation.

"Hey?" He gestures toward Batman and Iron Man doing hip circles in front of us. "Who do you think's faster?"

"I'm betting on Batman," I say. "The underwear over the pants just screams commitment."

He laughs. "You're funny."

You're not only solid, Chloe! You're funny!

The music gets louder, and Peppy Girl tells everyone to gather by the starting line.

While we maneuver through the rest of the runners, Miles says, "Just a heads-up. I don't really stop during fun runs."

"Me neither."

We find a spot close to the starting line and do some quick last-minute stretches.

"If I get too far ahead," he says, "I can run back and find you."

I stop my stretching. "What makes you think *you're* the one who's going to get ahead?"

He crouches and sets his right foot in front of his left. "I get really competitive."

"RUNNERS, ARE YOU READY?" Peppy Girl's voice suddenly booms through the speakers.

"Well, so do I." I plug in my earphones and see a glimmer of Miles's sexy smirk.

"FIVE, FOUR, THREE, TWO . . ." The starting pistol fires, and I, along with the rest of the crowd, surge forward. Ushers with flags direct the runners to the paths for the three-kilometer, five-kilometer, and ten-kilometer runs. I follow the superheroes headed toward the 10K flags.

I move past Miles, and he has to burst into a sprint to slide in front of me. I go faster, but he cuts me off again as soon as I come close to overtaking him. I go to his right, and he blocks me on the right. I go to his left, and he blocks me on the left.

Oh . . . okay.

He'll do anything to make sure he's ahead of me. He's a pretty boy *and* a petty boy.

Soon we're coming up to my favorite part of these fun runs, the refreshment stands. I always feel like one of those big-time race car drivers who get a whole crew to fuel them up during pit stops.

I'm about to pause for a drink when I notice Miles is watching me. As I slow down, he cuts his pace too. His eyes stay on me as I grab a cup, and he takes his own. I start sipping, and he straight up chugs his water.

"We're still competing here?" I laugh.

"Gotta get your head in the game, Chloe Elaine." He tosses the cup in the bin and starts running.

I go along with Miles and keep myself a few feet behind him.

After a while, he turns and smirks. "Tired?"

"Just getting started!" I shout back.

He swivels around and keeps running. We go through most of the course the same way—me trailing behind and him frequently checking on me. I almost get distracted when we run up a bridge that overlooks the city skyline. From here, you can see all the billboards with celebrities on them and the highway starting to fill up with the morning rush traffic. As the sun rises, it illuminates everything from the tips of the skyscrapers to the corrugated roofs of the houses below.

When I was writing my college essays, Ma arranged for me to meet with this counselor from the US. His advice was to do my best to "paint a picture of the poverty in the Philippines." Show how hard it was to come from a "third-world country," and how I was seeking a better life in America. But that was his story about my country, not mine.

People in America think that a ticket to their country is a

blessing from the gods that everyone in the world is praying for. They don't see the faces of Filipinos when they come back home. They don't see how big their smiles are once their plane touches down, how they burst out of the airport and soak up that familiar humidity, how they envelop both their families and their country in a hug. Sure, I want to go to college in the US, but it's not because I hate the Philippines. My country isn't perfect, but I don't think people love their home because it's perfect.

People love their home because it's home.

I snap a quick picture and then focus back on the run. Miles is a bit farther away, but I can feel that my lead is within reach. Especially now that his pace is slowing and his breaths are becoming labored.

We close in on an usher holding a sign that says LAST 50 METERS.

That sign is my cue.

I sidestep Miles and blow right past him. I can't help but smirk as I look back and ask, "Tired?"

I should do this smirking thing more often. It makes winning feel *so* much better.

I hear his grunts and his steps pounding behind me, but I keep building momentum. I turn a corner and spot the balloon arch that forms the finish line. The speakers blare the familiar voice, "GO, RUNNERS, GO!" Jesus, the Zumba instructor is my new hero. She has more stamina than all the runners combined.

I take a deep breath and sprint the last few meters. I know it sounds strange, but I actually love the feeling of sprinting.

Not the feeling after sprinting when you're dying and want to throw up, but that moment when all your surroundings blur and you're running as fast as you possibly can. I think it's the closest humans can get to flying.

I run through the finish line seconds ahead of Miles.

"Now I'm tired," I wheeze with my hands on my hips.

And instead of answering, he takes off his shirt.

Oh.

Hello.

Seriously. There should be some warning before he undresses like that.

He wipes his face and pulls me in for a side hug. "Nice race."

My heart almost skyrockets out of my chest.

Our moment is interrupted when Pa suddenly appears at the finish line. "There you two are! Ang bilis ninyo!" Pa imitates a car zooming with his hand. "How was the run?"

"Really good, Uncle," Miles says.

"Where's Auntie Queenie?" I ask.

"Ah, she took a power nap while waiting," Pa says, and pulls out his phone. "We should take a picture!"

Why does Pa always want to document moments when I'm gross and sweaty?

Miles and I follow Pa as he goes to the balloon arch because it's the most Instagrammable spot. I stand about a foot apart from Miles while Pa tries to find the best vantage point.

"Get closer, you two!" Pa says.

"I think you should be in the middle, Pa."

"No, no. I want to take a picture of just you young ones."

Never in my life has Pa not wanted to be in a photo.

Pa continues to direct us. "Closer, closer! Compress!"

Sure, I felt that we had a moment during the fun run, but I'm so not ready to be compressed to Miles's bare chest. He inches toward me, and I glue my arms to my sides.

"Chloe, why are you slouching?" Pa says. "Stand up straight! You two look like strangers! Miles, why don't you put your arm around Chloe?"

I groan. "Pa, just take the picture."

PLEASE.

"What's your username?" Pa asks Miles after he finally takes the shot. Pa always posts in real time.

Miles reaches for his phone and shows Pa his page.

"All right. What do you think?" Pa flashes us the picture with a caption that has ten hashtags.

Seconds later, I get a notification that @JeffreyLiang11 has tagged me in a post, and that @GoingTheExtraMiles now follows me on Instagram.

19

CIA SAYS THAT it's unhealthy for me to be checking my email every second. So I decide to be a little more patient and wait *two* seconds.

The festival website posted that the showcase finalists would get notified this week, and I keep refreshing my inbox hoping that a congratulations email will suddenly pop up.

Even on my call with Ma, I keep checking my phone on the side to make sure I don't miss anything.

My heart speeds up when my phone buzzes with a notification from @GoingTheExtraMiles.

Ever since the fun run, Miles has been replying to and commenting on my posts. Last night, he wrote **Solid show** when I posted a screenshot of the anime I was watching. Twelve-year-old me would freak if she knew anime could become a reason a guy would notice me. And this morning, when I posted a video of penguins dancing to "Formation," he asked me, **what's up?**

I replied, **aside from the ceiling?**

And just now, he wrote **lol**.

I think we're *actually* flirting.

"What are you smiling at?" Ma's voice snaps me out of my thoughts.

Whenever my parents would catch me smiling at my phone, I never understood why they always assumed I was talking to some boy. Who would have thought that I'd actually get caught smiling because of a real-life, nonfictional guy? I'm this close to gloating to my mother that there's someone in my DMs.

"Nothing." I tone the volume down on my joy and focus on the computer.

"Did you hear back about the showcase?"

I shake my head and refresh my inbox one more time.

"Don't worry, babes," she says. "It's still early. I was telling your dad we could get hot pot after to celebrate!"

I haven't told Ma about the whole kaishao madness or the fact that Pa might be the last person who'd want to celebrate anything animation related.

"What's wrong?" she asks.

"Nothing." I lift the corners of my mouth.

She purses her lips. "You know you can always talk to me, right?"

I hate it when people see through my polite smile.

"Yes, Ma."

"Even when I'm far away," she says. Then she adds, "We can talk outside of our weekly calls."

"I'm fine," I say. "Things have been really . . . hectic lately. Just been thinking a lot about leaving."

"How's your dad taking it?"

"Good!" I blurt out.

Ma squints at the screen. "Chloe, are you sure everything's okay?"

I nod. "Yup! Everything here is *great*."

My heart and mind are racing, telling me to end the conversation before I spill about Pa suggesting I stay home for school. The cardinal rule of having separated parents: Never complain about one parent to the other. Nothing hurts Pa and Ma more than when they feel like I'm picking one of them over the other. I love my parents, but I wish it didn't feel like I'm always choosing between two different teams.

I turn away from my laptop, pretending that I heard something. "Ah, sorry, Ma, I'm meeting Auntie Queenie for a debut thing. I'll talk to you soon, though!"

"Wait." She points her finger at the screen, and I freeze. "Promise you'll tell me what's going on when you're ready."

"Yes, Ma."

"Good." She nods. "And don't stress too much, babes. I'm proud of you no matter what."

I give her a genuine smile this time. "Love you, Ma."

"Love you too."

SOMEONE SHOULD'VE WARNED me that dancing is more tiring than running a 10K.

"Peter, my butt can't move that way."

For his "warm-up," Peter has been trying to make me do

this move where I have to kick my leg back like a horse trying to wallop someone in the face.

"It's hard when you're not used to it," he says, executing the move perfectly like some magical dancing unicorn. "Keep practicing, and you'll get closer to the desired results."

The only thing I'm getting closer to is a pulled ass cheek. I shake out and stretch my legs. "Why don't we move on to the actual dance?"

When I first arrived at the studio, I kept trying to tell Auntie Queenie that the debuts I've been to never had an additional dance number, but nothing registered. It was like I was talking to the studio mirror. Then she said she forgot something outside and stepped out, leaving me to warm up with Peter.

He plugs his phone in to the sound system and increases the volume. "This is all still a work in progress."

My jaw almost drops when the heavy bass of "Partition" starts to play. "You want me to dance to *this*?"

"You said you liked Beyoncé."

"Yes, but I'd rather not dance to a song about having sex in a limo."

Peter waves me off. "It's all about attitude, Chloe." He restarts the song and stations himself in front of the mirror. "It's very simple choreography."

I stand beside him, and he begins snapping.

Okay, I've snapped before. I can follow this.

"Then you pretend you're holding a steering wheel, but with purpose," he says while mimicking driving a car.

I follow the move, but with less purpose.

That's when his body starts going a million miles a minute. "One, two, three, four, five, six, seven, eight!" Peter counts as he performs a sequence of moves my body is not capable of.

I was already aware that Peter is a good dancer, and he's proving that fact a million times over with everything he's doing. It's physically impossible for me to follow, but he makes every step look so easy. There's this move where he pretends he's wiping sweat off his forehead, and he does it with so much swag. He's so good that he makes sweating look cool.

Just before the part of the song when a woman starts speaking in French, Peter says, "At this point, I was thinking you could do some freestyle." Then he slowly drops to the floor and gradually rolls every inch of his body from his head to his shoulders, hips, and toes.

When the song finishes, he turns to me. "What do you think?"

"*Great*. I think I'm ready to perform in front of your mom."

Peter gapes. "Really?"

"No," I firmly say. "Peter, you seriously thought I could follow all of *that*?"

"Which part of the dance was hard to follow?"

"Everything!" I say. "I thought you said you were going to teach simple choreography."

"It *is* simple."

"I was imagining something more like this." I pull out my go-to dance move: sidestepping and rolling my shoulders really quickly.

Peter watches like I'm the most appalling thing his eyes

have ever witnessed. I've never seen him resemble Auntie Queenie more.

"This is how you get the boys, Peter." I add a little shimmying to my shoulder-rolling and then break out my specialty—the shopping cart dance.

He laughs and crosses his arms. "No wonder you've needed my mom's help."

"Actually"—I beam—"I asked your mom during the fun run if we could hold off on the kaishaos."

He snorts like I said something unbelievable. "O-kay."

"I'm serious," I insist. It feels important that someone in my family knows I stood up to Auntie Queenie. "I told her I appreciated the effort, but I don't need any more potential roses." I leave out the fact that Miles sidetracked me from executing the full confrontation, but I *did* initiate it.

Peter tilts his head and stares at me like I've attempted to dance again. "You really told my mom how you feel?"

"Well, sort of."

"Like, how you *actually* feel? Not a filtered version?"

"Again, sort of."

"H-how?" he stammers.

"I don't know." I shrug. "It just came out."

"You don't just come out, Chloe." He slides his phone out of his pocket. "How do you even start that conversation?"

I look over at his screen and see that he wrote in the Notes app, **how to tell mom the truth**.

"Are you taking *notes*?" I ask.

His cheeks flush like two big Japanese peaches, which makes my heart crack open for my cousin.

"Hey." I poke him. "I don't think it has to be perfect. You can write and prepare a speech, but I think Auntie Queenie will listen if you speak from the heart."

Peter's mouth bunches to one side. "What does my heart sound like?"

Peter Liang Que: the king of asking questions I have no answers to.

Auntie Queenie suddenly bursts in, strutting over to us with her flats clicking on the studio floor. "I invited someone to help with the dance, but he's having trouble with parking." She puts her fan back in her bag and turns to Peter. "What's happening?"

"Nothing!" Peter stuffs his hands in his pockets. "Chloe and I were just going over the choreography."

"Oh! I have an exciting surprise for the performance!"

Surprises from Auntie Queenie are usually more frightening than exciting.

"I was talking to Martina, and she agreed to rent me her large venue projector for your debut!" Auntie Queenie clasps her hands. "Everyone can watch your dance number on the big screen—just like the movies!"

Who even asked for this?

She takes a break from describing the debut from hell when someone knocks on the door. "That must be him!"

And in walks none other than Miles Chua.

20

SOMEHOW, THE FIRST words my brain manages to come up with are "Nice to meet you."

I wonder if I'll ever be capable of saying a normal hello to this boy.

"Ah, Chloe, you two have met before!" Auntie Queenie laughs. "At the fun run, remember? When I bumped into Miles again, I knew he would be the perfect partner to start your roses program." She double-winks at me and whispers, "I usually advise to collect and select, but when the boy is this cute, Chloe, it's time to select and protect."

My cheeks are burning so much they feel like they're going to melt off my face.

"Peter here can fill you in on the dance moves." Auntie Queenie pats Miles on the shoulder. "My son was called a phenom in his dance crew. That reminds me, maybe I can ask Martina if they offer dancer discounts for the projector!"

Auntie Queenie hurries off, but not before telling Peter to help Miles and me with our "chemistry."

While the three of us stand there in awkward silence, I ask, "Where did you run into Auntie Queenie?"

"Oh, small world. Auntie bought some sponges from Andie's shop."

Andie, as in Miles's sister Andie. The same Andie who recently started selling cleaning supplies online. *I know this because we've been messaging and sharing personal information,* I want to tell Peter (and also everyone I know).

"Andie asked if I could deliver her orders that day," Miles continues, "and your aunt's place was my first stop."

I know I shouldn't be romanticizing things, but really, out of all the sponge stores in the world, what are the chances Auntie Queenie would pick Andie's? And on the day that Miles was in charge of deliveries?

"Why would my mom buy another sponge?" Peter says, interrupting my reverie. "We have so many at home."

"Not the point," I hiss. I smile at Miles. "My cousin Peter."

Miles nods. "The dance phenom."

"Have you learned choreography before?" Peter asks.

"I think I can handle it," Miles says in his silky ASMR voice.

Peter waits for Miles to set down his stuff before asking me, "Is he sick?"

"What?"

"He sounds like he has something in his throat."

"That's just his voice," I say. "I think it's relaxing."

"Yeah, he sounds stoned."

I roll my eyes and walk over to check if Miles needs anything. When I hear Peter setting up the music, it sinks in that he's supposed to teach Miles the acrobatic "Partition" dance.

"'Sup, Chloe Elaine?" he asks when he sees me approaching.

Ugh. How does he greet people so well?

"Hey." I smile. "Thanks for coming here and everything."

And for dealing with the several awkward situations my aunt has put you through.

"This dance is kinda complicated, though," I continue, "so you don't really need to learn it—"

"It's cool." He smirks and rolls up his sleeves. "Still have to avenge myself after that fun run."

"Dancing doesn't make you any faster, though."

He laughs at this. It's become one of my favorite things to do—making Miles laugh. He doesn't seem like the type of person to write out **lol** when he's really staring at his phone unamused. Whenever I get an **lol** from him, I have a feeling he's actually laughing out loud.

Our prolonged eye contact gets cut short when Peter claps his hands like some distressed penguin. "Ready to dance?" he calls out.

We return to the center of the dance floor, and Peter starts to guide Miles through the same stretches he (unsuccessfully) taught me.

Miles just stands there with his arms crossed. "I think I'm good, bro."

"I'm not teaching you the dance if you don't warm up."

"Maybe we can do shorter stretches?" I offer.

Peter isn't having it. "You know how many people get injured when they rush through stretching?"

"I'm fine," Miles says. "I mean, I'm the top recruit for the La Salle team."

"Yeah, but maybe you'd be better at your three-pointers if you warmed up," Peter counters.

My whole body goes numb. I mean, Miles seems nice, but isn't it some unspoken athlete bro rule that you're not supposed to make fun of their basketball skills?

Miles has his eyes narrowed at Peter, but it isn't a how-dare-you kind of expression. He actually looks . . . impressed? His little crooked sideways smirk is on full blast.

"This is the routine I learned from UP Streetdance," Peter says, moving on to his hip stretches. Of course, Peter finds a way to insert into the conversation that he's a scholar too.

This time, Miles goes along with Peter's warm-up, but he also shows off some things he does in basketball training. Peter keeps answering back with more exercises from his dance rehearsals. It's like the two of them are stuck in a scholar-mention battle.

Peter lines up the song again and asks me, "Do you want to practice too?"

"I'll review by watching."

I wish there was a way I could livestream the whole rehearsal for Cia.

Miles is a great basketball player, but he has the flexibility of a tree. There is no movement happening in his hips or torso. When Peter teaches him the steering wheel move,

Miles looks like a human windshield wiper. When he tries following Peter's body roll, it looks like he's breaking his back.

The choreography picks up, and Peter catches Miles by the elbows when he mixes his left foot with his right. "You okay?"

Miles stands and pulls the bottom of his shirt up to wipe the sweat off his forehead. "We should get you to train our team."

Peter grins and restarts the dance.

What he lacks in flexibility, coordination, and timing, Miles makes up for with sheer determination. Over the next hour, Peter keeps on repeating the steps over and over until Miles gets the routine—well, sort of. But it's a big improvement from where he started.

Miles's shirt is already soaked through when Peter calls for a water break.

"Want some?" Miles asks, offering me his jug.

My cheeks go warm. "I'm good."

I know it's drinking water, but this is the closest I've ever gotten to sharing saliva with a guy.

While Miles is still recovering, Peter starts doing jumping jacks on the other side of the room.

"I'm convinced that the entire Liang family can kick my ass," Miles says.

"Well, you've been keeping up with Peter," I point out. "Auntie Queenie is a whole different story."

Miles laughs. "Hey, we still need to have our rematch." He puts down his jug and tugs his sleeves even higher. "What're you up to this weekend? Maybe we could go for a run."

Did I . . . just get asked out? When I fantasize about my

first date, I always imagine dinner and a movie, not a wake up and run. But this still counts, right? Oh my god. I can't wait to tell Cia—

Shit. Cia. This weekend is her variety show.

"There's actually a school fair this weekend, and Cia's performing," I explain. "As the best friend, it's sort of mandatory that I'm there for moral support."

"Oh, the Mary Immaculate fair?"

"Yeah, that one!" And I suddenly hear myself say, "Do you wanna go?"

"To the fair?"

How did him asking me out turn into me asking him out?!

"Um, if you want to," I hurriedly say. "I was going to drop by the fair before the show, and I know it's kinda lame now that we've graduated—"

"No, it sounds cool." He thankfully cuts me off before I ramble on some more. "I'll message you later about the details?"

I smile and give him a thumbs-up.

"Solid," he answers with a smirk.

Super-duper solid.

21

HOW AM I already sweating?! I literally just stepped out of the shower, and there's already sweat dripping down my neck.

At first, I thought it was stress-induced sweat from my call with Auntie Queenie. After explaining that I'd never be able to come close to Peter's dancing ability, she finally agreed to call off the extra performance.

But then Cia messaged me that Manila is reaching a high of thirty-four degrees Celsius today. Whoever scheduled a school fair during the summer should never be in charge of making decisions ever again.

My beach crop top and shorts are the only clothes I have that don't make me look like a giant sweat stain.

Do you think I can sneak into school wearing shorts? I text Cia.

She replies, **This is the same school that had us measure the height of our socks.**

Good point. Every morning our teacher would have us

check if our socks were three fingers above our ankle bone, and Cia got reprimanded several times for showing too much ankle. I wish I could be meeting Miles without the restrictions of the Mary Immaculate dress code.

When I go downstairs to grab some water, my phone buzzes with another message from Cia: **Just a few MILES until we get there.** 😩

Right on cue, Raph messages: **this really feels like a day full of sMILES!**

It's my own fault. I knew that getting a ride from Raph and Cia meant being on the receiving end of all their Miles-related puns.

As I'm about to head back to my bedroom to change, I hear Pa's heavy footsteps approach the front door.

The door opens, and Pa pauses when he sees me. "Didn't know you were up already."

I can't even remember the last time Pa asked if I wanted to join him on his run. With debut planning and hanging out with Cia, I've been sleeping through his six o'clock alarms.

"Yeah, Cia's call time is pretty early," I say.

I'm not sure if he heard me because he's too busy scanning my clothes.

"You're going out with half a shirt on?" he says. Every single time he sees the crop top, we have the same conversation. "Did they run out of fabric to finish the actual shirt?"

"I'm going to change, Pa," I tell him while he continues to stare at me disapprovingly.

"Is that school secretly hosting a disco?"

I bite my tongue to stop myself from sighing. "No discos, Pa."

"You know there are boys that attend that fair."

If there are guys that get too distracted by crop tops, I don't see why that's *my* problem. I think about pointing this out to Pa when I realize this could also be a potential segue to bringing up Miles. Normally, I would never in a million years confide in him about a boy—but since he was involved in the whole kaishao chaos, would this make him happy?

"Pa—" I start, but I get interrupted when his ringtone goes off.

He picks up and immediately clicks his tongue. "I left the papers on my desk. It should be Nelson's turn to sign them."

Nope, nope, nope. Not ready for this level of father-daughter intimacy.

"See you later," I mouth, and make subtle backsteps toward my bedroom. Then I rush inside before he can say another word.

DESPITE THE SCORCHING heat, tons of people still show up for the school fair. All the streets leading to Mary Immaculate are filled with parked cars and parents walking with their kids. The closer we get to the school, the clearer I hear the music playing on the grounds.

Aside from the big banner that says WELCOME TO THE ENCHANTED SUMMER FAIR, everything still looks the same. The same tarpaulins advertising tutoring centers along the street, the same bust of Mother Mary hovering over the building, and the same billboard in front of the school with the motto WOMEN OF SERVICE. Graduation felt so momentous that I thought there would be some noticeable sign that I had left. But, no. The school moves on—with or without me.

Parking is so bad that Raph has been trying to find a spot a couple streets away from the school. Despite the whole kaishao-slash-Great-Wall incident, the two of them seem completely normal. Raph makes jokes; Cia laughs at jokes—typical Raph and Cia PDA. Whenever I ask Cia how things are going, she assures me that they've fixed everything.

At the moment, though, I can tell she's stressing out based on how often she's checking the clock on the dashboard.

"We're not going to be late," Raph assures her.

"You're just relaxed because your call time's at noon."

Some girl from the fair committee messaged Raph's channel and asked if he'd be interested in hosting the variety show. He has since made three videos documenting his "road to hosting" journey.

Raph groans when we turn onto another filled street. "So where are you meeting basketball boy?" he asks me.

"He said we can meet by the gate."

"Whew." Raph whistles. "A date by the gate."

Cia slumps in the passenger seat. "I wish we didn't have rehearsals. Then we could watch Chloe's first date."

"I wasn't this annoying when you two started going out," I remind them.

"Does she have her kilig smile on?" I hear Raph ask.

Cia turns in her seat. "Not yet."

"*What* kilig smile?"

"You know, that smile you do that's really big," Cia says,

like this is common knowledge. "It's how we know you're crushing on someone."

Raph flashes a huge Joker-esque smirk. "It's like you ate a protractor."

"It's not my fault that I'm a naturally smiley person," I say.

"Yeah, the smiling comes naturally when you're flirting," Cia says, giving me a smug grin. "It's nice seeing you happy, Chlo."

"Wait, about this kilig smile—"

I get cut off when Cia suddenly yells and points to a car that's leaving its spot. "Go, go, go!" Cia chants while Raph beats out the car behind us. It takes her only a second to unlatch her seat belt and start speed-walking to the school.

"Okay," I say, jogging beside her. "Your performance is at seven, right?"

"I start hosting at six." Raph pants as he catches up to us. "Is the dance troupe going after glee club?"

The way Cia's staring down the clock on her phone, I can tell she's no longer processing outside information. "We're officially going to be a minute late!"

"Good luck!" I yell as Cia yanks Raph's arm and they sprint toward the entrance.

With all the running and secondhand stress from Cia, I'm officially sweating through my pants. There should be a dress code exception for extreme heat. Schools should be more worried about their students getting heatstroke than seeing their scandalous kneecaps.

I'm rolling up the bottom of my pants when my phone buzzes in my pocket.

My heart sinks when I read the message from Miles: **Don't hate me . . . Coach just called for mandatory training, and he's saying everyone needs to go. Will make it up to you!!!!!!**

I type out: **Couldn't he have told you before I left the house???**

Delete, delete, delete.

No problem! 😊 have fun at training!

I mean, what else was I supposed to say? I get that training is important, but what about snow cones?!?

An idea crosses my mind and punches me in the gut. What if he made up the training excuse so he could bail? What if he left the dance rehearsal and realized he'd made a horrible mistake by agreeing to go to the fair with me?

Oof, don't go there, Chloe. It's way too hot to go down that slippery slope today.

Well, this isn't the school fair I wanted to risk evaporation for. Maybe I should go home and come back tonight for the variety show. Being the oldest person walking around the fair sounds way less appealing if I'm on my own.

Just when I'm about to turn around, I hear someone call out my name.

"Chloe!" Kuya Roger waves at me from the gate. I swear, I've never seen anyone as happy doing their job as Kuya Roger. He is a Mary Immaculate *legend*. No one knows how long he's been working as a security guard here, but even Auntie Queenie remembers him from her high school days.

"Kuya Roger! Kumusta ka?"

"Okay naman. Always happy to see students visit after graduation."

"Seeing you is the best part."

He gives me a wide smile. "Cia just flew through here. Are you performing in the variety show too?"

I shake my head. "Just a common audience member."

"Isn't that Cia's brother?" Kuya Roger asks. I turn around and see Jappy heading toward us carrying a huge box.

Jappy pants while he sets the box on the ground. "Hi, Kuya Roger," he says. Then he acknowledges me with a side-wave.

"*You're* going to the school fair?" I say.

When Cia offered him a variety show ticket, Jappy said he was allergic to school events.

"Please," Jappy huffs. "Ma asked me if I could drop off this very heavy box of equipment for Cia."

Jappy hands over his ticket, but Kuya Roger halts him at the turnstile. "Sorry, no shorts allowed on the grounds." Jappy laughs, but the smile on Kuya Roger's face says, *Yes, I'm very serious.*

"Kuya, sige na," Jappy says, realizing he's not getting in. "I didn't even go to this school, and I'm already nineteen."

"The dress code doesn't discriminate," Kuya Roger counters.

Jappy groans. "So the only way I can go in is if I wear pants?"

"Or a long skirt," I point out.

"Not helpful," he says.

Stress and sweat make Jappy's hair spike up even more than usual. It reminds me of the pineapple key chain I once lost.

"I might be able to help," I suggest.

"What's the catch?" He eyes me suspiciously.

I clutch my chest and gesture toward the school billboard. "I'm just doing my part as a woman of service."

After he's done staring me down with his judgy eyebrow, he relents. "Fine."

I turn to Kuya Roger. "Do you still have the lost-and-found box?"

He crouches down in the security booth and pulls out the cardboard box.

Ha! I knew there'd be leggings! I don't know how someone always manages to lose their pants, but they are a constant treasure in the lost and found. Right after hair ties and water bottles.

Jappy gawks at the leggings. "Why are you giving me those?"

"They're pants."

He backs up when I hand them to him.

"Do you think they're going to bite if you touch them?" I ask.

"They're the kind girls use for yoga." He stares at them like I'm handing him a thong.

"That means they're *comfortable*," I argue. "Jappy, either you keep lugging that box and driving back and forth from your place, or you put on these perfectly good pants."

He finally takes the leggings and retreats to the restroom.

When Jappy trudges back looking like the world's most miserable superhero, Kuya Roger exclaims, "Perfect fit!"

"See?" I say. "Comfortable *and* a great outfit."

Jappy pulls down his shirt so it covers his hips and darts his side-eye at me.

22

"JAPPY, NO ONE'S looking at your butt."

To get to the strip where the school fair is, we have to go up a long ramp that feels especially steep in this heat. Jappy's been making it harder on himself by carrying the box behind him. He's paranoid that the leggings are too tight and, to use his words, "grabbing his ass with each step."

"This wouldn't be a problem," he says, huffing shallow breaths, "if you didn't make me wear these pants."

"Hey, I was the reason you passed the dress code."

"The dress code isn't supposed to apply to me."

"If girls' legs are scandalous, then guys' legs are too." I take the box from him.

"I can carry it," he insists, despite the relieved look on his face that came with me sharing the burden.

"We can take turns, and you don't have to worry about shielding your butt." I shift my arms around the box to get a better grip. "What's in here, anyway?"

"Mainly mics and electrical equipment." He slips his glasses off and wipes the lenses on his shirt.

"So you're coming to the variety show too?"

He grunts. "No way."

"Why not?"

"I'm nineteen years old." He motions for the box, and I hand it over to him.

"You *love* pointing out your age."

"It's a great conversation starter."

We reach the top of the ramp, and the whole strip has a roof made out of tents and tarps. It's still incredibly hot, so someone has spread out a number of electric fans all over the place. There's a little stage in the middle of the strip, where the fair committee is stationed to play music and make announcements. Girls I recognize from the grades below me are walking around carrying posters advertising their different game booths.

It's different without Cia by my side, but I feel the same rush go through me when "I'll Make a Man Out of You" from *Mulan* comes on. I have no idea why they play this song every year, but it's impossible not to feel like you're preparing for battle with Li Shang hyping you up.

"Ready for the Enchanted Summer Fair?" I ask Jappy, karate chopping to the lyrics about being as swift as a coursing river.

"They should pay workers extra for turning schools into rip-off carnivals." He scoffs at the kids on the main stage playing a game where they have to race one another while balancing a calamansi with a spoon in their mouth.

"Come on. Those games are fun. Don't you want to go on

the rides? Snow cones?" I spread my arm toward the refreshment booth. "So many flavors of snow cones!"

"I was going to drop off the box and leave."

I groan. "Cia and Raph are stuck in rehearsals, and I don't want to be the only old person roaming the fair."

Also, I would rather not have the constant reminder that Miles bailed on me.

"Imagine these are computer games," I say, "but in 5-D!"

"I don't think they have 5-D games."

"Not my point." I put on my most convincing smile. "Don't be afraid to be happy, Jappy."

"Is the rhyming supposed to convince me?"

I nod and nudge his shoulders to make him loosen up. "Come on, Jappy. You owe me."

He throws me his judgmental eyebrow again. "Don't *you* owe *me* for being part of your roses?"

"Well . . . I drew you the characters for your model," I say. "And I did help you get past the dress code."

"I thought you were being a woman of service."

"Yes, and now I am asking you to reciprocate that service."

His face softens, and he glances at the fair strip. "What about the box?"

"You can drop it off with Cia while I get us ride tickets."

"You never take no for an answer."

"Nope," I say, tugging at his sleeve before he backs out.

AS WE MAKE our way through the booths, I notice the girls I know from lower grades giving me and Jappy double takes. I forgot that at an all-girls school, walking with a guy at the school fair amounts to announcing you're in a relationship.

I stop squirming under everyone's stares when he asks, "What should we get over with first?"

There are sounds of kids squealing and carts rumbling from the Caterpillar ride. I beam at Jappy. "We should go on the roller coaster!"

That makes him go all judgy again. "That is not a roller coaster. That is a worm-shaped train going around in a circle."

"It's perfect. The start of your fair experience before it blossoms into a beautiful butterfly." I convince him to squish in beside me in one of the tiny cars. "This is going to be the best ride ever!" I shake Jappy while he remains unamused.

The operator counts down until the ride slowly creeps along the tracks. Was it always this slow? Pa's driving is faster than this roller coaster. Pa's jogging—no, even his stroll—is faster than this.

Jappy turns to me. "Best. Ride. Ever."

"Hey, everyone used to line up for the Caterpillar."

"I'm sure," he says even more sarcastically. "It's amazing how it replicates the actual movement of the insect."

There's a tiny dip in the track ahead, and I raise my hands in preparation for the drop. "Whoa!" I say, even though riding an elevator feels more exciting than this.

Jappy continues to look like he's living his worst nightmare. "The ass-grabbing is even worse in tight quarters." He squirms in his seat and tugs on the leggings. "I can't believe we're at a school fair."

"Didn't you look forward to these in high school?"

"The only thing I looked forward to was high school ending."

"So you like college better?"

"Oh yeah. It's even more exciting than this *thrilling* Caterpillar ride."

"Okay." I angle my body toward him. "I'm going to make it my mission today to find something you enjoy."

"Why?"

"Because I believe everyone should get excited about *something*," I say. "Your life sounds really sad."

He scoffs. "Says the person who called this worm a roller coaster." He then shuts his eyes and pretends he's dozing off.

"On to the next one!" I cheer once we step off the Caterpillar. "How are we feeling about Anchors Away?" I point to the ship ride that swings back and forth.

Jappy shakes his head. "I get motion sickness."

"Inflatable slide?"

"High risk for wedgies with these leggings."

This boy thinks he's going to break me, but not even Jappy Torres is going to dampen my school fair spirit.

"Okay, food. You can't say no to food; I've seen you eat." I head toward the snow cone station before he has time to argue.

While we wait in line, Jappy complains that we're paying for shaved ice with flavored syrup drizzled on it.

"Well, that's the essence of a snow cone," I point out.

"Why would I pay for something I can make myself?"

"With that logic, you could talk yourself out of buying anything."

"But this is literally ice and sugar."

"That's essentially ice cream too."

"Ice cream involves elaborate preparation—plus milk and cream and stuff."

"How would you know? You don't even cook!"

We get to the front of the line, and I see him pointing to the vanilla flavor.

"No." I swat his hand away. "You're not making your snow cone that bland."

He flexes his hand, pretending he's hurt. "You women of service are so bossy."

I order us both the blue raspberry flavor.

We dig in eagerly before the snow cones melt, and halfway through, I look at Jappy and laugh.

"What?" He looks up.

"Your lips are blue."

"So are yours," he argues. "Even your tongue is blue."

"Yours is bluer."

"No way." Jappy laughs and shakes his head. "You've always been a messy eater."

"I'm not!"

"The lasagna they served at your prom? More cheese went on your face than in your mouth."

I roll my eyes and point toward the photo booth. "Let's get a picture taken and see who's right."

"I'm not sure if you heard, but phones have cameras now."

His sarcasm doesn't stop me from rushing over when I see the booth is empty. I insert coins into the machine as Jappy pushes through the curtain and slides in next to me.

"Choose your background!" a voice chirps while different options flash on the screen.

. . . Why do all of them have hearts?

Right. I forgot that photo booth pictures are a "couple thing."

My cheeks flush at the sight of one that has Cupid shooting arrows and the phrase "This Is What Love Looks Like!"

Jappy clears his throat and scrolls to the background that has us sitting in a house on fire with a speech bubble that says "This is fine" floating above our heads. "This best describes our friendship," he says.

I groan to hide my relief. "Okay, get ready . . ." I click the fire theme. "Stick out your tongue!" I nudge him.

"Oh, are we still practicing porn dialogue?"

"Ew! Jesus, Jappy." And my disgust wastes a photo frame.

For the last two shots, I actually get Jappy to cooperate, and we get definitive proof that my tongue is a lighter shade of blue than his.

"Ha! Told you!" I say, rubbing the photo booth print in his face.

"You get excited about very boring things."

"I guess that's why I spend so much time with you."

His two dimples flash on his face, and I get a weird sinking feeling in my gut.

"Keep it," I tell him when he hands me the photo strip. "A reminder that I'm usually always right."

He grunts and gazes at the rest of the fair. "Wanna play some games?"

I wait for a snarky comment, but it doesn't come. "Seriously?"

"Aren't games part of your beloved fair experience?"

Yeah, but . . ." I fold my arms. "Aren't you going to give me some lecture about how these games rip you off?"

"Oh, they do." He pauses and grins. "But I'm legendary at them."

WHILE JAPPY INSISTS on paying for the game, the girl in the booth hands me some darts to throw at the balloons.

"How do I get the poop emoji?" I point at the stuffed toy hanging in the back.

The girl checks her prize chart. "You just need to pop three balloons!"

"Why do you want a toy shaped like shit?" I hear Jappy ask behind me.

"It's cute."

I offer a dart to Jappy, and he motions for me to go ahead. I position the dart at the optimum angle and flick my wrist perfectly, which makes me . . .

Miss terribly.

"Womp, womp," Jappy taunts behind me.

"I was *close*."

"Sure you were," he says, annoying me with the most patronizing smile. He grabs a dart and tells me to step aside. "It's okay, Chlo. Not everyone has the gift of masterful aim, the flair of precision."

Jappy stops his gloating and throws. The dart nudges a balloon, then falls to the ground like a limp noodle.

"Womp, womp," I say even louder than he did.

"That was an accident," he argues.

"But how can there be accidents when you possess masterful aim and the *flair* of precision?" I scoot him aside and take the last dart.

Okay, Chloe. This is it. You're Katniss with her bow and arrow. Spider-Man with his webs. Your dentist, who always manages to find exactly where your cavity is, no matter how hard you try to hide it.

"Yes!" I pump my fist when the balloon bursts.

The girls manning the booth cheer and ask me which prize I want to claim.

"What do you want?" I ask Jappy.

"Oh, we're not stopping until we get that poop toy," he says, already paying for another round.

Wow. I never knew Jappy shared my inclination for winning.

I tell him to go ahead when my phone pings with an alert. My heart squeezes once I see the email subject line: **Your Entry to the Philippine Animation Festival Student Showcase.**

Dear Applicant,

This message is to inform you that your entry has not been selected for the next round of deliberation in the 18 and under category. We received an overwhelming number of submissions this year, and the competition was incredibly steep. We will announce the twenty finalists and the top five winners by the end of the month. Thank you so much for sharing your work!

That's it. A form response with a generic "Dear Applicant" greeting. I didn't even make it through the first round of judging. And after all that hype Pa built up around the showcase, my whole family's going to think I'm an even bigger fraud. Shit. How am I going to break the news to Ma?

My thoughts stop spiraling when I hear Jappy's voice. "Hey, you okay?" he asks.

I shove my phone back in my pocket and feel the stinging in my eyes. "Yeah! I just, um . . . am not feeling too well." I turn away from him and blink back the tears. "Thanks for going around with me, but I—I really have to go."

He says something else, but I'm already rushing to hide in the nearest restroom. Hopefully a little kid forgot their Vicks VapoRub jar in a stall.

23

FREAKING OUT IN a bathroom is pathetic. Freaking out in a bathroom that has toilets that barely fit my butt is a whole new low. But the first-grade restroom had the shortest line, and therefore would allow a longer window for a melt-down.

The HOW TO USE THE TOILET PROPERLY diagram on the stall door really drives home how sad this is even more.

A few minutes after I panic-call her, Cia finally texts me: **Sorry, just finished another run-through. You ok?**

I stop myself from dialing her number again and quickly message that it was a butt-dial. God. I can't even deal with rejection on my own.

You're not Chloe in America. You're just Chloe who has melt-downs on tiny toilets.

When I manage to gather the guts to exit the restroom, I see Jappy being crowded by girls selling T-shirts that have FAIREST OF THEM ALL printed on them. It's like watching the supervillain from *Despicable Me* getting overwhelmed by tiny yellow minions.

"Sorry, I don't think my friend is interested," I tell the girl who's holding a shirt up to Jappy's chest.

"But it goes so well with his leggings!" she points out.

I shoo them away, and the girls finally disperse. "Having fun shopping?" I ask Jappy.

"I do identify with being the fairest of them all," he says. After a beat, he adds, "And one of them had puppy-dog eyes and cute cheeks, which made it really hard to say no. It was like rejecting a baby panda."

I laugh. "So the baby panda trapped you at the fair?"

He ruffles his hair. "I wanted to see if you were okay."

"Oh."

"Yeah, you looked kinda freaked."

"Yeah, I got this stomachache . . . Y'know, the urgent kind when you have to rush to the nearest restroom to avoid a big disaster . . ."

His perplexed expression makes me realize that I avoided talking about the showcase by discussing my bowel movements.

"Well, since we're on the subject." Jappy reaches into a paper bag and pulls out the poop-shaped stuffed toy.

"How'd you get that?"

His brow scrunches. "Didn't we spend a ton of my money trying to win this thing?"

"First of all, you offered," I point out. "Second, *how* did you hit three balloons in a row?"

"Pure skill."

I roll my eyes, and his gaze darts to the prize he's holding. "So? Do you still want this piece of shit?"

At that, I give him *my* judgy look.

"What?" he says. "I'm calling it what it is."

I smile and take the stuffed toy.

He eyes the ground and shifts his feet. "It's my thank-you for putting up with me. Didn't mean to ruin the fair for you."

"You didn't."

"Really?" He looks up at me.

"Well, not completely." I grin. "There's still the variety show."

"Yeah, it starts soon, right?" He hesitates. "Do you need someone to go with you?"

"Are you offering because you feel sorry for me?"

"Little bit," he says. "You did just hide out in the first-grade restroom."

I laugh. "Fine. I guess you could come. We can cheer on Raph and Cia together."

He grunts. "Raph is performing?"

"*And* your sister. You can't quit the school spirit train now. The first step is winning a prize from a game booth. The second step is watching high schoolers do interpretative dance."

"Great," he says sarcastically. "I was worried they were going to skip my favorite kind of dance."

"I know, and with the leggings, you'll fit right in."

The dimples on his cheeks flicker, and the weird gurgling sensation in my gut appears again.

24

THE STAGE LOOKS like it belongs more on Broadway than in our high school gym. A huge marquee flashes the variety show name, ILLUMINATE, and there are stars all over the gym that look like they're twinkling. While Jappy goes backstage to check if Cia got the equipment, I scout for good seats.

Most of the seats near the front are already taken by actual high school students. By the time I find two empty ones, Raph is storming onto the stage.

"Gooooood evening, Mary Immaculate!" His voice carries through the gym. "I'm Raphael Siy, and I'm so excited to be hosting ILLUMINATE."

He encourages the crowd, and they start cheering louder and louder.

When Jappy finds me, Raph is already midway through his monologue.

"I'm a big fan of this year's theme," Raph says. "The committee spent days searching for a star who would make the decorations shine—and *that's* why they hired me."

Jappy grunts. "They couldn't find anyone else?"

"Hey," I say, "Raph's actually pretty good."

Most of the crowd came here for the singing and the dancing, but Raph's energy gets people's attention.

"What's your grudge against him, anyway?" I ask.

"Nothing." Jappy folds his arms and huffs.

"I know not all his jokes land, but—"

"You know I haven't heard him have one conversation without trying to be funny?" He ruffles his hair, and I settle in for another Jappy Torres rant. "The first time he came over to the house, he made some joke to Ma about her turon. They instantly loved him." Jappy leans forward and rests his elbows on his knees. "Dating my sister isn't a joke. My parents are committed to loving everyone they meet, but he still needs to prove he's good enough for my sister."

"Is there *really* anyone good enough for Cia, though?"

"There was some guy who made the news for creating a software tool that detects cancer," Jappy offers. "He seems all right."

"Sounds like an underachiever," I counter, grinning.

He snorts and smiles back. "Or maybe, like, Tom Hanks."

"What?" I laugh.

"A younger version. Whenever I watch his movies, I always think he's the nicest guy in the world." Jappy glances at me. "You're going to call me a weirdo again, aren't you?"

I nod, and he smirks.

"Grabe talaga 'tong stage!" Raph exclaims. "When I got

here, I told the fair committee that these decorations reminded me of going stargazing. One time, I was lying in bed looking up at the stars, and I was thinking"—he pauses and squints—"Wait. Where did my ceiling go?"

From the corner of my eye, I see Jappy snort.

"Did you just laugh?" I ask.

"What?" he says, getting all defensive. "I was coughing."

"Hey"—I tap his foot with mine—"Raph does make a lot of jokes, but I think he cares about Cia."

"We'll see." Jappy slumps in his seat. "And don't tell Cia I care this much."

"I don't know," I tease. "With you being overprotective *and* showing up to her variety show, people might mistake you for a supportive brother."

Then Raph's voice booms through the gym. "Ladies and gentlemen! To start off the festivities tonight, we have the one, the only, Mary Immaculate glee club!"

The lights dim, and the curtains draw open. People in the front start screaming their heads off when the glee club walks onstage in their red polos and jeans. If you want a support system, you should get friends from Mary Immaculate. There's a special volume level that's only reached by cheering students from an all-girls high school. The performance hasn't even started, and a girl's already losing her voice from yelling, "Go, Janine!"

I nudge Jappy and point to Cia, who's standing in front of the girls, in the conductor's spot.

"Are they doing 'Don't Stop Believin'' again?" Jappy asks.

"Probably."

The glee club moderator has been always addicted to the show *Glee* and loves paying homage to the pilot episode. Cia says the moderator is also the one who chooses their outfits. Maybe the moderator should explore other TV shows, or at least watch the other performances on *Glee*.

I lower my voice. "I do have a soft spot for the a cappella harmonies they do in the beginning."

We cheer Cia as she approaches the mic. I yell out her name and clap until my hands are sore.

"Hi! I'm Patricia Torres. Since we're celebrating Mary Immaculate's seventy-fifth anniversary this year, we prepared a special performance."

She counts them down, and they start vocalizing the familiar *dun, dun, dun* intro. But instead of Cia singing about being a small-town girl, she begins to . . . rap?

"Does this always happen?" Jappy asks.

I shake my head. "This is very new." I spot the glee club moderator rushing to the stage and having an even worse freak-out than during the holiday-concert incident.

Another girl joins in while some members begin to beatbox. It turns out to be a mash-up of the usual Journey song and one of Cia's hype songs: Nicki Minaj's verse in "Monster." People in the audience cheer when Cia changes "bad bitch that came from Sri Lanka" to "bad bitch that came from Manila."

Jappy's mouth is open, and his eyes are practically popping out of his head.

I laugh and nudge him. "You okay?"

"I'm not seeing things, right? That's . . . my shobe? And she's singing about being a monster?"

"A *motherfuckin'* monster," I correct him.

Then he switches on judgy Jappy mode. "Isn't she going to get into trouble?"

"Hey"—I lightly knock his skull—"you have my permission to judge anyone else, but my best friend is off-limits." I watch Cia take over the bridge and completely own the song. "Look how much fun she's having."

His face softens, and he keeps his eyes on the stage. After another verse, he says, "She does sound good."

I nod and yell out, "That's my best friend!!!"

Jappy starts to dorkily clap along and bob his head. I whoop when Cia hits a high note, and he cheers, "Yeah!" when the whole club joins in for the last chorus.

I switch my attention between Cia onstage and stage brother Jappy. Because, I mean, it's kind of adorable.

When they finish the song, there's a thunderous roar from the audience. But they've got nothing on me and Jappy. I'm screaming my head off, and Jappy keeps shouting, "That's my sister!"

Even if the moderator stages the biggest meltdown in the history of Mary Immaculate, the glee club has the whole gym on their side.

25

"DO YOU WANNA stay?" I ask Jappy after we watch the dance troupes go on. "I don't think Cia has any more surprise performances."

"Who's up next?"

"They got Ben&Ben this year."

"*Excuse* me?"

"They're an OPM band—"

"Why didn't you tell me Ben&Ben is performing?"

"I didn't know you knew them?"

He sits up, and his eyes dart to every corner of the gym. "Ben&Ben is really here? Like, *here*? They're going to perform on that stage? In front of us?"

I laugh. "Are you fanboying?"

"It's *Ben&Ben*!" He rises to his feet.

Total fanboying.

Jappy is so excited that he actually cheers when Raph

appears. "So I ran into this band backstage," Raph says. "I think they were called Ben?"

People in the audience start going wild and getting up from their seats. Jappy motions for me to stand too.

"MARY IMMACULATE!" Raph bellows. "ARE YOU READY FOR BEN&BEN?"

The ILLUMINATE marquee blinks in different colors, and the curtains open to show the band onstage. The people in front of us take out their phones and raise their arms to film, obstructing most of our view.

Jappy's face falls, and he bends and swerves to get a better look.

"Hey"—I tap Jappy's shoulder—"I know where we can go."

THE ART ROOM is on the second floor on the left side of the gym. And only those who have spent a lot of time there would know you can pop out one of the windows and climb onto a mini balcony that overlooks the stage. It's useful if you want to people-watch—or in this case, get an unobstructed view of Ben&Ben.

Jappy hesitates before climbing out the window. "Are we breaking some kind of rule?"

I shrug. "You're the one who said the rules shouldn't apply to you."

After a little more coaxing, he finally follows me and leans over the railing. I watch as he slowly bobs his head and mouths along to the words. As the song goes on, the smile on his face gets bigger, and he starts losing himself completely to the music.

I don't think I've ever seen him this happy.

Seeing everyone dance and sing in the school gym makes me think of all the variety shows and assemblies I've attended over the years, even my graduation.

Jappy taps me. "What's wrong?"

"Nothing." I swallow hard and give him my polite smile.

He waves his hand around my forehead. "Zero poker face."

A moment passes as he waits for a response.

"Fine," I say, hating that he can see through my polite smile too. "I got a little sad thinking about how this isn't my life anymore." I cross my arms and lean on the railing. "It sounds stupid."

While Ben&Ben croon their next song, Jappy says, "I don't think it's stupid."

"Let's not forget that I hid out in the first-grade restroom today."

"Those toilets are too small for anyone to use anyway." He tilts his palms up. "They're more practical for meltdowns."

I can't help but laugh. It's weird—I've known Jappy for most of my life, but I never really realized how easy he is to talk to.

"You want to know the reason for my freak-out earlier?" I ask.

He nods, and I take a deep breath.

"I applied to this showcase that's supposed to pick the top five student animators in the country. Well, I wasn't in the top five." I scoff. "I wasn't even good enough for the top twenty. And if a whole panel of judges tells me I'm not a good animator, shouldn't I be listening?"

"It's just one contest," he says.

"Yeah, but I was wait-listed at USC. I was their second choice. My dad and my aunties and all these signs are telling me I'm not cut out for this." I sigh and face him. "How do you do it?"

He arches his eyebrow. "Do what?"

"You always do your own thing." I angle my body toward him. "You don't waste time looking back and missing things like high school. You're like one of those horses with blinders on—you don't care about what anyone thinks. I wish I was like that."

"Chlo." He grunts and shakes his head. "I care what *everyone* thinks. You remember my parents' story about how they were both star students?" he asks. "I always feel like I got the recessive genes in the family."

"You know more about computers than anyone I know."

"But I suck at school." He fidgets and wraps his fingers around the railings. "I always panic when it comes to tests. Even when I pull an all-nighter, my mind just keeps spiraling. It's either *oh, what if I forget this?* or *what if I run out of time?* or *what if I studied the wrong thing?*" Jappy pauses and exhales. "Since high school wasn't great for me, I thought I could make up for it later in life. That's what happens in those success stories, right? Steve Jobs started Apple after dropping out of college."

I bite back a smile. Referring to Steve Jobs is the most Jappy thing ever.

He's quiet for a moment and grips the railing even tighter. "But what happens to the people who suck at high school and find out they suck as adults too?"

"Jappy, come on."

And then he says, "I didn't get into any of the colleges I applied to." There's a dip in his voice that breaks my heart a little. "I got panic attacks during all those entrance exams and found out one by one that I didn't pass. The only reason I got into UST is because I wrote an appeal letter for them to reconsider my case."

"Sorry," I tell him. "I didn't know."

He shrugs and rests his arms on the railing. "I guess that's why I don't like going to these things. Always makes me think I deserve some 'biggest loser' award."

He keeps his gaze fixed on the stage, and his words hang in the air while the band continues to play.

"Hey"—I bump him with my elbow—"there are way cooler awards that fit you more."

"Yeah?"

"Like, most likely to go on a church date, or blandest taste in ice cream. Lots of possibilities in the *kwe-we*." I get a hint of a smile from him and keep going. "And as seen by today's events, fairly good balloon popper."

"Confession." He pauses and presses his lips together. "I paid the girls at the booth to get the stuffed toy."

"You *cheated*?"

"Different methods, same result." He shrugs. "It's like USC admissions. Some kids they pick right away. With you, they needed a little more time to decide if your alarming devotion to snow cones was worth it."

I bite my lip, holding back a laugh. "For a second, I forgot how annoying you are. Thanks for the reminder."

"Always a pleasure," he says with a small bow. A silence stretches between us. "And in case it wasn't clear . . ." Jappy bops me with his elbow. "I think it's gutsy that you're going for your dream."

"Doesn't feel like it," I say. "I can't even show my mom any of my work."

"Why not?"

"I don't know." I squeeze my shoe into the space at the bottom of the railing. "It's . . ."

"Scary?"

I nod.

"It's normal to be scared. It's a natural reaction when you're going for something you really want."

I tilt my head at him. "What do you want?"

"Hm?"

"You're telling me it's normal to be scared when you want something." I poke his arm. "What are you scared of, then?"

"That I'll never get to see One Direction reunited."

"Ah, the dream of millions." I roll my eyes.

I think he's about to change the topic when he mutters, "I did think about architecture."

"Really?"

"It's stupid."

"It's not!" I nudge him. "I think you'd make a great architect! Your 3-D model looks like it was made by someone who knows what they're doing. Designing houses clearly runs in your blood."

"Got the recessive genes, remember?" He snorts and his eyes fall to the ground. "I'm fine making models on my own.

But I can't do what you or my parents do. My mind doesn't . . ."
He does spirit fingers near his face.

"What was that?" I ask, laughing.

"It symbolizes the creative process."

"Well, I think you're capable of *this*," I say, mimicking his spirit fingers.

He cracks a full-dimpled smile. I'm about to say something else when Jappy's jaw literally drops.

"This is. My. Song," he says.

"Really? You made this?"

He's too busy freaking out to notice my joke. Ben&Ben are playing "Pagtingin," and Jappy starts swaying and singing along. It's very impressive how he manages to miss every single note.

"What?" he asks when he catches me staring.

I shake my head. "I never expected you to be a Ben&Ben fan."

"What kind of music did you think I listened to?"

"I don't know," I say. "Intellectual classical stuff? Like Mozart and Beethoven."

Jappy turns away from Ben&Ben and gawks at me like I just slapped him in the face. "You really think I'm that boring?"

"I said *intellectual*."

"That's just a nicer way of saying boring."

I laugh. "Ben&Ben's songs are about romance, love, and all those feelings. It seemed like you'd think it was cheesy."

"You call it cheesy; I call it art," he says. "So many people only listen to artists from other countries and sleep on the ones we have here. Every single one of Ben&Ben's songs is a master class in songwriting and tugging at a listener's emotions. Plus, there's something about hearing lyrics in Tagalog that makes you feel things on another level, and—" He stops and stares at me. "Why are you smiling?"

"I was taken aback by the passion." I bump his shoulder. "Do any of your gamer friends know you like these love songs?"

"Nope." He hesitates and meets my eye. "Just you."

That weird sinking feeling reappears in the pit of my stomach. I should really get my body checked. I break our gaze and move back from the railing. "We should probably start heading down before someone catches us."

But instead of following me, Jappy suddenly starts snapping and bouncing his knees.

"Jappy, what are you doing?" I ask, laughing.

He points at me and clutches his heart as the band builds up to the chorus. "Proving to you that I'm not boring!"

"I never said *boring*!"

He then starts belting out the song. He shuts his eyes, and his voice cracks when he tries to hit the high notes. Damn. In terms of vocal cords, he *did* get the recessive genes in the Torres family.

Jappy catches his breath as the crowd downstairs cheers for an encore. When "Pagtingin" starts to play again, Jappy looks at me. "You're really going to abandon me during my performance?"

"I don't sing."

"Ohhhh." He nods. "You're going to choke again?"

"Wow, you're gonna go there?"

"I get it," he says with a shrug. "I choke during tests, and you choke during singing."

Jappy resumes singing while darting glances my way, as though challenging me to join in. All right. If Jappy has the confidence to sing at a hearing-loss-inducing volume, I can hum. I mouth along to the chorus, and Jappy bumps my hip and pumps his fist as if we're partying to a DJ Tofu song.

Most of the crowd joins in the singing, and it's like a movie scene when the song playing in the background gives you goose bumps because it matches the moment so perfectly. I smile and raise my voice as the harmonies of "Pagtingin" echo through the Mary Immaculate gym.

Jappy and I spend the rest of the concert swaying and singing lyrics about loving when you're ready and confessing your hidden feelings.

It's all so wonderfully, wonderfully cheesy.

WHEN THE SHOW finishes and we climb down from the art room, Jappy asks what my plans are.

"Gonna say hi to Cia backstage and wait for them to finish celebrating. You?"

"Heading back home with Ma's equipment," he says. "Do you need a ride?"

"It's not out of the way?"

The glee club girls are all super friendly, but hanging out with them after their shows always feels like I'm intruding.

Jappy shakes his head. "I could use the help with the box too."

"So you're offering me a ride in exchange for labor?"

"Pretty much." He smiles, and my insides start to feel all jumbled again.

We reach the gym, and Jappy tells me he'll meet me by the fair strip.

"Wait." I stop him when I see a poster of the concert lineup. "Stand over there."

He scrunches his brow. "Why?"

"I want to take a picture so you can remember seeing Ben&Ben."

"My memory is fine without the photo."

"Well, mine's not." I tell him to scooch until he finally steps closer to the poster. He folds his arms and glares at my phone's camera. "Can you try less serial killer and more excited fanboy?"

Jappy maintains the scowl, but he at least throws up a peace sign.

"You know what would be cute? If you formed a heart with your hands over the—"

He cuts me off with a grunt. "Chlo, take the picture."

After I manage to get a couple photos—and actually get Jappy to show some teeth in one of them—Raph suddenly jumps in and poses next to him.

"This should be your phone wallpaper," I say when I snap a picture of Raph slinging his arm around Jappy, who's giving me an even more severe I-want-to-melt-your-phone scowl. I wonder how many more photos I can take before Jappy actually snatches my phone.

"Kuya Jappy!" Raph beams at him. "I didn't know you were coming. Did you see my set?"

As Jappy morphs into his grumpy mode, I shoot him a look that says, *Be nice.*

And with the enthusiasm of someone getting a tooth pulled, he mutters, "I liked the joke about the stars."

Raph's face lights up brighter than the whole stage. "I have a notebook filled with jokes. I had to narrow them down, but I can show you my backups if you want!"

While Raph starts skimming through the Notes app on his phone, Jappy glares at me and mouths, "Your fault."

"Hey, Raph," I say before he can read his entire monologue. "Have you seen Cia?"

"I think she's still backstage." He faces Jappy. "Do you wanna join? The glee club's having an afterparty at Pancake House."

"We're good," Jappy and I say in unison.

Raph looks back and forth between the two of us. "You're both good?"

"Yeah, I'm dropping Chloe off," Jappy says.

"*Interesting,*" Raph says.

Before Raph can interrogate Jappy further about this ride home, Jappy says he has to go gather the equipment. He gives me a side-wave, and I return it with a side-wave of my own.

Once Jappy leaves, Raph wiggles his eyebrows at me. "I see the date went well."

"Miles didn't show."

"Yeah, so you found tall, dark, and moody instead." He wiggles his eyebrows even more intensely.

"Jappy is Cia's *brother.*"

"Oh, I know. That was the first time he didn't look like he wanted to rip my head off."

"Maybe he finally found one of your jokes funny."

"Or maybe he's basking in that falling-in-love glow."

I groan. "Why don't we go look for Cia?"

We navigate through people clearing the chairs and the fair committee taking selfies next to the stage, and then I spot Cia huddled with the glee club.

"Chlo!" Cia cries out when she sees me.

As I make my way toward her, I play "Monster" on my phone, and she starts dancing.

"Make way! Make way!" Raph announces to the few people left. "Glee club legend coming through!"

Cia beams. "You liked the performance?"

Raph starts rapping, but thankfully only lasts a few bars.

"You didn't see me?" I ask. "I lost my voice cheering for you out there."

"Those lights onstage make it impossible to see anything." She pauses. It looks like she's inspecting my face.

"What are you doing?" I ask, laughing.

"Ha!" She points at me. "Kilig smile."

"Told you," Raph adds.

I suddenly feel my cheeks go warm. "This is my normal expression."

Cia's eyes grow wider, and she points her lips at something behind me. "The source of your kilig is approaching."

"I am *not* getting kilig over—" I turn around and freeze when I see Miles making his way toward us.

"'Sup, Chloe?" He gives me a side-hug paired with a beso.

"Wh-what are you doing here?" I ask once I've regained the ability to speak.

"I told my teammates about the variety show, and we wanted to check it out." He fist-bumps Cia. "Officially my new favorite rapper."

"You know, *Chloe* says that to me all the time too!"

It reminds me of the kaishaos when Auntie Queenie and Pa would loudly point out all the wonderful things I had in common with their setups.

"Oh!" Cia acts like she just remembered something. "Sorry, we have to go to a quick variety show debriefing session." She reaches for Raph's hand and shoots me a very loud wink: *Have fun.*

So I'm really just getting set up by everybody these days.

As Cia pulls Raph away for their fake debriefing, Miles says, "Hey, I'm sorry that I couldn't make it this morning."

"It's okay. It was fun," I say, and I really mean it. Halfway through the fair, I forgot that I was even supposed to be with Miles.

"What did you end up doing?"

"Just the usual fair stuff."

Like helping Jappy bypass the dress code, riding the Caterpillar, eating snow cones, taking photo booth pictures, winning a stuffed toy, watching the variety show . . .

Shit.

Was I on a date?

"Sorry?" I say when I realize I completely missed the last minute of our conversation.

"My friends and I were gonna get some wings if you wanted to join," Miles says, his mouth bunching to the side with his little smirk.

"Oh, I—" I stop when my phone lights up with a message.

It's from Kaishao Boy: **Got the box!**

How in the world am I conflicted about this? It's fried

chicken and Miles! If I still wrote fan fiction, that's the exact combo I would be writing about. But I already told Jappy I would go with him . . .

And part of me feels kind of excited about seeing him again.

27

I AM NOT *getting kilig over Jappy Torres,* I keep telling myself as I march down the ramp to the fairgrounds. *So you turned down Miles to go help Jappy carry a box. That's just you being a good friend, Chloe. You have strong principles—you keep your promises and your commitments. This is indicative of your upstanding moral character.*

"Gago ass shit!" I hear a voice yell out and then a crash.

I follow the noise and see Jappy staring down at a broken box on the ground. His hair is puffed up, and even when he's obviously steaming mad, he still looks kinda . . .

Oh my god. What's wrong with me?!

I am. Not. Attracted. To. Jappy. Torres.

Even if I did have a "kilig smile," it wouldn't be triggered by *Jappy.* Kilig is supposed to leave you speechless and send your heart flying. But words flow naturally when I'm with Jappy, which is the complete opposite of what happens when I'm crushing on someone.

As I walk toward him, he's still grumbling and trying to piece together the broken cardboard.

"Need help?" I ask.

Jappy startles and bumps his head on a game booth wheel. He grunts and massages the back of his head. "Did anyone ever tell you how quiet your footsteps are?"

I do two big stomps on the ground. "Better?"

"Much," he says.

"Let me," I offer, taking some of the equipment so he doesn't have to cradle ten microphones in his arms.

While he grabs the rest of the stuff and starts making his way toward the gate, I get a strong whiff of a fresh, earthy smell.

Rain.

"Do you mind if we wait a bit?" I ask.

He scans the empty fairgrounds. "Does this thing have a late-night shift?"

"No, I'm—" Will Jappy find it weird if I tell him the truth? Although I've already said way weirder things to him in the past. "Waiting for the rain," I finish.

His puzzled eyes search mine. On second thought, this rain-smelling thing might be a little too weird.

"I have this thing where I can sense when it's going to rain," I explain. "And I like waiting until it starts."

He pauses. "You're asking me to stay here so that I, along with my mom's electrical equipment and my cardboard box that's already falling apart, can get soaked in the rain?"

"Yes?"

He heads over to the deserted booth area and sets down the equipment under one of the still-assembled tents.

"What're you doing?" I ask.

"If I'm waiting for your psychic rain," he says, "I'm staying dry."

"A little rain won't kill you," I say.

"The twenty typhoons that hit this country every year say otherwise." He whips his head around the booth and walks toward a wooden crate tucked in the back. When he lifts it, I notice how his upper arms flex. Since when does Jappy have arm muscles? Does playing video games give you nice arms? He slides the crate next to me. "In case you wanted to sit."

"Oh, thanks," I say, feeling that weird floating sensation in my gut. He takes another crate and slides it beside mine.

Is this . . .

No. I'm not getting kilig. This is me projecting Raph's assumptions onto things that aren't actually happening. This weird stomach stuff stems from digestive issues, not romantic feelings.

I scoot over on the crate and sit near the edge opposite Jappy. We're purely platonic, but it can't hurt to leave some space so my body doesn't get confused.

Although seeing him trying to cover his butt is helping ease the confusion.

"How are you still bothered by the leggings?" I ask.

"Why do they make girls' pants so tight?" he grumbles while shifting on the crate. "There's no room for anything, and you don't even have pockets. It's unfair."

"Wait until you hear about childbirth."

His eyes flit to the sky. "How much longer before it starts?"

"I don't know," I say with a shrug. "I can't tell exactly when it's going to happen."

He laughs and stretches his hand outside the tent. "So you watch the sky until the rain comes? How do you get anything done during the rainy season?"

"I don't sit and watch the rain all the time."

"Well, you draw rainy scenes a lot."

"Every scene gets better when you add rain to it," I say. "Sad scene? Have the character crying in the rain. Happy scene? Have them skip frivolously through a storm. Haven't you noticed how many music videos have singers walking through the rain?"

"Or how many movies and TV shows have characters making out in the rain."

"Yeah, I never really got those scenes," I mumble. "Their clothes must be soaking wet, and they're for sure gonna get sick right after."

He shrugs. "Guess all the kissing keeps their mind off things."

I feel my cheeks go warm when my mind starts connecting Jappy with the concept of making out.

"Wait." I turn to face him. "How do you know what I draw?"

"You talk about them."

"No, I don't."

"Maybe I'm psychic too."

"Jappy."

His hair sticks way up as he squirms on his seat. "I was browsing online and stumbled upon your Vimeo page."

"How do you *stumble upon* it?"

"It's easy when you . . . type 'Chloe Liang art' in the search engine."

"Oh." I hesitate, trying to remember how to articulate sentences. "What did you think?"

"Well, obviously, none of the drawings were at the same level as the one you made of me."

"I should go back in and make the head bigger," I say.

He smiles. "I've always liked your videos, even the one you showed at your prom."

"You watched that?" I didn't even know anyone was paying attention.

"Yeah, it played again after you left me to go get sermoned by your teacher," he says. "It was odd."

"*Odd*?" I repeat.

"I mean it as a compliment."

"How is that a compliment?"

"The video felt different from other cartoons."

"Yes, you did mention it being *odd*."

"That came out wrong." He sighs and ruffles his hair. "All your videos have your specific kind of humor, and I like how your style feels like a mix of those classic cartoons and the ones I see now, but not like those movies that always have the same dopey boy character."

"What movies?"

"You know, the ones with those Tom Holland look-alikes. White guy with a big nose. Think about how many characters look like the guy from *Ratatouille*."

Huh. He does have a point.

"And even if you draw dogs dancing to K-pop—"

"Corgis," I correct him.

"Fine, corgis," he relents. "I can tell they're inspired by

things in your life. Everything on your page looks like some-thing only you could've made." He bumps me with his knee. "It's cool."

After a long pause, I mumble, "Thanks."

There was some more bubbling in my gut that happened while I was listening to him. I cover my stomach with my arm in case it makes any weird noises.

And then I hear the soft pattering of rain on the tent above us.

"Wow," he says, every letter dripping with sarcasm. "It's so much different than all the other rain I've seen throughout my life."

I watch the water slowly coat the grounds. "Doesn't it feel special when the thing you've been waiting for actually hap-pens?"

"Yeah, the extra-sticky sweat from the humidity feels very special."

"Does the light get sapped out of everything when you turn nineteen?"

"Things get dimmer," he admits. "I think they go com-pletely dark when you hit thirty."

His face breaks into a smile, and I nudge him back with my knee. This time, his knee stays pressed against mine.

My heartbeats start synchronizing with the pounding rain above, and all that swirling and fluttering in my gut hits me ten times harder. I'm not sure if he's doing this on purpose, but I kind of don't want him to move away.

Shit. I think I'm getting kilig.

28

FOR THE NEXT few days, I find solace in adding more frames to my video. It doesn't matter that I didn't make the showcase.

I haven't told my parents about the rejection. Pa keeps posting countdowns to the festival, and I've been acting like I haven't heard back yet.

Still, I think I'm being very mature about the whole thing. So what if I haven't come clean to my family? Would a non-grown-up take her art so seriously that she would draw without the promise of outside validation?! Don't think so.

I sketch Ma writing one of her articles.

Then I sketch Jappy.

I draw my cousin Missy with her baby.

Then I draw Jappy.

I animate Pa running.

Then I animate Jappy and me touching knees.

See? *Super* focused.

Jappy's mixed messages are also *not* helping. It's annoying how my heart jolts whenever my phone buzzes.

I keep reading his latest text over and over trying to figure out the hidden meaning: **Hey.**

What does it *mean*? There aren't even any emojis for me to analyze.

Wait. Is the lack of emojis the part I'm supposed to be reading into?

My phone almost runs out of battery while I try composing my reply.

First, I select the waving emoji. Then I reconsider and pick the monkey-covering-its-eyes emoji.

Next, I type out: **Hi! Thinking about the school fair and how I felt some weird tension between us. Do you agree/disagree with that observation?**

Delete, delete, delete!

Finally, I settle on **Nothing much. Going to my auntie's house for more debut planning.** 🙃

Is the upside-down smile a flirty emoji?

When I hear the familiar sliding of Auntie Queenie's footsteps, I shake off all thoughts of Jappy Torres. It's physically impossible for my body to worry about Jappy *and* pleasing Auntie Queenie at the same time.

"Chloe!" Auntie Queenie says when she answers the door. "What are you doing here?"

I stand there speechless while my mind tries to process the fact that the lady standing in front of me is Auntie Queenie. I've never seen her look so disheveled. I mean, she looks like me when I've just woken up, but Auntie Queenie isn't the type of person who rolls out of bed and answers the door. She always looks like she's ready to host a fancy dinner party. This is the first time I've ever seen her without makeup on and wearing . . . baggy yellow shorts?

Auntie Queenie wearing shorts is the equivalent of my dad wearing a crop top.

I snap out of my daze. "You asked me to drop by to discuss the theme?"

She stares at me blankly like I was speaking in French. "What theme?"

"For the debut?"

"Oh, right, right," she mumbles, and walks back inside.

Weird. She's usually sending me messages every hour about my debut.

Once I slip off my shoes and close the door, I notice the craft explosion in her living room. There are scissors, glue sticks, stickers, and stationery all over the place. I haven't seen this much glitter since I was in kindergarten.

"New project, Auntie?"

She crouches down to pick some photos up from the floor. "I was working on my scrapbook."

"You make scrapbooks?"

Auntie Queenie puts her hands on her hips. "Crafting is a delightful way to pass time, Chloe."

Adding that to my collection of "Auntie Queenie's Words of Wisdom."

I help her gather the photos, and it's like I'm preparing a shrine to Peter. There are photos of him dancing onstage where he looks barely six years old, pictures of his graduation, clippings of school articles about him. If Pa documents his memories on his Instagram feed, I guess Auntie Queenie stores hers in her scrapbooks.

"I was working on this." Auntie Queenie places the heaviest album on the table. I hover next to her, and she flips to a page with pictures of Peter holding his UP acceptance letter. There are Spider-Man stickers everywhere and a shiny purple glitter border. "I was the first person Peter called when he got that scholarship." Auntie Queenie smiles.

As she flips the pages of the scrapbook, I hear a little sniffle. I turn to see Auntie Queenie dabbing the corners of her eyes.

"Auntie," I carefully ask, "are you okay?"

"Of course I am," she says with a click of her tongue. But when her eyes continue to water, she barks at me to fetch her the tissues.

I hand her the box, and she turns away to wipe her eyes. I can tell she's trying to hold in the tears, but it only makes her breaths more ragged and her whimpers sound like mouse squeaks.

This is really freaking me out. I thought Auntie Queenie only had two emotions—pleased or disappointed. I've spent my whole life trying to handle her two feelings, and I have no idea how to grasp this new one.

"Peter told me about him and Pauline," she says quietly. "That they weren't really dating."

"Oh."

Wow. Good for Peter.

"Has he talked to you about this?" she asks.

I'm not sure how much Auntie Queenie knows, but what I *am* sure of is that Peter's secrets aren't mine to tell.

"About what, Auntie?" I ask, avoiding eye contact.

She clicks her tongue again. "You're a worse liar than your father." She takes a deep breath. "Did Peter tell you that he's gay?"

"Um." I pause and then admit, "Only recently."

"Is anyone hurting him? Is he okay?"

I shake my head. "Peter's really brave."

Her eyes go to her scrapbook, and she lets out a heavy sigh. "I don't know why he only told me now."

"Maybe he was worried about how you'd react, Auntie," I try explaining. "Because of what people would think?"

"Did Peter say he was scared?"

I remain quiet because I don't know if I can lie to a crying auntie.

She stares into space and says, "Our world is already so tough on people who are different, Chloe. My job as a parent is to shield my son from the things he fears in this world, not add to them." She stops and shakes her head. "But what do I do when I'm the one he's afraid of?" Her voice breaks, and she covers her mouth and weeps into her hand.

I stroke her back and feel her whole body heaving. "Auntie," I say once her crying calms down. "Peter loves you."

"But he didn't tell me."

I hesitate and try to choose my words carefully. "Sometimes it's harder to say things to the people we love the most."

She wipes her eyes. "Is that why you keep things from Jeffrey?"

"I—I . . ." Does she know that I haven't told him about the showcase? "I don't keep things from him . . . most of the time."

Auntie Queenie gives me a sad smile and places her hand on the one I'm holding her with. "If you and my son aren't ready to talk to your parents yet, promise that you'll look out for each other." She gives my hand a little squeeze, and I nod.

"Okay, Auntie."

She gives me a double-wink and lets out a breath as she pulls out another scrapbook. It has the words *Chloe's 18th* on the front.

"I've been meaning to share this with you," she says. "These are some mood boards I made for your debut." Auntie Queenie flips through the book, and every page has a cutout picture of me standing in the middle of a party. There's an Under the Sea theme, where I'm wearing a mermaid costume; a Parisian theme, where I'm wearing a dress shaped like the Eiffel Tower; a Hunger Games theme, which could be either really cool or *really* terrifying. With all the design and detail, this scrapbook must have taken ages to put together.

"Auntie, when did you make this?"

"Ah, I add a page here and there during my spare time." She tuts. "When I found out Ahia was going to have a daughter, I knew he would need all the help he could get."

She's been planning this since I was born?

I can't believe it. Before even *meeting* me, she thought I was worth celebrating.

"I think the mermaid outfit would have been very pretty on you." Auntie Queenie scans my body up and down. "The seashell bra might have been tricky to get past your father, but we could've worked something out. We would've had to modify it anyway so it would stay up during the program."

I guess all this effort is Auntie Queenie's love language.

29

"YOU'RE SURE WE didn't burn it?" Raph asks me for the millionth time as he parks his car.

Raph said he would give me a ride to Tita Gretchen and Tito Vince's anniversary party at Lily Bakery. Hours before he was supposed to pick me up, he called panicking about his gift for Cia's parents. When I got to his place, he was freaking out because he had tried to replace cream cheese with mozzarella in a cheesecake recipe.

It was like the worst baker in the world collaborating with the second-worst baker in the world. Despite how many times we reread the instructions online, the top ended up covered with cracks. And before sliding the cake in the oven, Raph decided to experiment with some pink food coloring. Between the huge crater in the middle and the pink food coloring oozing out of random cracks—we basically baked Cia's parents a giant popped pimple.

"Just curious," I say when he keeps eyeing the box we

stuffed the cake in. "Why make a cake if they're celebrating at a bakery?"

"So it's a gift they won't expect." He smiles and taps his temple. "Is Jappy already there?"

"I don't know." I let out a laugh that sounds fake even to my ears. "Why would I be talking to Jappy?"

Fine. My brain may have squealed when Jappy asked me earlier if I was going to the anniversary party, but that doesn't mean we're *talking*.

Raph answers me with a smirk. "Nag MOMOL kayo, 'no?"

"God. We did not make out," I say, feeling my cheeks burn.

But why did Raph jump to that conclusion? Does he know something I don't?

I focus my gaze on the cake on my lap. "Why do you think we did?"

"I saw you two at the fair," he says. "When there are sparks, I can feel it. Detecting romantic tension is my fifth sense."

"Don't you mean sixth sense?"

"I suck at smelling things, so I don't count my sense of smell."

I groan. "Jappy and I are just friends."

"You two never had a moment? Maybe one time he was in his room busy with his video games, and he turned to you and said . . ." Raph lowers his voice and bites his lip. "I'd rather play with *you*, Chloe Liang."

"Ew!" I shove Raph away, and he laughs.

"Okay, if it wasn't making out," he says, "what did happen?"

"Well . . ." I can't believe I'm actually considering asking Raph for advice. The only person I'd ever turn to about guys is

Cia, but her being Jappy's sister is making this extremely difficult. "There was *sort of* something after the variety show. Our knees touched."

Raph's face scrunches up. "Huh?"

I bump my knees together to demonstrate. "We did that."

"Ohhhh," he says, smiling. "Knee-touching."

"You had to be there."

"You want to spoil my innocent eyes with premarital knee-touching?" He gasps and shields his eyes. "And you did it in a high school with *children* present? You two must've been really . . . hor-knee."

Ugh. I should've seen this coming.

"Never mind," I say. "I'm imagining things. Jappy doesn't see me that way."

"Aw, Chloe. Stop overthinking it," Raph reassures me. "Maybe the whole knee thing is Jappy's way of flirting." He does his little jumps in his seat. "You should try doing a grand gesture!"

"A what?"

"Something romantic," he says, and points to the cake on my lap. "Like baking something for him! Or writing him a love letter."

I imagine Jappy judging like he's never judged before. He may like Ben&Ben, but he's never going to be the type of guy who goes for some cheesy romantic gesture.

"Does Cia also think there's something between me and Jappy?" I ask.

He shakes his head. "She's convinced you're on your way to becoming Mrs. Basketball Boy."

The thought of facing Jappy again makes my whole body clam up. If I run into him, I might panic and have to hide in another restroom.

"Do you think it'd be okay if I skip the anniversary party this year?" I ask.

Raph considers me, then reaches for the cake and hops out of the car.

"What're you doing?" I ask as he walks around to my side and pulls open the door.

He crouches down to face me. "Remember that time we watched *Into the Spider-Verse*?"

"Great movie."

"You remember that scene when Miles Morales takes a leap of faith and finally claims his role as Spider-Man?"

"God. The animation there was *breathtaking*. That split second when they turned the frame upside down—"

"Didn't mean to get all technical here," Raph says, cutting off my fangirling. "You know how Miles Morales wasn't one hundred percent sure he was ready to be Spider-Man, but he still jumped off the building?"

I nod.

"Having feelings for someone for the first time is sort of like that. It's taking a leap of faith. You'll never know if the person you like likes you back if you don't jump off the building." Raph cringes. "That sounded more morbid than I had planned."

I smile and say, "I got the message."

He's right. I'm never going to figure out this whole Jappy situation if I never see him again. If Peter had the guts to tell the truth to Auntie Queenie, I should be able to face Jappy. Also, what's more wholesome than seeing each other in a bakery? I can't embarrass myself too much if I'm in a room filled with bread and pastries.

I draw a deep breath and get out of the car. This whole thing could be all in my head. I mean, maybe the knee-touching was an accident. Jappy Torres could simply be my best friend's brother who was once in close proximity to my knee—and nothing more.

We get closer to the bakery and hear loud music playing.

"Are you sure it's open?" I ask Raph. It looks like all the lights are switched off.

"I think the music's coming from inside . . ." He pushes open the door.

Janet Jackson's "Together Again" is blasting through the two-story bakery, and the whole place has turned into a dance floor. The tables and chairs that are usually set up are gone, and the counter that typically displays baked goods now showcases a selection of cocktails. Both levels are crowded with Tita and Tito's friends, who are all ballroom dancing. There's even a dance instructor who's spinning Tita Gretchen around. To top it all off, a huge disco ball is dangling from the ceiling.

"Welcome to Lily Bakery's Disco Night!" The DJ's voice booms through the room. "Where we'll be spinning all the classic hits from the seventies to the two thousands."

My dad's worst nightmare came true—I actually ended up at a disco.

30

I TRY ADJUSTING my ponytail higher, and my hair tie snaps in my hand. Great. The one time I have my hair down is when I'm stuffed in a bar with all the titas and titos of Manila.

"Cia said she got a table upstairs!" Raph yells above the music.

We swerve through the crowd—and turn down multiple offers to join in the ballroom dancing—and make our way to the second floor. Everyone up here is either talking or dancing. Then I see Jappy sitting by himself in a booth near the back. I almost bolt downstairs when he notices us and side-waves.

"Don't worry." Raph winks and nudges me with the cake box. "My fifth sense gotchu." He shimmies over to Jappy and points a finger gun at the drink on the table. "Nice one, Kuya Jappy! Is that vodka, gin, tequila?"

I try not to stare at Jappy as Raph lists every alcoholic beverage ever made.

Jappy grunts and nods at me. "Hey."

My heart and my mouth say hey back.

"So much passion beneath the grunts," Raph whispers to me, and I shush him.

Jappy explains that Tito Vince called Cia to go downstairs and makes room for us to join him in the booth. Raph gestures for me to sit, and I insist that he go in first. The farther I am from Jappy's knees, the better. So the three of us end up squeezed in the booth with Raph taking up most of the space with his elbows.

"What's in the box?" Jappy asks.

"Cheesecake. Chloe and I made it for your parents." Raph smiles and offers it to him. "Want some?"

Jappy narrows his eyes at the zit dessert. "It's pink."

"Maybe we shouldn't be offering this to other people," I tell Raph.

"This cake is our masterpiece, Chloe." Raph scoops out a whole spoonful. But as soon as he stuffs it in his mouth, he grabs a napkin and spits it out.

I stop laughing when Raph's phone buzzes with a message and he starts stress-scrolling.

"What's wrong?" I ask.

He closes the box and gathers his things. "I gotta get a new cake."

"Raph, I really don't think you need to," I say.

Even Jappy agrees with me. "My parents are way too focused on dancing to eat anything."

Raph ignores us and asks if I can step out so he can leave the booth. He slides off the bench, and I follow him to the stairs. "Hey, what's up?"

"My brother just messaged that he saw my car parked outside." The words and panic tumble out of his mouth. "They had this whole family dinner planned, and I said I couldn't make it. I didn't know they were going to be eating right next door."

"I'm assuming they don't know you're here for Cia's parents?"

He shakes his head.

"Okay," I say, trying to calm him down. "Maybe you can say that you dropped by a friend's party. They don't have to know who's celebrating."

His shoulders relax. "Right, right."

"You want me to go with you?"

"I got this." Raph is suddenly all smiles again and lifts his nonexistent glass. "You stay here and take your leap of faith."

"There will be no leaping."

"Yeah, okay." He points at my legs. "Just watch your knees."

Raph's knee buckles when I kick the back of his leg. "Watch yours."

The ladies at the bottom of the steps erupt into cheers when the DJ starts playing "Dancing Queen." I take a peek downstairs and see Tito Vince taking Tita Gretchen from the instructor and beginning their own dance. I glance back at the table and see Jappy bobbing his head to the song too.

"Hey." Jappy raises his eyebrows when I take the seat across from him. "How's Raph?"

"Usual Raph," I say. "How's being young and sweet, only seventeen?"

"I stand by ABBA." He blinks and takes a sip from his drink. "Hey, your hair's down."

"Oh." I tuck a loose strand behind my ear. "Yeah, that happens when it's not up."

I should just stick to reciting ABBA lyrics for the rest of my life.

He nods and gives no further commentary. God. There he goes again, throwing me off by bringing up my hair.

"Do you want a drink?" I hear Jappy ask. "Their tea is pretty good."

I peer at his glass. "You ordered tea?"

"It's a bakery. I usually order tea when me and my friends come for Disco Night."

I shake my head, laughing. "You've been to other Disco Nights?"

"The pastries are good, and the music's not bad. People who like disco are less annoying."

The disco ball downstairs spins and flashes. Even the second floor is getting packed with more people dancing. "I thought you hated parties."

"It's not as bad if I'm around people I'm comfortable with." He motions around the bakery-slash-bar. "By myself? I hate crowds. Usually too many people in them." He takes a sip of his tea. "It's like the kaishao stuff with your auntie."

"What do you mean?"

"You sacrificed for your family by getting set up." He points to himself. "I sacrifice for my family by attending parties."

"That doesn't sound as selfless as you make it out to be," I say, and he laughs.

Did he bring the kaishao up on purpose? Maybe this is the segue to the leap of faith Raph was talking about.

Before I can say anything, Jappy stands to greet a couple of aunties approaching our table. I recognize one of them as Tita Vicky, Tita Gretchen's sister who always wears three pearl necklaces.

"Ah, look how gwapo my pamangkin is!" Tita Vicky reaches out and pinches Jappy's cheeks. She boasts to the ladies around her that she has the most handsome nephew. I bite back a laugh when Jappy side-eyes me.

"Nice to see you, Tita," he says.

"Wow, ah. You brought a date pa to your parents' anniversary party." My cheeks go warm when Tita Vicky gestures to me. "Girlfriend mo?"

"No, Tita," Jappy immediately answers. "We're not together. Chloe is Cia's friend."

Wow. I wasn't even friend-zoned. I was friend-of-sister-zoned. I guess that's my answer to the whole leap-of-faith question.

After I beso Tita Vicky and the rest of her friends, Jappy offers for them to take our table.

"Sorry," he tells me. "Ma would sermon me for days if she knew I didn't give up my seat for Tita Vicky."

"No problem," I say.

I guess all that stuff was in my head. The fair, variety show, the whole knees-touching moment—was that just him being nice? Maybe Jappy just puts up with me because I'm Cia's best friend.

"I think that's an empty table!" Jappy points to the other end of the room.

My heart squeezes when I feel his hand on the curve of my back.

"You good?" he asks as he leads me through the sea of dancing people. I nod and try to concentrate on the shimmying going on around me instead of Jappy's hand.

But when we approach the booth, we see another group has already beaten us to it.

Jappy lets go and wipes his brow. "Are you okay with standing?"

"Yeah," I say, trying to forget how the room felt ten times hotter when Jappy was touching my back. I really need to stop overthinking these things. Rom-coms never have back-touching or knee-touching as big declarations of love.

The crowd cheers again when the DJ switches the song to "Ever After" by Bonnie Bailey. Whenever we go on road trips, Ma always has this on. Even though the singer isn't Filipino, Ma insists that "Ever After" is honorary OPM, based on how much it gets played here.

The song even gets Jappy to start swaying.

"Should I get ready for another Jappy Torres performance?" I ask.

He shakes his head, laughing. "*That* was a once-in-a-lifetime experience."

Someone pushes me in the back, and I bump right into Jappy's chest. My breath hitches as I'm pressed up against him.

"Hi," he says, and I get a full close-up look at his dimples.

"Hey," I exhale.

I can smell the detergent on his shirt, the familiar scent of his cologne. My whole body stills when I feel his hand rest on the back of my waist. I lift my eyes to meet his, and he holds my gaze. I don't think anyone has ever looked at me like this before.

He dips his head and brings his lips closer to my ear.

"Chlo?" he whispers.

His eyes drift to my hand, and I realize my phone's ringing with a call from Raph.

"Sorry." I snap out of it and step away from Jappy. "I should probably go see what's up."

"Do you want me to—"

"No, you should stay and enjoy the party." I dive back into the crowd and gulp down all the swirling feelings in my stomach.

I RUSH OUTSIDE and take a minute to clear my head. Note to self: Avoid cramped spaces with loud music when I'm with Jappy.

I'm about to call Raph back when I hear someone call my name. I turn and see it's—

"Uncle Dennis!" I say. I give him a beso.

"Funny, I just saw Raphael," he says. "Were you two at the same dinner?"

"That's, uh . . . That's a good question."

Before I can figure out what to say, Uncle Dennis sees Raph and Cia walk out of the bakery.

"Raphael!" Uncle Dennis calls out. "Look, it's Chloe!"

By the time he and Cia reach us, all color has officially drained from Raph's face.

I look at Cia for some clue as to what we should do, but her focus is completely on Raph's dad.

"I thought you said you were going home?" Uncle Dennis asks Raph.

"Yeah, I was just . . ." He tugs on his hat. "I made a quick detour for cake," he says, lifting the pink box.

Uncle Dennis chuckles and wags his finger at Raph and me. "I know what you two are up to." His mustache perks up with a big smile. "You and Chloe are on a date!"

Oh, dear god, no.

Raph shakes his head so hard some of the cake spills out. "Dad, no. This isn't a date, and I'm not dating Chloe. I'm—" His eyes drift to Cia. "We're with . . . our friend Patricia."

Uncle Dennis reaches out and shakes Cia's hand. "Are you trying to get these two lovebirds together too?"

She answers with a slight smile. I see her eyes wrinkle with hurt, and chomping guilt churns my gut.

"Do you and Chloe want to join us for dessert?" Uncle Dennis smiles. "Raph's mom just ordered some of the best Nutella crepes."

My mind is too distracted to even scramble for a good alibi.

Raph thankfully steps in. "I think we were going to head out soon."

"Right," Uncle Dennis agrees. "We'll get those crepes next time, then! This place makes their own customized Nutella. Do you wanna know what their secret ingredient is?"

"Uh . . . sure, Uncle," I say.

"Maybe I shouldn't tell you. You guys might *spread* it." Uncle Dennis's head bobs as he laughs. "Get it? Like how you spread Nutella?"

I smile and squeeze out a polite laugh. "Good one, Uncle."

"I'll see you at home," Raph says, and we all beso Uncle Dennis goodbye.

For most of our friendship, I've usually been able to read what's going on in Cia's head. There were even times when I'd say "bless you" before she sneezed. But right now, I have no idea what she's thinking.

MUSIC IS SUPPOSED to be the window to one's soul. If that's the case, Raph's soul must be the most chaotic place in the universe. Being in Raph's car with his DJ Tofu mix playing is the equivalent of getting strapped to a dental chair and being forced to listen to someone's teeth getting drilled.

After the disaster with Uncle Dennis, Cia told Raph that he should probably head home. When I tried asking her if she was okay, she just said that I should probably go too, since Raph was my ride.

"Did you know there was a cake shop right across the street?" Raph asks. "Like, why would they put two bakeries right next to each other?"

"Cool." I nod while he keeps bobbing to the bass that's literally shaking the car. I start typing out a message to Cia to tell her that I'm sorry about Uncle Dennis when my phone runs out of battery. "Shit."

"What's up?" he asks.

I mean, Raph and I are friends. What if I just ask him about what happened?

"So, your dad . . ."

"Sorry about his jokes," he says. "He's been watching Ali Wong specials and got inspired." The song ends and skips to another earthquake-inducing ballad.

"Oh, I don't mind the jokes," I say. "I was just . . . Is Cia really okay with your family not knowing about her?"

His eyes cut to me. "Did Cia tell you something?"

"She keeps saying she's fine."

"And you think she's not?"

I shake my head.

He lets out a heavy sigh. "I've been trying to make Cia feel better about all of it. Like maybe it wouldn't matter as much if I put in more effort with everything else."

"That's why you were so stressed about the cake."

He nods and pauses. "What would you do if your parents disapproved of the person you were with? Like, what if they hated Jappy?"

My neck starts growing hot. "Jappy and I aren't together."

"Okay, fine," Raph says. "Picture another hypothetical tall, dark, and moody guy, then. What would you do if your parents didn't like the guy you loved?"

His question hangs in the air until I admit, "I don't know."

I'm only on the brink of liking someone right now, and it already feels overwhelming. It feels like it takes so much to reach the point of *loving* someone. And if you get there—if you find a person worthy of the magnitude of the word *love*—how are you supposed to give that up?

"If it was me," I finally say, "I guess I would stay with the guy because I loved him."

"My brother would say"—Raph pauses and exhales—"that

you should break up with them because you're supposed to love your family more."

"I don't think it's selfish for you to love Cia."

His head turns in my direction. "But it is selfish for me to keep hiding her when I know she's hurting." Raph's voice catches, and his eyes look like he's blinking back tears.

For the rest of the ride, we avoid talking and let DJ Tofu fill the empty space.

I don't have the heart to agree with him out loud.

EVER SINCE THE anniversary party, Cia has been dodging my questions. Every time I message her about Raph, she sends me a link to a new rap song.

I have enough songs for a "Cia Being Evasive" playlist.

So I figured that if I happened to drop by, it'd be easier to check how she's *really* doing.

"Hi, Tita." I give Tita Gretchen a beso when she opens the door.

"You just missed Cia!" she says. "She went to the mall with some of the glee club girls. I think they were planning to watch a movie, if you want to catch up with them."

"Oh, it's okay, Tita." I smile. "Sorry, I should've texted. I'll come back when she's home."

"Ah, you're welcome here anytime, Chloe." She waves for me to come in, and my mouth waters when I get a whiff of the fried bananas. Cia is the baking expert, but Tita Gretchen has really mastered the perfect turon. "Come have some merienda first," she says as if she can read my mind.

When we get to the kitchen, I spy *Got 2 Believe* paused on the small TV by the fridge. Tita Gretchen goes to the stove and drizzles the turon with her special sauce and then plates it with a scoop of vanilla ice cream.

I take my first bite, and my teeth sink into the crunchy lumpia wrapper while the sugared banana and ice cream melt in my mouth. Tita resumes the movie, and it's the ending scene when the guy says he didn't believe in forever until he found forever in her.

Tita Gretchen clutches the dish towel to her chest and mouths the girl's exact lines: "You never say sorry for loving someone. You never say sorry for loving me." She lets out a squeal when the two hug and the cheesy love song plays in the background.

I finish eating, and Tita pauses the movie on a shot of Rico Yan whispering into Claudine Barretto's ear.

"If a guy with a face like that tells you he wants to marry you, kikiligin ka rin." Tita Gretchen blows a kiss at the TV and reaches for my plate. I tell her I can take care of it and walk to the sink to help out with the dishes.

While Tita wipes off the dining table, I ask, "Did Tito Vince ever give you a speech like that?"

"Vince?" She laughs. "I used to tease him that he should be more like the guys in the teleseryes. Very shy yung tito mo when we were younger. He spoke more with his actions. I think Jappy got that from him."

"Oh." I scrub another plate in the sink, wondering whether I should ask the question on my mind. "How did you know you wanted to go from friends to . . . more than friends?"

She tilts her head at me. "Why do you ask?"

"I like love stories," I say innocently.

"Talaga ba?" Tita looks at me skeptically. "Well, it's like the story your tito always tells. We had the same classes during college."

"And it's true that you didn't get together until years later?"

She nods, and I notice her eyes sort of twinkle. "We were the only new hires in our first job. He was older but still felt like the same Vince I knew in college." Tita shakes her head. "He was already so cheesy back then." She slides in next to me at the sink to wash her hands. "There's some water there," she says, pointing her lips to the fridge.

While getting the pitcher, I glance back at the couple hugging on the TV. These local rom-coms always make this romance stuff look so easy, like two people can actually fall in love within the span of two hours.

Tita Gretchen hands me two glasses, and I blurt out, "What made you say yes, though, Tita?" She eyes me curiously, and I quickly focus my attention on pouring the water. "Um . . . like in *Got 2 Believe*, doesn't the movie say that if you love someone, you'll *really* know if you get the hiccups?"

She laughs again. "The movie also says that a woman will be cursed to be 'single for life' if she's not married by twenty-five."

"So you weren't waiting for any signs before you got together with Tito?"

"I already liked your tito when we were in college, but I never told him. I kept thinking there was going to be a more perfect time, a moment when I felt more ready, and then I suddenly had to move away. When I saw him again at work, I guess I stopped thinking." She takes a deep breath. "All I knew was that I wanted to be with the person who made me happy."

"But there has to be more to it than that, right?" I ask. "People must get together and fall in love for more important reasons than making each other happy."

Tita pauses and squeezes my shoulder. "Is your happiness not important?" Before I can answer, she plates another turon for me. "Is this sudden interest in love stories inspired by a recent development in your love life?"

Does Tita know about my feelings for Jappy?

Wow, look how quickly the sweat glands on my palms open up.

"Um." I gulp. "There might be . . . something going on. I'm not really sure."

"Well, whoever it is, they should know you're too good for them." She nods and smiles at me. "By the way, I'm so happy you and Jappy are still hanging out. Honestly, I'm still shocked that he volunteered for Queenie's setup."

I almost drop the plate when Tita hands me the turon.

"Volunteered?"

"Queenie dropped by here with invitations to your debut and asked if Jappy had any friends he could introduce you to," Tita says. "When Jappy overheard our conversation, he said he would go on the date with you."

Tita is hurling way too much new information at me for me to process.

So Jappy knew the church thing was going to be a setup? And why the hell would he *volunteer* to go on a kaishao?!

While I'm having what feels like a stroke, Tita keeps on talking. "I thought the church was a strange place to go on a date, but I guess church is a good place to get to know someone. Anyway, despite how things turned out, I'm glad you two are still friends."

After a moment of gathering my thoughts, I slowly nod. "Yeah . . . still friends."

33

THIS ISN'T SOME scene from a love story. I am not walking into some romantic grand gesture where a guy eloquently professes his deep feelings for me.

The only reason I came upstairs was to check on my good old friend Jappy. And the reason I lied and said I needed help with some design software was because I wanted advice from my good old friend Jappy.

"Jesus, Chlo. Check your messages." Jappy grunts while pointing out the fact I have five hundred unread emails.

Is that his coded way of telling me to look out for the messages he's been sending me?

"I think the issue is coming from your firewall." He clicks through my computer settings. "I'll turn it off and try re-launching Animate."

Maybe *that* is code for *We need to break down the walls between us.*

After realizing that I haven't said anything since I got to Jappy's room, I squeak out, "Cool."

He pulls his other rolling chair in front of me. "Want to sit down?"

Sitting next to Jappy means my knees would be next to Jappy, which means the very loud question in my head—*Why would Jappy ever volunteer for a kaishao?*—would be even louder.

"I'm good." My feet (and knees) back away from the chair. "I'll walk around and let you focus."

He answers me with his judgy look, but he leaves it at that.

I should not be attracted to a guy who uses his headboard as a drying rack for his socks. This whole room should be immediate Jappy Torres repellent to me by now. He has a poster that says NO STUPID PEOPLE BEYOND THIS POINT and another with a giant taco saying SOMETIMES I FALL APART. Those should be red flags of emotional baggage, not shit I find funny.

As I smooth a corner of a poster that's sticking out, I notice a book called *The Architecture of Happiness* placed next to the mounds of paper scattered on his dresser. I open it to the section he bookmarked and see a photo booth strip tucked between the pages. It's the one of us at the fair with both our blue tongues sticking out.

"I think I fixed it!" He swivels his chair toward me. "You're lucky that you're friends with a computer genius—" He stops talking when he sees me holding the photo strip.

My brain is working so hard to formulate coherent thoughts that all my mouth manages to say is "Why?"

"Huh?"

"Wh-why do you use this as a bookmark?"

"I lose track of what page I'm on." He shrugs and focuses back on my computer.

You're jumping to conclusions, Chloe. Maybe Jappy uses random things for bookmarks all the time. Maybe his last bookmark was a used tissue. This is absolutely, completely, totally not about you. Let it go. Let. It. Go.

Then I hear myself word-vomit, "Did you volunteer to get kaishao-ed with me?" His shoulders tense up, and I keep talking before I lose my nerve. "Tita Gretchen told me that you wanted to go on the kaishao."

My words hang in the air as he turns in my direction. I think he's about to shrug me off again when he says, "Maybe."

Maybe?

"Wh-why didn't you tell me?"

"Because I didn't know your dad ambushed you without your consent." He hesitates and squirms in his seat. "Also, that whole thing about the mountain."

"What mountain?"

"The mountain metaphor." His pineapple hair flares out in full force. "All that stuff about how dating should be like climbing Mount Everest and how getting set up felt like walking."

"Well, I didn't know you wanted to walk." I gulp, feeling my heart fluttering wildly in my chest.

His eyebrows knit together. "Am I walking on the mountain or a hill?"

I groan. "Jappy, forget about the metaphor."

He's quiet for a moment and rests his hands on his lap. "Whether I volunteered or not, it doesn't really matter."

I fold my arms over my gut. "It might . . . matter."

His eyes widen. "Really?"

"Maybe," I say. "Does it matter to you?"

"I asked you first."

"You were the one who lied about the kaishao in the first place."

"How was I supposed to know you weren't in on the plan?" he asks, throwing his hands to his sides.

"It was in a church, Jappy. Who plans a date to the church?"

"Religious people!"

I bite my lip, and I catch a flicker of a dimple on his cheek.

After a beat, he asks me, without any figurative language about landforms, "So, you *did* want to go on that church date?"

"No . . . not really."

"Oh. Cool, cool." He tenses his jaw, and his eyes fall back to the screen. "Your license for this software is about to expire."

"Jappy." I touch his shoulder to stop him from swiveling away from me. "I didn't want to be ambushed in church that day, but . . ." I take a deep breath and ball my hands into fists when I feel them clamming up. "If the person I got set up with wanted to maybe hang out sometime in a non-kaishao scenario . . . without any of my relatives monitoring . . . I might be open to a possible date . . . that's not in a church . . ."

Oh my god. This is the longest sentence uttered by anyone. Ever.

Jappy's watching me as one naturally would when faced with a rambling idiot.

Say you want to go out with him. Say that you think you like him. Say . . . something!

"I'll be right back," I yelp, and scramble to the safety of the bathroom.

If by some miracle I do end up in a relationship, my sweat is going to start smelling like Vicks VapoRub.

Out of all the things I could think of while I'm massaging the ointment on my forehead, the image that flashes in my mind is the *Into the Spider-Verse* scene. This might be the leap of faith that Raph was talking about.

I don't know if I'll ever get a handle on all the intricacies of liking someone, but I guess the point isn't waiting for some big sign like getting the hiccups. You can't control how you meet a person—whether it's some magical earth-shattering rom-com moment or an awkward matchmaking attempt by your auntie.

Maybe no one really knows for certain if they're going to have an epic happily-ever-after kind of love with the person they like. Maybe everyone has to start with a leap of faith.

Once I gather up the courage, I put back the Vicks and head to Jappy's room.

Leap of faith, Chloe. Leap of faith.

I'm about to knock on Jappy's door when I notice the usual anti-inspirational quote on his whiteboard is gone.

Instead it says:

Will you go out with me?
(NOT TO A CHURCH!)

34

HOW DO I impress somebody who's seen almost all my life's awkward stages?

This is a guy who's seen me at prom, graduation, that one Halloween when Cia and I went as a fruit bowl. What if the searing image of me in a banana costume is the only thing Jappy can think of during our date?

I really didn't want to have to explain Jappy to Pa yet, so I told Jappy I wanted to keep our parents out of this whole thing for now. He understood that they would all blow this up into a way bigger deal than it needs to be.

But as the hours go by, I'm starting to feel like this *is* a big deal. I'm going on a date. An actual date with a guy I think I like and who seems to like me back. When I sing along to "Love on Top," the "you" in the song might start referring to an actual person.

For the hundredth time, I think about messaging Cia, but I keep stressing over how she'll react about Jappy. Cia still wasn't home when I left their place, and things have been weird since the anniversary party. What if she freaks out even more that I'm going on a date with her brother? That must be against some sort of friend code, right?

There's a knock, and my bedroom door flies open. Pa's whole knocking-and-entering thing is why I was trained from an early age to change in the bathroom.

Pa scans my outfit. "Where is Cia taking you, again?"

I told him a tiny white lie that I'm going somewhere with Cia. I mean, she's also a Torres, so it's even whiter than a white lie.

"Just dinner at the mall," I say.

"Good." He nods. "You can go after our merienda with Peter."

Excuse me?

"Pa, Cia and I are going to eat soon."

"And Peter's waiting downstairs," he says. "It's important that we honor our commitments to family, Chloe."

This is literally the first time I'm hearing about this particular commitment.

"Can't I catch up with him during our family lunch tomorrow?" Or any other Sunday that I already spend sitting next to Peter?

With his frustrated tongue click, I already know there's zero room for me to argue.

IT'S VERY HARD to stay pissed when there's a perfectly juicy piece of Chickenjoy in front of me. But great fried chicken aside, I have no idea why this merienda is so urgent. It doesn't help that Pa is taking ten times longer than usual to say anything.

Case in point: Pa has been slicing the same piece of chicken for the past five minutes.

"Peter, is there anything new with you?" he finally says.

Peter looks up and wipes the gravy off his mouth. "Been busy preparing for my first day at UP, Uncle. I went to National Bookstore to laminate some maps yesterday."

"Maps?" I say.

"I want to be prepared for my first day, so I printed out campus maps so I can attach them to my ID."

"Why don't you use the maps in your phone?"

"This is in case my phone dies or doesn't have a signal, and I can study the maps better when they're printed copies."

Pa beams at Peter. "That kind of forward thinking is what made you a scholar."

Only Peter would find a way to be an overachiever even before college starts.

Then, out of nowhere, Pa segues the conversation with the most random question: "Have you seen the post about the two chickens?" Peter and I remain quiet, waiting for more context from my father.

"I don't get the joke," Peter says, glancing at me.

"While going through my feed," Pa continues, "I read about this woman in the UK who adopted two hens named Domino and Michelle. Even though Michelle was the bigger hen out of the two, she was easily scared by her shadow and was picked on by the other chickens . . ."

What kind of accounts does Pa follow?

"And then Domino, the smaller hen, would come to Michelle's defense and put her wing around her. She'd bring her food so they could eat separately from the rest of the chickens. After consulting with a breeder, the woman found out that Domino's behavior was similar to a rooster wooing a hen."

"So Michelle and Domino were a couple?" Peter asks.

"Seems like it. And they were two hens. Do you know what hens are?" He turns to me like a teacher calling on a student who didn't even raise their hand.

"Female chickens?" I say.

"Right!"

Peter and I startle from Pa's enthusiasm.

"Two female chickens who took care of each other, and if they came to this house, they'd be welcome here." He turns to my cousin. "You understand that, Peter?"

That's the moment both Peter and I realize that Pa is addressing Peter's coming out. And despite the heavy poultry content, I don't think I've ever respected my father more.

Peter smiles back at Pa and says, "Got it, Uncle."

PA MIGHT BE all supportive of chickens in love, but he's still insisting I go out with a chaperone. Even though I repeatedly insisted that I already had a ride, Pa basically shoved me into Peter's car.

This is fine. Instead of meeting down the street from my house, I'll ask Jappy to pick me up outside Peter's dance training.

Once Peter turns the engine on, the stereo announces that he has a new message from Miles. He switches off the volume and quickly disconnects his phone.

"Miles as in . . . Miles Chua?"

"Uh . . . yeah." He fidgets and adjusts the mirror. "He sometimes messages about workout stuff."

"I didn't know you guys were friends."

Peter quickly changes the subject. "Where are you and Cia going?"

"Oh, I can ask her to meet me wherever your training is."

"It's pretty far, and Uncle Jeffrey said that I should bring you to your dinner."

Crap. If Peter sees Jappy picking me up, he's for sure going to tell Pa.

I message Jappy: **Change of plans. Meet at Wilson Plaza instead!!!**

Once we're near, I tell Peter he can drop me off by the Starbucks.

"Uncle Jeffrey told me that I shouldn't leave until I see Cia," he says.

"Oh, she's not coming until later."

"I don't mind waiting." He grabs his wallet. "I needed one more coffee order for my rewards card."

"We were actually going to meet in Pancake House first," I say, hoping Peter takes the hint.

"Pancakes sound good too."

I sigh. There's never an easy way when it comes to Peter.

"Okay." I turn to face him. "I know my dad is the Iron Man to your Spider-Man, but can you please, please keep this a secret?" After I confide in him everything about the kai-shaos and Jappy, I quickly add, "And not to hang this over your head, but I did keep your secret about Pauline."

Silence floats around us until Peter asks, "Wait, you're not interested in Miles?"

"I'm dating Jappy." I stop and correct myself: "Well, going on *a* date with Jappy."

"Oh, I thought maybe you were into Miles."

"Did he tell you that?" I ask.

"No . . ." He turns away, unable to look me in the eye.

"Peter, what is it?"

He blinks and slouches in his seat. This might be the only time I've seen him break his perfect posture. "You know when you told my mom that you wanted to cancel the dance performance for your debut?"

I nod.

"So . . . I never passed on the message," he says slowly. "I lied to Miles and said that the performance was still on. I was going to meet him after this, not my street dance club."

"Wait, how often have you been practicing?"

"Just, like . . . every other day?"

"Peter!" I spin to face him. "What were you going to tell Miles when he showed up to the debut and there was no performance?"

He hunches his shoulders. "That I wanted to spend time with him?"

Okay, fair. Points for being straightforward and honest, I guess.

And then Peter adds, "He asked me out last night."

"Wait, what?!"

"Well, I think he did."

"What did Miles say?"

Peter pulls out his phone and shows me the message: **Do you want to go out with me?**

"Yeah, I'm *pretty* sure he asked you out," I tell him. "Wow, I guess I just always assumed Miles was straight."

"After I came out to him, he told me that he's dated both guys and girls. He really understood what I was going through, since he came out as bi to his friends last year."

"Gotcha." I nod and poke Peter's arm. "So, is tonight the big date?"

He sighs and stares up at the roof of the car. "I said no."

"Huh? Why?" I ask. "I thought you were into him."

"I thought *you* were into him." Peter throws up his hands. "I didn't want to come between you two if you had something going on."

"There's nothing going on," I assure him.

"Sure." Peter scoffs. "I could smell how much Vicks you put on at Cia's party."

"Fine. I did have a crush on him before, but it's totally gone now," I say. "And also, I appreciate you considering my feelings, but you could have just talked to me about it. God, even Auntie Queenie would be pissed if she found out you turned down someone that hot."

He frowns and lets out another deep sigh. "I think I blew it."

"Hey, you never know." I slide closer to him. "Like my dad would say, maybe it's not too late to get your chicken."

That gets a small smile out of Peter. "Why aren't you telling Uncle Jeffrey about Jappy?"

"Because I'd rather finish my date before my dad kills the guy."

"I think Uncle would understand." He shrugs. "You heard the chicken story."

"Well, he's different with me."

Peter gets the version of Pa that shares parables about chickens in love. I get the version that zones out as soon as I open my mouth.

"Is this Jappy a good guy?" Peter asks.

"No, he's the son of Satan," I deadpan.

"But what are his credentials?"

"Peter, I didn't tell my dad so I could avoid the interrogation."

"Which is why I need to make sure you know what you're doing."

I reassure him that I'm going to take care of myself, and he clicks his tongue. "At least tell me he's a better dancer than you."

"Hey, I'm not that bad."

"You struggle with the most basic steps."

"Oh, yeah? Could a bad dancer do this?" And I bust out my shopping cart dance in the car until Peter caves in and follows my moves.

AMONG THE HIGH schoolers hanging around Wilson Plaza, I have no trouble spotting Jappy.

The things I automatically notice:

1. His smile and those dimples.
2. His hair. It looks like he actually used gel to smooth it down.
3. Peter parked by the milk tea stand, being the complete opposite of subtle.

Peter's crouching down in his seat, but I can still see his humongous eyes spying on me through the car window.

As Jappy walks toward me, I shoot my cousin a message: **PLS LEAVE**.

Peter immediately replies: **I need to make sure you're not dating a criminal!**

I start to type, **IF YOU DON'T LEAVE RIGHT NOW**—but I don't get to send my follow-up threat because Jappy is already standing in front of me.

"Hey," he says, giving me his side-wave.

Before I do anything else, I check to make sure Peter is leaving. Thank god his car is finally moving.

"What are you looking at?" Jappy asks, following my gaze.

"Nothing!" I grab his face to turn it back to me. Then I quickly remove my hand because, wow, one minute into the date, and I'm already touching his face.

He takes his hand from behind his back and holds out a sunflower. "I got this for . . . you."

"Oh. Wow." My mind races, trying to remember any movie or show that taught me the proper way to accept flowers. All I end up saying is "So bright . . . like the sun."

I GUESS MY comment about the sunflower was the premature nail in the coffin of this date. We've been in this Sunrise Buckets booth for five minutes, and it feels like we've been here for hours. We've been sitting in silence for so long that I've counted how many surfboards are displayed on the walls, how many Polaroid pictures of couples are tacked onto the specials board, and how many times the guy seated across from us orders a water refill.

Jappy clears his throat. "Is that a new top?"

"Oh." I suddenly feel very self-conscious about my outfit. "I've had this for a while, but I don't wear it that often."

"It's nice." He squirms and adds, "Really suits you."

"Uh, thanks."

After another painful pause, Jappy leans forward. "Does this feel weird to you?"

"Yes!" I blurt out. For a second, I worry that I said it a bit too enthusiastically until a smile crawls across his lips.

"We're on one of those awkward dates that people point to and say, 'Glad we're not those two.'"

"Wouldn't want to be that guy either." I motion to the guy who has now grabbed the entire water pitcher for his table. His whole face is dripping with sweat, and he keeps panting after each bite of his chicken wing. Meanwhile, the girl seated across from him is chilling and nibbling every wing to the bone.

"Your face turned that red too," Jappy says.

Before my taste buds developed their current (very resilient) spice tolerance, I was used to Pa's diet, which prohibits anything spicy. So when Cia invited me to her house when we were kids and Tita Gretchen served dan dan noodles, I was expecting the watered-down version Pa orders in restaurants. Tita considered taking me to the hospital because of how flushed my face got.

"That was one time," I argue. "And I've gotten stronger since then."

"Suuuuuure."

In defiance, I order the ultimate crazy hot wings, which features four chili pepper icons next to it on the menu.

"Kuya, for drinks, is it possible to get a glass of just milk?" Jappy asks the waiter and then glances at me. "She's a little weak with the spice."

I roll my eyes and shove the menu back at him.

Jappy laughs and shakes his head. "Thank god. I thought we were going to keep up the weird polite conversation all night."

"It's your fault," I point out. "You were the one who got the flower and started complimenting my outfit."

"We're on a date. That's how people act on dates."

"But that's not how *we* act." And then I'm blessed with another metaphor epiphany. "It's like how I built up my spice tolerance. I couldn't jump from zero to four chili peppers straightaway. It had to be gradual."

He raises his eyebrow and gives me his judgy look, which I'm suddenly finding extremely cute. "So are we at zero chili peppers now?"

"Maybe at . . ." I hold up one finger and fidget in my seat. "But the start of the night felt like we were rushing to a four right away . . . I need some more time to, uh . . . get adjusted."

Wow, Chloe. Way to plaster your pathetic lack of experience all over your face.

But instead of laughing, Jappy meets my eyes and nods. "Okay. Sige."

I smile back at him. "Sige."

We're interrupted when the waiter serves us our order of chili cheese fries. Jappy reaches for the sriracha bottle and pours some on his plate. He offers the bottle to me, and I put up my hand. I love spicy food, but that crosses the line into overkill. "You're dipping chili fries in sriracha?" I ask.

"Only way to do it."

I cringe when he soaks the fry until it's all soggy. "Gross."

"Weak." He grins at me smugly.

We take turns grabbing fries, and midway through the basket, his finger brushes against mine.

"Sorry." He retracts his hand. "Didn't mean to . . . That must have been like jumping from zero to three chili peppers . . ."

Seeing him so nervous makes me realize how special it is to find someone who's so careful about holding my hand.

"It's okay." I interrupt his apology and hook my pinkie with his.

He considers me and then intertwines our hands. "Too soon?"

I shake my head and smile.

Jappy smiles too and holds my hand underneath the table as we keep eating fries and joking about who else is on an awkward first date in this place.

WE DON'T NOTICE that we're the only ones left in the restaurant until the waiter serves us our bill. While Jappy insists on paying, I start plotting how to get back to my house without Pa figuring out the whole lie.

Is it weird that we stopped holding hands? How long do people usually hold hands? Is he not holding my hand because he's too nice to admit my palms were super gross and sweaty? Away from the sanctuary of the restaurant table, the whole PDA thing feels like such a foreign concept.

Once we leave Sunrise Buckets, we revert to awkward silence again.

"Do you want to chill for a bit?" Jappy suddenly asks.

"Oh, sure." I scan for the places that are still open. "We could get some milk tea? Or hang at Starbucks?"

"Arcade?" he suggests. Before I can even answer, he asks, "What?"

"I didn't say anything."

"You were giving me your judgy look."

"I don't have a judgy look," I say as he gives me *his* judgy look.

"What? You aren't in the mood for me to win you a prize?"

"I'd rather not win by cheating."

He then starts marching toward the arcade.

"Where are you going?" I call out.

"Proving to you I can win!"

CALLING THE WILSON Plaza arcade an arcade is very generous. It's a tiny room that squeezes in two basketball games and a claw machine. If you come here after school lets out, it sometimes takes an hour to get both basketball games free at the same time. Luckily, Jappy and I are the only ones here.

On a less lucky note, I hate to admit that Jappy is . . . crushing me. He's like some arcade basketball whisperer. He barely flicks his wrist, and the ball always manages to swoosh into the net. This would've been very useful knowledge to have had before I agreed to our bet.

For every round, the winner gets to ask the loser any question, and they're required to answer 100 percent truthfully.

Round one Jappy question: "First childhood crush?"

"Zuko."

"The Airbender cartoon?" he asks with an accompanying judgy eyebrow.

"Have you seen him?"

Round two Jappy question: "Thing you're most looking forward to in college."

"The cinematic arts library."

He shoots me with an even judgier look. "You're going to a completely different country by yourself, and you're most excited about a *library*?"

"Do you know how many iconic scripts and drawings they have archived there?"

We go back and forth, with him getting more and more astounded by my answers and me getting increasingly frustrated that I keep losing.

I curse and bounce the ball off the backboard when I lose a round by one basket.

"Sayang." Jappy shakes his head and taunts me. "That last shot could've been good if it had gone in . . . but it didn't." He keeps going. "And if you had made that last shot, we could've been tied . . . but you didn't."

"If you keep this up, I'm counting this as a question," I say through gritted teeth.

He's silent for a moment to prolong the torture. "Was I your best kaishao date?"

Ugh. I hate that my answer is going to fuel the fire of his rapidly growing ego.

"So . . ." He cocks his head when I don't reply. "You're saying that I was the best."

I groan and tap our game card on both machines.

My body must have absorbed something through osmosis from all those times Pa forced me to watch basketball games.

In the last minute of the round, when all the baskets count as three-pointers, it's like I've been miraculously blessed with Steph Curry's talent. The machine, which cheers "You did it!" after each successful shot, can't even keep up with how many baskets I'm making. Even my attempt to chuck two balls at the basket at once somehow gets in, quadrupling the point bonus. The buzzer rings, and I manage to not only beat Jappy but also nab the machine's highest score.

"Boom!" I open my fist, imitating a mic drop.

Jappy grunts and rolls out his arm. "Rematch."

"No, no, no." I wag my finger at him. "Unlike you, I know how to quit when I'm ahead. You could've left here unbeaten, unrivaled . . . but you didn't. If you weren't so cocky, this arcade could've been renamed in your honor. Wilson Plaza could've been Jappy's Plaza—"

"One win and she's acting like she's Bea Daez." After a beat, Jappy adds, "She's a basketball player."

"I know who she is," I say.

I don't.

He folds his arms. "Which team did she play for?"

"You know . . . a basketball team." Before he makes this into another "kwe-we" situation, I say, "Aren't we supposed to be talking about the bet you just lost?"

Jappy gives an exasperated grunt, but I still see a hint of a smile on his lips. "What's my punishment, then?"

There is one question that I've been wondering about all night. I wait a moment and ask, "What made you want to go on the kaishao with me?"

He raises his shoulders and pulls out his usual deadpan

tone. "I was hoping to be a kaishao success story. Be the inspirational Filipino guy who bested the Chinese Filipino ones."

I fight my disappointment in his answer. I mean, it's what I expected. For as long as I've known him, Jappy Torres has always been the guy with walls built up around him. The trouble with liking someone who's that guarded is that every time they shut down and refuse to feel anything, you wonder how easy it'll be for them to refuse their feelings for you.

37

JAPPY IS SILENT when I tell him I should do most of the talking with the guard by the village entrance in case Pa asks who I was riding with.

I think he's about to pull out of the parking lot when he unlatches his seat belt.

"Um . . . did you forget something?"

He's staring down at his lap when he finally starts to talk. "Remember during the school fair when you said that everyone should feel excited about something?"

"I did?"

Jappy nods and still doesn't meet my eye. "I don't like caring so much about things. If it's not a big deal, then it's all easier. The last time I tried really hard for something was getting into college . . . and I messed that up." He blinks and takes a deep breath. "You're one of my favorite people, Chlo. I keep thinking that you're my friend, my sister's friend . . . just generally thinking about you." He looks up and meets my eye. "With you, I care about everything, and I'm scared about messing it up." Before I can come up with a suitable response for something as beautiful as that, he grunts and shakes his hair. "Sorry, I'm not that great at the whole sincere confession thing."

I smile and squeeze his hand. "That was pretty good."

He looks at me for a weirdly long time with his insanely adorable dimples, and slowly leans in . . .

Ohmygodohmygodohmygod. This is happening. He's going to kiss me.

Except, I bump his forehead with mine, and his glasses fall on my nose.

"Ow," we both mutter.

I guess movies lie about first kisses. All the first-kiss scenes I've watched come with a perfectly timed musical cue and, like, fireworks bursting in the sky. The only thing I'm getting from my first kiss is an injury.

"Sorry," he says once I pass him his glasses.

"No, I was the one who crashed into you."

Despite everything, he's still smiling at me. "Take two?"

I grin back at him and nod.

This time, he pecks me on the lips, and it lasts for mere seconds.

Huh. So, that's it. My first kiss.

"Um. How was that?" Jappy asks me.

"It was great!" I hurriedly say. "Really, uh . . . pleasant."

"Pleasant?"

"*Pleasant* is a good word."

"It's not how you should describe a kiss. I didn't want to rush things, and I was trying to not go too far on that chili pepper scale—"

"It was a good kiss," I insist, and gesture toward the road. "Maybe we should get going."

"Wait." He angles his body toward me and removes his glasses. "Take three."

"Jappy, it's okay. We don't need to—"

Before I can finish, he pulls me in, and his mouth melts into mine. He kisses me so softly that it sends shivers through my whole body. I feel his hands travel from my shoulders down to my back, and I run my fingers through his hair. Everything he touches feels *electric*.

I have no idea what the hell I'm doing, but I suddenly don't care.

If touching his knee made my heart flutter, kissing him is making my heart soar. Actually, no. It's more than flying. My heart has hijacked a rocket and is blasting to the freaking moon.

This is why movies make first kisses epic with fireworks bursting in the sky. Because that's exactly what kissing Jappy feels like—fireworks.

He unlocks my seat belt, and I press harder into his body. He leans forward, wraps his arm around me, and kisses me urgently.

How can a boy I've known my whole life make my heart want to explode?

"Is it okay that we jumped from one to four?" I hear him whisper, and I feel his smile against my lips.

"I think we can go up to five, maybe six." I laugh, and he leans in again. And I know I could spend hours and days kissing this boy. I also know falling for someone like Jappy Torres has suddenly become the easiest thing in the world.

38

I ALWAYS FOUND it weird when couples spend so much time together. If you like someone, aren't you supposed to leave some room for that person to miss you? With Jappy, though, I totally get it. Whenever we're together, I feel like I'm already excited for the next time I'm going to see him.

For our date tonight, Jappy said he had something really special planned out. But I think it would be way more romantic if he'd give me at least *one* hint about where we're going.

So . . . where are you taking me? I message him for the millionth time.

Patience is a virtue. 😌

A virtue I never really cared about.

I told Pa that I was hanging out with Peter, and I'm about to stealthily sneak out when I hear someone ring the doorbell.

To my horror, I open the door and see Jappy holding a bouquet of chicken wings. "Wh-what are you doing here?"

"Picking you up." He extends the wing bouquet to me.

"Knew you weren't a fan of flowers, so I got a better alternative."

Before I can even react, Pa calls out, "Who's at the door?"

Shit.

"So let's go?" I say, pushing Jappy out the door, chicken wings and all.

"Wait, I need to say hi to Tito Jeffrey."

"Why?"

My heart stops when I hear Pa say, "Jappy?"

I stand there helplessly as Jappy reaches out his hand to Pa. "Hi, Tito, I hope it's okay that I'm taking Chloe out."

Shit. Shit. Shit.

Pa looks at Jappy like he's trying to peer into his soul. "Taking her out?"

"Uh, on a date, po," Jappy says, pulling his hand back.

If we were in a cartoon, there'd be question marks floating atop both of their heads.

"Um . . ." I start.

Say something. Anything!

"We're just friends, Pa."

Guilt swirls through my chest when I see the hurt on Jappy's face and the disappointment on my dad's.

"Jappy, maybe we should just reschedule," I say quietly.

He nods and says goodbye to Pa, who's still glaring at us wordlessly.

After I walk Jappy to his car, Pa is waiting for me in the kitchen. I can feel his eyes on me as I store the chicken bouquet in the fridge.

When he doesn't say anything, I slide closer to the stair-case. "I'm gonna go to bed . . ."

Pa clicks his tongue. "How long have you been seeing Jappy?"

My brain screams at me to lie. *Say this has never happened before! That you* were *really planning on hanging out with Peter.*

But maybe Peter has a point. What if Pa *would* understand? What if Pa is only hurt because I didn't tell him? What happened with Peter and Auntie Queenie could happen with me and Pa. I might even get a heartwarming story about chickens.

"This was our . . . eighth date."

Pa's face shifts from anger to confusion. "Eighth?"

I nod, praying that my father doesn't lock me in this house forever. "That time I told you I was going somewhere with Cia last week? I was with . . . Jappy."

A moment passes without him saying anything.

"Pa?"

"So you've been going out with random boys behind my back?"

"Just one guy—"

"Do you know how dangerous it is for me not to know where you are or who you're with?"

"Sorry, Pa."

He scoffs. "So when you go to Gretchen's house, is that an excuse to spend time with Jappy?"

"No, I—"

"Sneaking around with a boy. You know what kind of impression that gives off?"

"I wasn't doing anything bad."

No surprise, Pa completely misses my point. "Sasagot ka pa?"

I try not to roll my eyes. Every time I try to express my opinion, I get accused of talking back.

"You're still a member of this community, Chloe. It matters what people think of you."

"Yeah," I grumble. "Didn't you want this to happen? You helped Auntie Queenie set me up with the guy."

Pa's eyes widen, but then he shakes his head and clicks his tongue again. "You don't get it. You're getting too—"

If he says "Americanized," I swear to god . . .

"Americanized," he finishes. "Just because you are going abroad, you think you can do anything now?" He watches me with the coldest look on his face. "Going to America is getting to your head." He says *America* like it's a bad word.

"That has nothing to do with this!" I groan. It's like talking to a freaking brick wall. "Ma wouldn't live there if it were that bad."

"Okay, go, then! Join your mother where it's so much better!" He opens the refrigerator door with so much force that it shakes. "After you fly out, don't even bother coming back."

"That's not what I meant!"

He grumbles and twists the cap off a Gatorade bottle so roughly that the drink spills onto the counter. "You think the US is so great? I've been there, Chloe, and not once did I feel like I belonged. When you go to America, you know what's going to happen? That boy you've been sneaking around with is going to forget about you. You're so quick to turn your back on your home for a country that will never want you."

I open my mouth to say something else, but there aren't any arguments left in me that he hasn't heard before.

Out of the corner of my eye, I catch a glimpse of an Instagram post framed on the wall. It's Pa's **#ChristmasBestmas** photo from last year—the one where we're posing next to our Christmas tree. I remember right after that photo, Pa quickly wiped off his smile and gave me a sermon on how I didn't greet my aunties properly.

"Pa." I pause and swallow the lump in my throat. "Why is it so much easier for you with Peter? You're there for him—like, really there for him—and you tell him you're always going to be there no matter what happens. With me, you never seemed that . . . sure. I know it's probably my fault that I'm a disappointment to you, but I'm always scared that I'm one strike away from you giving up on me completely."

His face softens, and I avert my eyes because I know one look from Pa would tip me over the edge and make me fully crumble into tears.

"I'm really sorry about lying to you," I choke out before running up to my room.

39

IT'S MIDNIGHT WHEN I get a call from Cia.

"Hello?" I pick up, clearing my throat.

The call is silent until I hear shuddering gasps spilling into full-on sobs. I give her time to cry and let her breathing calm down.

"Sorry for calling you this late," she finally says. "It just happened, and I needed someone to talk to . . ."

"Cia, what's wrong?"

After a long pause, she says, "Raph and I broke up."

I ask if she's okay and let her ramble on the phone.

"It's been hours, and I can't stop crying. And my eyelids are all puffy. My eyes aren't my best feature, but I look much hotter when they're not all red and swollen . . ."

I stay on the line and listen, even though she gets more and more off topic.

Then she stops, and her voice catches. "I—I really need my best friend."

And I say with no hesitation, "I'm on my way."

"Wait," Cia says. "I don't mean *now* now. It's almost one in the morning."

"I'll be right there," I say, hanging up before she can protest any further.

That's when I realize there's no way in hell that Pa is going to let me go to Cia's house at this hour, especially after the fight we just had.

His bedroom is dark when I peek out my door. I quickly change into leggings and sneak downstairs. I can do this—I've seen all those shows where teenagers stealthily tiptoe out of the house. I try making my feet as light as possible, yet somehow my version of tiptoeing makes my footsteps extremely loud.

Once I reach for my shoes at the bottom of the stairs, the living room lights switch on.

"Chloe?" Pa steps out of his study and catches me red-handed. "Where are you going?"

"I'm—"

Going for a midnight jog? Hanging with Peter somewhere that's magically open at this hour? There isn't a single believable excuse that I could use right now.

So I tell the truth.

"Cia needs me," I say. "She just called, and she's going through something. I promise I'm not going there for Jappy, but she's my best friend, and I—"

I stop rambling when he moves to slip on his shoes.

What's happening?

Pa grabs his keys and reminds me to spray on some mosquito repellent. "I'll drive you there."

"LOOK! THAT CAR looks suspicious," I say, trying to zoom in with Cia's toy binoculars.

Since Pa told me that I could stay over, I keep checking the roads outside Cia's house to make sure he isn't secretly spying on us.

"Chlo, that's my mom's car."

"Well, he must be hiding somewhere . . ."

Cia takes the binoculars from me. "It's two in the morning. Wild thought, but what if Tito Jeffrey actually meant it when he said you could sleep over?"

"No way. Not after . . ."

"What?"

Not after I lied about going out with your brother . . . and making out with your brother multiple times.

"We just had a weird night," I say, and segue to what really matters. I climb next to her on the bed and cross my legs. "Do you wanna talk about it?"

When I got here, Cia was gathering snacks and choosing what movie we should watch like our whole phone call had never happened.

"I was single before. I'll just go back to being single again," Cia answers with a shrug. She reaches for her laptop and asks if I want to finish our last rewatch of *Four Sisters and a Wedding*.

"Sure," I say.

I have no idea how a breakup feels, but I do know that Cia likes dealing with things on her own time. The movie plays, and I notice that Cia isn't reciting the lines like she usually does. By the time we reach the final wedding scene, she fully succumbs to a crying attack.

"What if I made a mistake?" she asks in between gasps.

"What happened?"

"Nothing. I just got . . . tired." She reaches for the tissue box on her bedside table. "That night at the bakery, when we saw Raph's dad, it was like my mind left my body. It was like I was someone else watching what was going on, and my mind kept wondering, *what* is this person doing? This girl's been with this guy for more than a year. Why isn't she saying anything? Why is she being so fucking pathetic?"

"You aren't pathetic," I say softly.

"But I felt that way," Cia insists. "I feel like I've been holding my breath this whole time, just waiting for his family to find out. And if I'm not worried about that, I'm always being so careful about what I'm doing, what I'm saying, constantly terrified that Raph will see another reason why he shouldn't introduce me."

"I'm so sorry, Cia."

She blinks hard. "Being in a relationship isn't supposed to make you feel worse about yourself, right?" She sniffles and rubs her eyes. "But maybe I overreacted . . . It's not Raph's fault that he has a Great Wall or that his family broke up his brother's relationship. He makes me laugh and tries really hard. Did you see the cake he made for my parents?"

"Yeah, I saw the cake."

She faces me. "Was I too hard on him?"

"I think you're trying hard to make excuses for him."

"Then I'm right for breaking up with Raph?"

"Cia, I can't answer that."

"Ha!" She points at me. "So you're implying that I *shouldn't* have broken up with him."

"Maybe you should consider law instead of medicine." I shift in my seat and hold her forearm. "Do you think you deserve better?"

She goes quiet and nods.

"I think you do too."

Cia wipes her face with her palms when she starts sobbing again. "Sorry. Your first sleepover, and I'm wasting the whole time crying."

I lean over to grab my bag and hand her the "SOS" friendship coupon she made me. "I'm here for you always. Even without the coupons."

She groans and covers her face. "You're just making me cry more."

I grab some more tissues for her and lean on her shoulder while she sobs. We stay like that for a while until, out of nowhere, she asks, "Have you told your parents about the showcase?"

"Nope, tonight is all about you."

"Come on. At least you're stressing over real problems. How many times have you seen me crying over a dumb boy?"

Welp. If Cia only knew . . .

She shoots daggers at me and raises a questioning eyebrow. *What are you hiding?*

Dear Lord, why didn't you grant me a good poker face?

"Please don't be mad," I say.

A concerned look spreads over Cia's face. Probably not the best way to start this confession.

"I've been kinda, um . . . dating your brother."

Cia's whole body freezes. She stares at me with the same expression she had when our classmate once said Ed Sheeran was her favorite rapper.

"Cia?" I wave my hands across her face. "Yoo-hoo!"

And then everything suddenly registers. "My brother?"

"I'm sorry. I should've told you, and I really crossed the line—"

"My *brother*?!" The fact that she can reach that pitch this late is very impressive. "You find my brother *sexy*?"

I'm about to give a cool and detached answer when my body suddenly rings with the memory of Jappy's lips on mine. "Um."

"Oh my god." She freaks out. "You've had sex with my brother?!"

"God! Cia, no!" I lower my voice. "You asked me if I found him sexy."

"Which is one letter away from sex!" She covers her eyes. "What could you possibly find attractive about my brother?"

"I think it's best if I don't answer that question."

She rubs her temples like she's trying to massage the thought away. "Are you two . . . together now?"

Are we? Did we break up? Were we even together in the first place? We never really talked about that, and we haven't talked yet since Pa caught us.

"I don't know," I admit.

Her frown deepens. "Okay, if I'm going to have this

conversation, I need to pretend you're talking about someone else." She shakes her head as if clearing it of all thought and then meets my eye. "Tell me about Rudolph."

"What?" I ask, laughing.

"First name that came to my mind." She waves me off. "Now, what's been going on with you and Rudolph?"

"Um, I guess it all started with that kaishao . . ."

Cia's horror morphs into fascination the further I get into the story. She even lets out a tiny squeal when I tell her how he actually volunteered to get set up.

"Wow," she says when I finish.

"Yeah."

"He really likes you."

"I mean, I don't know."

"No, Chlo," she emphasizes, "he *really* likes you. Spending the whole day at the fair, getting you flowers, taking you out on all those dates—I've never seen Kuya put that much effort into . . . anything."

"But if this is already a lot for him, what about a long-distance thing?" I voice the thought that has been growing in the back of my mind. "Do you think he can handle that?"

Cia's face falls. "I don't know. All this relationship stuff is hard enough without literal oceans standing between you."

I lie down and groan into my pillow.

"You really like him too, huh?"

"Why is it so hard, though?" I sigh. "What are the chances that I'll go to college and meet a perfect, complications-free guy named Rudolph?"

"If you find him, ask if he has a brother based in Manila."

She laughs and plops her head on the pillow next to me. "Maybe the two of us deserve something easy."

"Maybe." I stare at the date flashing on my phone. "I can't believe I'm leaving in two weeks."

"Me neither."

"Hey"—I bop her with my elbow—"are you okay with me leaving?"

Her head swings to my direction. "Are *you* okay with leaving?"

"No." I let out a heavy sigh. "But I guess I have to be."

"Then I will be too." She nudges me. "Plus, maybe it'd be healthy for us to get some distance."

"Sorry, but even if I'm far away or, like, getting married to Rudolph, you're stuck with me for life."

"Back at you." She smiles. "You know what our friendship is like?"

"We were having such a pure moment without a metaphor."

"Our friendship is like a big shit," she continues anyway. "Even though there may be times when you try your hardest to hold it in, it'll still find a way to come through."

"That was surprisingly more sweet than gross."

"And everyone around us will be jealous because they'll smell the strength of its persistence."

It gets grosser and grosser the more Cia elaborates on the metaphor. We keep talking and laughing until we see the sun peeking through her window blinds.

I don't remember when exactly we drifted off to sleep. What I do remember is thinking that I wouldn't trade this shitty friendship for the world.

JAPPY HAS BEEN weirdly quiet this whole morning. When I ordered Spam with my breakfast sandwich, he didn't once lecture me about preservatives or sodium content.

It turns out that the special thing he had planned for the other night was taking me to an art fair. I asked if we could meet up at Wilson Plaza like we usually do, since I still have no idea how to navigate this situation with Pa. Jappy agreed and asked no further questions.

When we get in his car after picking up breakfast, the only thing he asks is "Did you go to the fair last year?"

I shake my head.

"Cool. They have an animation exhibit I thought you'd like, but the line's always long, so we'll have to wait a bit."

"No problem."

He ends the conversation there. Nothing about what happened with Pa or the fact that we haven't spoken for a whole week. I keep replaying my talk with Cia in my head—is everything too much for Jappy to handle?

"Hey," I blurt out. "I'm sorry for what happened with my dad last week."

"It's fine," he says.

"I haven't really told him about us, so that was where the whole 'just friends' comment came from."

Jappy lets out a heavy breath. "I don't want to talk about this now, Chlo."

"Oh," I mumble. "All right." He's started to talk about the exhibit more when I cut him off: "I think we should talk about it, though. Not talking about things makes everything worse. Look at Cia and Raph."

His eyes cut to me. "What do you mean?"

"Oh, they broke up."

Jappy immediately stops the car. "What did he do?"

I take a deep breath and explain that Raph was one of the guys I got kaishao-ed with. I paint the whole catastrophe of crashing his family lunch, even getting caught by Uncle Dennis outside Lily Bakery. Then I tell Jappy about his Great Wall and how he's been keeping their relationship a secret.

By the time I finish, Jappy's face is full-on scowling.

"What?" I ask.

All he does is grunt at me wordlessly. Ugh. Sometimes he's impossible to talk to.

I tilt my head at him. "You're really not going to talk to me?"

His grip on the wheel tightens. "Well, you just told me that you've been helping Raph keep my sister a secret."

"It was complicated," I say.

"Because his family was nice to you?"

"That's not why I . . ." My throat tightens. Maybe I should've said something to Raph when I sensed that Cia was getting hurt. I could've told the truth when Uncle Dennis saw us outside the bakery. Should I have done more to be there for Cia? "I didn't know what to do."

He sighs and runs his hands through his hair. "Sorry. I didn't mean to blame you." There's this silence, and his voice turns quiet. "Is that why you haven't told your dad about me?" he asks. "Because I'm not Chinese?"

"Jappy, of course not." I reach over and squeeze his arm. "I don't have a Great Wall, and my auntie was the one who set us up in the first place."

My heart twists when he shrugs off my hand. "Let's just go."

"Oh." I nod and say okay, even though things are far from it.

Is he going to keep shutting me out if I keep pushing him? Maybe I should give him time to process things . . . but I'm *leaving* next week.

Has he even thought about me leaving?

"Um, Jappy?" I ask before he starts the car again. "What's going to happen . . . after August?"

He shrugs. "Based on past experience, September."

"No, like"—I sigh, trying to grasp at the right words— "when I leave."

"Ah."

"Do you think this . . . thing between us is going to last if I'm away?"

My words hang in the air until he finally says, "I don't know."

When people in movies say that their heart is breaking, I always thought they were describing some weird stomachache. But right now, this aching feeling in my chest is precisely that—my heart breaking. It wasn't like I was expecting Jappy to say we'd be linked forever after a couple dates, but when I asked the guy I really like if we're going to last, I was really hoping he would say yes.

He blinks and shifts his hands along the steering wheel. "I can't tell with the distance and the time difference, and I don't want to say anything that'll let you down."

"I get it," I say before he says anything more.

He presses his lips together. "Sorry." His voice sounds detached. "This thing between you and me . . . It's harder than I thought it would be."

There's this long pause, and I keep waiting for Jappy to give me a "but." *It's harder than I thought,* but *this is worth it. It's harder than I thought,* but *I want to try.* But it never comes.

I swallow the lump in my throat as I feel my heart crumbling more. "Do you mind if we go to the art fair some other time instead?"

"You don't want to wait for the exhibit?"

"I'm okay."

He doesn't argue when I step out of the car. It suddenly feels pointless to wait for something when you know how it's going to end anyway.

WITH FURTHER ANALYSIS, I'm convinced that *Got 2 Believe* is more of a cautionary tale than a love story. First of all, the guy doesn't even realize he has feelings for the girl until *after* she starts dating someone else. Second, how does a guy go from someone who preaches that "love is a nightmare" to proposing within the span of the movie?

This has been my third rewatch today, and I've already gone through two buckets of cheese popcorn. When the two main characters hug and confess their feelings for each other, I throw a kernel at my laptop screen.

"You'll break up eventually," I grumble.

The movie pauses when my computer pings with a message alert. I quickly exit the window and silence all notifications.

Ever since I told Auntie Queenie that I wanted to cancel the entire program segment of my debut, she's been calling nonstop. In between the calls, she's been flooding my messages with emojis of candles and roses.

I know how much planning she put into this, but I don't think I can go through with it. How can I face a slow dance with Jappy? I've hardly even replied to his messages. He already said what he needed to say—I don't need a replay of that conversation.

My phone buzzes with a video call from Ma. With everything happening, I completely forgot about our weekly call. I click on the screen, and Ma's face appears.

"Hey, babes!" She hesitates. "Are you okay?"

I glance at my camera feed, and wow, I look like a mess. My eyes are puffy from all the crying, and there's cheese powder on my face.

"Yeah!" I rub my cheeks and turn on my polite smile. "Just watching some movie."

"Ooh, same here. I finally started the *Bao* video you recommended!" She flips her phone, and I see a frame of the cartoon dumpling suddenly growing arms and legs. "It's so cute!"

"It's going to get really sad," I tell her.

She ignores my warning and goes on about the cute dumpling. "It reminds me of the drawings you had in your sketchbooks when you were younger." She beams. "I'm so excited to see what you came up with for the festival."

Great. I get to have my heart broken *and* break Ma's heart, all within twenty-four hours.

"Ma?" I gulp. "I didn't get selected for the showcase."

"Oh, babes." My eyes start misting over when I hear the concern in her voice. "Are you okay?"

"I'll get over it," I mumble.

Wow, that didn't even sound convincing to *me*.

"You know most artists aren't overnight successes," she points out. "You'll get here and have amazing professors and new opportunities. You'll get tons of experience. When one door closes, another opens. This is the beginning of something great for you, Chloe."

But what if it's not? The showcase was supposed to be the way for me to prove to everyone that I can make it, but that didn't happen. Going abroad means I'm leaving Cia, Pa, Jappy—everyone that's been there for me my whole life.

What if leaving means I'm letting go of something great?

"Ma, would you be mad if I don't go?" I ask. "Like, if I stay here instead of going to USC?"

Her brow furrows as she listens. I brace myself for the Chloe Elaine Ang Liang tough-love speech.

But instead of uttering my whole name, Ma says, "Of course I wouldn't be mad. Are you having second thoughts?"

Ma has been nothing but supportive about my drawings. When I got into cartoons, she was the one who would find more movies for me to watch. She bought me my first set of art supplies, gave me my tablet. She was the first person I called when I got off the wait list.

"It's okay if you don't want to go abroad," she continues. "If you want to stay in Manila and study something else, I'm all in for that too."

"I just don't think I can do it," I admit, trying not to let my voice tremble too much.

That's when Ma calls me out with my full name. "The question is never whether you can do it or not—because, babes, you'll never know until you try. All those big dreams you have? I've always believed you could reach them. You should be asking what will make you happy."

I feel like I'll start crying if I say anything, so I simply nod.

"You have options, babes," she adds. "This is the start of a new chapter in your life! The whole world is at your fingertips."

I appreciate Ma trying to switch the conversation from depressing to upbeat. The problem is, I'm still stuck on the first emotion.

"Thanks." I force a smile. "Sorry, Ma. I should probably go."

"Are you feeling better?"

"Yeah, yeah. The debut is next week, so I have to get some things ready."

"Don't get too down on yourself, okay? There's no wrong decision here."

I nod.

"Love you, babes," she says, blowing me a kiss.

I blow her a kiss back. "Love you, Ma."

When she ends the call, I sigh and unpause *Got 2 Believe*. But all I hear are Ma's words. I exit out of the movie and pull up the showcase video I've been working on.

God. Everything looks so freaking stiff. All of my

animations—scenes of my family and my friends and Jappy—
they don't pop like they usually do. I can't believe I thought
this was good enough to show to other animators.

When I asked Ma if I should still go to USC, I thought
she'd tell me 100 percent yes. Now I have no idea what I'm
supposed to do.

Maybe *I'm* the problem. Maybe I'm just not good enough.

I slump further down in my bed and stare at all the drawings on my walls. This is the only thing I've ever dreamed of.

When I was a kid, I would watch animated movies and
copy the characters in my sketchbook. My drawings would
come to life in my mind like they did on the screen. And when
I watch movies now and the end credits come on, I imagine
the day when I'll see my name listed. It sounds like a little
kid's stupid dream, but I fantasize about working at Disney or
Nickelodeon or even creating my own studio. It's a one-in-a-
million chance . . . Am I being delusional about all this? I
hardly see female animators leading the industry—and there
are even fewer female animators from the Philippines. What
makes *me* the one in a million?

I grab my tablet and open my latest draft. I pick up the pen
and scrawl a huge X over my work. With every stroke, the
color bleeds over each curve and line I drew. I don't stop until
the page is nothing but black.

Maybe I'm not someone who's meant to dream big.

42

AFTER HOURS OF research and emailing the admissions office, I make my decision.

I brace myself and knock on the door to Pa's study. Moments later, he still hasn't answered. The door to his study has always been a designated border in our house. Once Pa crosses the border, I know that he's gone into his separate world, and I usually retreat to mine. But I know this talk has to be in person.

When he still doesn't answer after another knock, I push the door open. Pa is at his desk, bent over a massive pile of papers with his hands on his temples. The table is shaking from how much he's bouncing his legs.

Throughout my almost eighteen years in this world, this study has not changed one bit. Pa still has the same brown rolling chair, which he refuses to change despite its tattered arms. His desk is still cluttered with all the pens he's "borrowed" from different hotels and restaurants over the years.

Every time Pa signs a check, he pockets the pen. The man has never bought a pen in his life.

The one difference is the frame on his desk. Rather than keeping it taped on the wall, he had the drawing I made of our family back in the first grade framed. Seeing it makes me even more sure of my decision.

"Pa?"

"Not now, Chloe. I'm busy," he answers while jotting something down.

"I need to talk to you about something," I say.

He still doesn't look at me.

"I don't want to go to USC."

That's when he drops his pen.

I take a deep breath. "My work didn't get chosen for the showcase . . . and it got me thinking that I'll fit in much better going to college here."

"You didn't get into the festival?" he asks with his eyebrows furrowed.

I shake my head. "I talked to someone in the admissions office, and she said she might be able to refund my deposit. I talked to Ma about it a little, and I think she'd understand. You're right. Colleges here can give me a great education too. I don't know if it's too late for the school here to take me back, but I can help you out with the business until I can start classes. It would give me more time to research business courses."

I can't read Pa's face. I can't tell if he's happy, mad, or disappointed. It's like looking at a blank page.

"If the refund doesn't work out," I say, "I can also work to pay it off."

His eyes meet mine. "Are you sure?"

My throat tightens when I think about how this is going to change my life. I'm not going to walk through the court-yard of the School of Cinematic Arts, which I've seen a million times through the USC campus virtual tour. I'm not going to be living near Hollywood or be surrounded by people who aspire to be artists and filmmakers. There's never going to be a Chloe in America. The dream I've had ever since I was a little kid is going to stay just that—a dream.

But I push back those thoughts, along with my tears. That life isn't meant for me.

"Yes, I'm sure."

43

LAST NIGHT, I dreamed of sitting in a huge USC lecture taught by Professor Hayao Miyazaki. I woke up right as he asked me if I wanted to work as an animator on *Spirited Away 2*.

Worst dream of my life.

It would be so much easier to move on from my dream if my subconscious dreams would cooperate.

Even my bedroom walls are taunting me, with almost every inch covered by my drawings. If I'm ever going to move on, I can't have all this surrounding me.

I need to let go.

I take down my drawings from fifth grade, then fourth grade . . . At first, I do it carefully and slowly. Every time I remove a picture, it feels like I'm ripping a piece of my soul away. But then I go faster. I push back the memories of the rush I felt whenever I worked on a sketch. I tear everything away until the only reminders of my art are the bright spots they leave behind.

But if I really want a clean slate, I can't stop with my room.

I log on to my Vimeo page and go to my account settings. I hover over the option that says **Delete account**.

Suck it up, Chloe. It's not like someone's actually torturing you.

It's going to be a million times harder to start over if I have this online reminder of everything I used to dream of. Plus, there are *way* more painful things I might experience. Like . . . giving birth. Pushing a literal human being out of my body is going to hurt way freaking more than deleting my Vimeo page.

An email notification distracts me from imagining how excruciating childbirth is. It's a message from my school's withdrawal coordinator.

> **Hi Chloe,**
>
> **Sorry again to hear you're thinking about withdrawing your admission. Though we were very pleased to hear from your family that we'll be seeing you soon. Have you reconsidered your decision?**

My family?! When did they talk to my family?

I'm in the middle of typing my response when I hear my door open.

"I'm not signing this," Pa says, handing me the envelope with the letter I printed out inside. It's the one I wrote to USC explaining my reasons for withdrawing.

"Okay . . ." I say, taking it back.

"You're going to USC."

"But—"

"I didn't pay all that money for you to go to college just so you could drop out."

"But they might give us a refund."

"Don't trust people when they say they're going to give you a refund."

"We get refunds all the time. You got a refund on those pants—"

He clicks his tongue and cuts me off. "Basta. You're going."

"Wait!" I hop off my bed before he closes the door on another unfinished conversation. "Pa, I told you I want to stay."

"And I'm telling you you're going."

Ugh. Why does he never listen to me?!

"I'm almost eighteen! I don't need your permission for everything!"

"You do for this." He scans my walls and clicks his tongue again. "Fix your room."

Wow. I can't believe he's ignoring my wishes *and* insulting my room.

I'm on the brink of delivering a very convincing, well-thought-out argument when Pa walks out of my bedroom and closes the door.

WE ARE NOT DONE HERE.

I collapse on my bed and bury my face in my pillow.

Isn't this what he wanted? I'm finally becoming the daughter he asked for. I'm going to follow in his footsteps and embrace his plan for me.

Pa didn't even bother to replace the envelope that he

ripped open. But just because he doesn't want to sign the letter, doesn't mean that I'm not going to send it.

I open the envelope, and my first grade drawing is tucked inside.

A familiar scribble stares at me when I flip it over.

Kaya mo 'yan.

You can do it.

I MADE A promise to Cia that I would have a heartfelt conversation with Pa and tell him that he'd convinced me to study abroad.

The problem is, whenever Pa sees me, he reacts by playing a basketball video at full volume, and I get the sudden urge to go running. I guess my aversion to confrontation is another thing I got from my father. On the plus side, my calves are getting really fit from all the extra jogging I've been doing.

Unfortunately, our evasive father-daughter routine comes to a screeching halt with the chaotic arrival of Auntie Queenie.

"Heeeey, Auntie Queenie," I say when she storms into our house.

Before I can even beso her, she shoots me the iciest stare I've ever seen. "Are those running shoes?" She points to the Nikes I'm holding.

"Um. Yes?" I finally squeak out.

"Don't. You. Even. Think. That you're going to go running

right now." She puts her bag on the couch. "Where's your father?"

"Uh . . ."

"JEFFREY!" Auntie Queenie shrieks, and all the hairs on my arms immediately stand up.

Pa bursts out of his study with the collar of his polo sticking up. "Anong nangyari?" He looks back and forth between me and Auntie Queenie. "What's wrong?"

Auntie Queenie points her finger at Pa. "You haven't been replying to any of my messages about the debut."

Pa groans. "Shobe, I thought someone died."

"Someone will if the two of you don't help me," she says. "Am I the only one who cares that we only have days until this debut?"

Yes.

Auntie Queenie faces me, and I panic that my auntie now has mind-reading abilities. "Go turn on the TV."

"Huh?"

"I have a slideshow of all your beautiful childhood memories here, and I want to see if it works on another monitor," she says.

"But—"

Auntie Queenie places her hand on my shoulder. "Chloe, I've already limited this debut to a sad number of people, agreed to remove the roses and candles, axed my lovely theme after you rejected it . . ."

She messaged me last night that she wanted the theme to be "bohemian rustic chic," and I still have no idea what any of those words, individually or together, even mean. I replied that maybe we should try something simpler and more personal.

"For the sake of your auntie's state of mind, switch on the damn TV."

Hearing Auntie Queenie utter "damn" is enough to make Pa and me shut up and follow orders.

The three of us end up squished together on the couch watching the slideshow. A song about having the time of your life plays while pictures of baby me flash on the screen.

"I was thinking we could play the video right before we serve the food," Auntie Queenie says. "That way, we'll have everyone's attention."

I glance at Pa. I can't even tell if he's enjoying any of the photos. He's staring at the TV with his resting bored face.

When the slideshow gets to some pictures of me and Pa crossing the finish line of a father-daughter fun run, Pa gets up from the couch. He clears his throat. "I have some calls to attend to."

"Can't it wait until we're done with the video?" Auntie Queenie asks.

He scoffs. "Chloe doesn't listen to my opinions anyway."

See? How am I supposed to be grateful when he's this petty?

He retreats back to his study without saying anything about the slideshow.

Auntie Queenie keeps glancing at me while I pretend to stay focused on the TV.

"Don't be mad at your father," she says.

"I'm not." I cross my arms, pushing down my anger.

"I've spent many, many years fighting with my brother. I know what being mad at him looks like." She double-winks. "You capture it perfectly."

I groan. "He's just so hard to talk to."

Auntie Queenie pauses the video and turns to me. "Oh, Chloe. You have to understand that your father doesn't handle emotions well. You have no idea how hard these past few months have been on him."

"Why? Did something happen with the business?"

She shakes her head. "Ahia's not stressed about work. Well, he's *always* stressed about work, but no more than usual." She tucks a strand of hair behind my ear. "He's been stressed ever since you got off the wait list. That's why I agreed to help him kaishao you."

Wait. *What?!*

"It was his idea?"

"He kept going on about how you'll stay in the States forever and never come back, so I said he should entice you with a man! Clearly, he did a horrible job since you canceled your roses program—"

"That's why he's been setting me up on dates?" I ask. "He thinks I'm going to give up something I've wanted my whole life for some guy?"

She hesitates and studies my face. "Ahia made me promise not to show this to anyone, but I think you should see it."

Auntie Queenie takes out a worn red notebook and hands it to me. Its elastic strap is stretched thin from all the extra notes tucked inside the pages. My heart squeezes when I recognize Pa's handwriting.

"When I was asking for advice about what you would want for your debut, Ahia gave me this and told me that everything he knew about you was written in this notebook. He said he started taking notes after he and your mom decided you were going to grow up here."

Make sure to request the thigh part when ordering Chloe Jollibee chicken. Watch out that she doesn't only eat the chicken skin.

Stock up on drawing paper in the house. Chloe doesn't like the oslo texture. Check Diane's recommendation for best colored pencils.

Cia and Patricia are the same person.

Big fan of Beyoncé singer. "Slay" and "Red Lobster" do not seem to be malicious disco sex words. That one "Schoolin' Life" song is catchy.

Chloe doesn't want to go to school after Diane leaves. She feels better when you tell her "kaya mo 'yan."

I can't believe I forgot about that. Whenever Ma left after a visit, I'd lock myself in my room and claim that I wouldn't come out until she came back. Pa wouldn't say anything, but when he handed me my lunch for school, there would be a little folded paper underneath that said *Kaya mo 'yan.*

"Chloe." Auntie Queenie turns to me. "Your father tried so hard to find a reason for you to stay because his heart was breaking at the thought of you leaving."

WHEN I GO downstairs, Pa is sitting at the foot of the staircase putting on his running shoes. "Pa, can I—"

He interrupts me before I finish. "Chloe, I already told you that you're going."

"I know," I say. "I was gonna ask if I could join you for your run."

"Oh." His face flickers with a confused look. "Okay."

On my runs with Pa, we usually take about ten minutes to warm up before we start jogging. This time, we circle around the village loop for almost an hour. Running in silence is perfectly fine, but I'm worried that there's no foreseeable end to our wordless walking.

"Diane was always better at this," Pa says, finally breaking the silence.

My heart lurches at the mention of Ma. Pa hardly ever brings her up.

"I have a hard time picking the right words to say. Your

grandfather told me what to do, and I did it, and your aunties did enough talking in the house for me."

I can totally see that.

"Before she left for the States, we thought it'd be best if you went with her."

"What?" I turn to Pa. I've never heard this story before.

He nods. "We'd already shipped some of your clothes and even gotten you a ticket. It seemed right for a daughter to be with her mother. But when you were about to leave, you ran to me and latched on to my leg. You wouldn't let go and kept crying, saying that you wanted to stay with Papa."

Pa pauses to pull me to the inner side of the sidewalk. I let him point out the turn, and for some reason, it doesn't bother me as much this time.

"I've always wondered if Diane and I made the right decision," he says, staring off into the distance.

To be honest, there were many moments in my life when I wished I could be with Ma. I've had multiple fantasies (and made a lot of drawings) of what my life could've been if I were in California with her. One time after a really big argument with Pa, I had a dream that I ran away and took the first flight I could find. But when I woke up, I remember feeling so much relief that I was still here—that I was still home.

I reach out for Pa and hold his arm. "It was the right decision."

He answers by gently putting his arm around my shoulder. It's Pa's version of a hug. "You remind me so much of your mother," he says, shaking his head.

It's been a long time since someone has said that I remind them of Ma and meant it as a compliment.

"Sobrang tigas ng ulo," he adds.

I take that back. Calling me "hardheaded" isn't technically a compliment.

"She hated it when anyone told her she couldn't do something. If I told her something was risky, she'd be even more motivated to go do it. That wasn't how I was brought up." He turns to look at me. "Did you know your grandfather wanted to be an accountant?"

I shake my head.

"That was his dream, but during his time, Chinese people in the Philippines couldn't get citizenship. To be a professional and get a license as an accountant, you needed to be a citizen."

"But wasn't Angkong born here?"

"Yes, but it was still very difficult for him to get naturalized," he says. "That's why he decided to go into business instead. It was his best option to support his family."

"I had no idea."

Pa nods. "I want to make things easier for you. A business here is stable, something you can rely on. My father worked hard for me and my siblings, and I work hard so that you will have something to inherit."

"I'm sorry." For the first time, the guilt inside me is flowing out instead of swallowing me whole. "I see how hard you work, and I know you want me to stay home so I can study business and help out with the company. But . . . when I draw, it feels like it's what I'm meant to do. I don't want to give up on animation without giving it a shot."

If this were like the million conversations Pa and I have had before, he would reply by saying that I need to be more practical and realistic. Instead, he says, "I didn't ask you to stay close to home because I wanted you to help me with the business. I asked because . . . the house feels empty without you."

Ideally, I'd answer with an equally beautiful and heart-warming message to my father, if I wasn't so choked up from what he just said.

"You can do your cartoon thing as long as you promise to come home."

I have to restrain myself from jumping on Pa and hugging him. "I promise, Pa."

"And if you tell me what's going on with you and the Torres boy."

"Uh . . ."

How can I give Pa an answer to something I'm not really sure about myself?

"I . . . don't really know." I say.

He shoots me the same puzzled look he gave me when I first tried explaining animation to him. "You don't know?"

"Yeah . . . I still have to talk to Jappy. I haven't clarified the whole long-distance situation yet."

Pa scratches the back of his head. "Hay, Chloe. You're already gambling on your career. You can't gamble on your love life too."

I can't stop myself from laughing. Who'd have thought that I'd be getting love advice from my father?

"Tawa ka pa." He grins and pats me on the shoulder. "See? My kaishaos worked!"

"Pa, please, *please*, never kaishao anyone again."

"Why? I'm good at it! I bet I'm better than the Tinder!"

I groan and shake my head.

"We should head back to the house. You still have a lot of packing to do. You really shouldn't leave everything to the last minute."

"But we still haven't done our run yet."

His eyebrows shoot up. "You're not busy?"

"I'm not going to leave without beating you one last time."

"Okay." He puffs his chest out.

"And, Pa," I say before we start, "I don't need a guy to get me to come home. You're always going to be the reason I want to come back."

He clicks his tongue and leans forward, getting ready to run. "Next thing I know, you're going to bring home an American boyfriend."

Before I can answer, Pa takes off.

I sprint after him and yell, "That was cheating!"

And he shouts back, "You have to get used to long distance!"

Wait.

Did Pa just tease me about Jappy?

I don't even mind that I'm falling behind or that I can't think of a good enough comeback. It's been too long since I last heard Pa laugh this much.

46

CIA MANAGED TO do the impossible. She showed up wearing something even more bizarre than my highlighter debut dress.

When I answer the door, I have to do a double take to make sure it's her. She's wearing this high bun and a baby-blue dress that reminds me of the ones we wore for our First Holy Communion. Even Pa takes notice and tells Cia she looks really "proper."

There's nothing wrong with the dress—it's just not Cia at all.

I hold my tongue until she asks me if the collar on her dress is too revealing.

"It's a collar!" I snap. "There's nothing revealing about a collar."

"Wow, okay." She holds up her hands. "Just asking for an opinion."

"Why do you look like my dad dressed you?"

"Hey, your dad used to pick out your clothes all the time."

"It's common knowledge that I'm the unfashionable one in this friendship."

"You're not unfashionable," she grumbles. "You even pull off the banana dress. Sort of."

Cia peeks at her reflection and makes her bun even tighter. "I knew Raph was going to your debut, and I thought I should be more low-key."

"And by low-key, you mean you decided to dress for a convent?"

She glances at me. "Was the bun too much?"

I exhale and ignore how my dress pinches my waist. "A wise person once told me that finding the perfect dress is like getting your first period." We're both quiet as I wait for her to fill in the blanks. "I was hoping you would finish the rest of the metaphor."

"You know, I didn't really know where I was going with that one."

"Well, I find it very profound," I argue. "Like how a period can be painful, and how you have to grow into it. And with all the blood—"

Cia starts laughing, and I soon join her.

"Fine, forget the metaphors," I say. "I just think you've been acting 'low-key' because of Raph and his family, even now when you're broken up." I shrug. "You've always been a high-key person."

She smiles and checks herself out in the mirror. "High-key person. I like that."

Cia lets down her hair and unbuttons the dress collar. "Mind if I borrow your earrings?"

A few minutes later, she's managed to go from on the way to church to on the way to a fashion show.

"How did you make that blue dress cool?" I ask, bewildered.

Cia casually tosses her hair. "It's all about attitude and accessories. Debuts do have lots of eligible bachelors."

"You do know that Auntie Queenie promised she'd limit the guest list to family. The only bachelor our age is Peter."

"What about Jappy?" She not-so-subtly smirks at me.

"I love you, but I really can't approve of incest."

She shakes her head and notices my smudged eyeliner. "Did he greet you, at least?"

I hand her my phone while I step closer to the mirror to fix my makeup.

happy bday chlo!

That was it. Those were the only words that Jappy came up with to greet me on my eighteenth birthday. He didn't even bother capitalizing any letters or spelling out the word *birthday*. I know we're in some limbo without labels or anything, but I feel like it's standard etiquette that if you occasionally make out with someone, you should at least have the common courtesy to spell out all the words in a birthday message.

ty!!! is all I replied. If he's not going to spell out words, *I'm* not going to spell out words.

"My idiot brother," Cia grumbles. "He didn't deserve your exclamation points."

"Sayang, he missed the chance to see me in . . . this."

Even though looking at this dress for too long starts to feel like staring at the sun, Auntie Queenie insisted it was the "perfect" dress. I eventually gave in and played along, pretending that I was in love with the dress too. She'd already bent over backward compromising with me for the debut. I figured it was worth getting my ribs crushed for one night if I could keep Auntie Queenie's feelings from getting crushed again.

Then I hear Auntie Queenie's ballet flats hammering toward us.

"Chloe!" she exclaims as she enters my room.

Wow, she has worse knocking etiquette than Pa.

Auntie Queenie squeezes my shoulders. "Someone wants to greet you a happy birthday."

My polite smile slowly switches to a cringe. Oh god. Is this a last-minute kaishao?

"Happy birthday, babes," I hear.

That's when I see her walk into my room. I knew she was coming, but seeing her *actually* here feels too good to be true.

Auntie Queenie gives a curt nod to Ma. "Diane."

Ma replies with a curt nod of her own. "Queenie."

That's the most affection I've ever seen between the two of them.

"Patricia, is that you?" Ma asks Cia. "I feel like it was only yesterday that you and Chloe were having One Direction birthday parties!"

"We still do," Cia jokes, and pecks Ma on the cheek. "So great to see you again, Tita."

Meanwhile, my body is still in shock, and my mind reverts to that spinning computer wheel.

This is my mother, the woman who gave me life, and she is now in front of me, not on a phone or computer screen.

"Babes?" Ma places her palm against my forehead. "Are you okay? You look a little pale."

Feeling her touch finally jolts me into action. I wrap my arms around her so tight, as if I'm afraid that she'll vanish if I let go. "I can't believe you're here."

47

IS THE THEME for my debut . . . fruits?

Auntie Queenie rented out the event space at the club-house in our village. I've been here before for tons of birthday parties, but it's never been this, well . . . yellow. Banners that have lemons and limes printed on them are hanging from the ceiling. There are different designs and sizes of lemon stickers decorating the walls. All the tables have giant lemon center-pieces and . . . lemon-shaped hats? My god. How did Auntie Queenie make the room smell like lemons?

"What do you think?" Auntie Queenie gestures excitedly at the room of citrus.

"Um." I try to take it all in. "I—I don't know what to say."

"Ahia said you really love lemonade and keep going on about how it's iconic and a masterpiece." Auntie Queenie double-winks. "You should consider going into the fruit or juice business if you feel this passionately."

I think about telling her that *Lemonade* is the title of a

Beyoncé album, but I decide to let it go. This might be the funniest and sweetest misunderstanding ever.

At least the sight of my relatives' heads looking like giant lemons makes sitting onstage in front of my whole family feel less daunting. I wanted to sit next to Cia or Ma, but Auntie Queenie insisted that the celebrant should be front and center.

Auntie Queenie steps up to the podium in front and taps the mic. "Good evening, everyone!" Her voice roars through the room. "Thank you for joining us in the celebration of our dear Chloe's eighteenth birthday!"

She pauses, seemingly waiting for applause. All she gets is some late clapping from my cousins and a random "Whoop!" from Cia. But that doesn't stop Auntie Queenie. She goes on with her speech as if she's hosting the biggest event in the country.

"As all of you know, a girl's debut marks a turning point in her life. At eighteen, Chloe is moving on to bigger things. College, adulthood, dating." Auntie Queenie manages to give me a double-wink when she says that, and I see Pa uncomfortably squirm in his chair as he's taking a video with his phone (of course). "As we all know, Chloe has always marched to her own drum. While the established debut program is a shining beacon of our culture, Chloe would rather do away with certain traditions."

Jobert, who for some reason is the DJ for the night, punctuates the awkwardness with a sad "womp, womp" trombone sound effect.

I wish Auntie Queenie had warned me about this guilt trip before I got onstage.

"Since she opted out of the traditional dance with the eighteen roses," Auntie Queenie continues, "Chloe's roses have decided to dance on their own!"

Huh?

"Auntie, *what* roses?" I ask, leaning toward her.

She ignores me and pushes me to stand. I keep trying to ask her what's going on as she moves me to the side of the stage.

Then the door to the clubhouse suddenly opens. My relatives (mostly my aunties) clap when Peter, Raph, Miles, and Jappy march in. They're wearing suits and doing some weird choreographed shimmy-walking (only Peter is making it look like dancing) to the dance floor by the stage.

Once they get there, they bow their heads, and Jobert starts to play "Partition."

Ho-

Ly.

Shit.

They're doing the choreography that Peter attempted to teach me. But while Peter looks like a cool, sultry peacock, my "roses" look more like lost pigeons.

Peter is the only one who looks like he knows what he's doing, and he's keeping count to help Miles, Raph, and Jappy.

"Five, six, seven, eight," Peter calls out as the others try to keep up in the background.

When Peter drops down and does a smooth body roll, the other three collapse to the floor and look like they're wriggling worms. Miles does seem to have memorized all the steps, but his every move is like a stiff, rigid version of Peter's.

But I don't care. I can't believe Peter and all my "kaishao boys" are willing to do a dance for me in front of my entire family. This might even top watching Beyoncé perform the song (not really, but close).

I cheer when Peter does a flip and when Jappy sort of rolls around on the floor. By the middle of the song, Raph gives up on the choreography and ends up doing his own flailing moves.

Once the song ends and the four boys bow, I give them a standing ovation.

"What an . . . interesting performance!" Auntie Queenie says as she returns to the stage. "Do you have a message for the birthday girl?" She shoves the mic in front of Jappy's face, and he freezes in the spotlight.

"Uh." He clears his throat. "Happy birthday, Chloe." I feel my heart flutter when his eyes find mine.

"Let's give another round of applause to the roses!" Auntie Queenie says, then she shoos them off the dance floor and goes back to her podium. "Now the beautiful women who would've been in Chloe's eighteen candles—if Chloe actually agreed to have a proper program—also have something special prepared for tonight."

Auntie Queenie slips off her heels and waves Cia over. Cia walks up and takes the mic while the rest of my aunties follow. Even . . . Ma(?!) stands up.

The room gives the loudest roar when my aunties and Ma assemble onstage. Auntie Queenie points at Jobert, and he plays the punchy drum instrumental, then Cia starts singing Beyoncé's "Single Ladies."

All my aunties start twirling their hands and feeling themselves like they're teaching a Zumba class. Auntie Queenie, of course, assumes the role of the lead dancer. She almost knocks Auntie Sandy out with her elbows when she does the punching steps in the chorus. Ma also gives her 100 percent, but she has to cover her face when Auntie Queenie pulls out her sexy hip moves.

I didn't think it was possible for anything to beat the "Partition" performance, but here we are.

Pa is laughing so hard that he can't even hold his phone still. While my aunties do some sort of freestyle dance-off, Ma breaks from the circle and pulls me in to join them. Cia keeps repeating the "whoa oh oh" part until I eventually give in and follow the steps.

This might be the weirdest . . . and best debut I've ever been to.

48

"IF YOU LIKED it, then you should have put a ring on it,"
Cia sings for the millionth time.

"Cia, I'm trying to pee!" I call out from the stall.

She sang on our way to the restroom, she sang as she
peed, and now she's singing as she washes her hands.

Once I get out of the stall, Cia keeps singing as she shimmies up against me and rolls her hips.

"So"—I maneuver around her so I can wash my hands—
"how long have you been planning your Beyoncé concert?"

"When you canceled your debut program, your auntie
called us in for an immediate boot-camp rehearsal. Your mom
even joined over Zoom," Cia says while imitating Auntie
Queenie's aggressive hand twirling.

I turn on the faucet and reach for the soap. "And she told
you about the guys' dance too?"

There's a noticeable tamping down of her dancing. "She
might've mentioned it."

"Are you okay with Raph being here?"

"You're really being a killjoy at your own birthday." She flicks some water from the faucet in my direction. "Stop worrying."

Before I can splash water back at her, Auntie Queenie storms into the restroom. "Chloe! What have you been doing?"

Probably the worst question to ask in a restroom.

"Um. Peeing?"

"The slideshow isn't working!"

"Oh no!" I say, trying to sound as devastated as she does.

"I don't know what to do. It says the file is corrupted!"

Auntie Queenie's phone rings. She answers it and starts barking at the person she hired as the "event coordinator" to uncorrupt the video.

"Uh, Auntie," I say carefully. "Maybe we don't need to do the slideshow."

She clicks her tongue. "Then what are people going to do while they eat?"

While Cia tries her hand at calming Auntie Queenie down, I remember the note Pa gave me: *Kaya mo 'yan.* If I'm really going abroad, switching on full-blown Chloe-in-America mode, I can't wait for other people to boost my confidence. Auntie Queenie wanted me to give a performance for my debut, so I'm going to show off a talent that I actually enjoy doing.

I clear my throat. "I might have a video I could show."

Auntie Queenie whips her head toward me. "You do?"

Before I can explain further, Auntie Queenie is already dragging me out of the restroom. "Where are these videos?"

"Um. I just need to sign on to someone's computer."

Auntie Queenie takes out her phone again and asks the event coordinator to double-check that the computer connected to the projector is working.

"Is everything okay?" Ma approaches us, probably alarmed that she could hear Auntie Queenie's voice from the other end of the room.

"Diane, go help Chloe set up her video," Auntie Queenie says with another click of her tongue. "I need to go check that they didn't mess up the food servings."

As soon as Auntie Queenie scurries away, Ma says, "I always thought your auntie would do well as a high-powered executive . . . or a ruthless Zumba instructor." But everything she says is lost on me as I suddenly realize that Ma is going to be in the audience. "What's this video you need help with?"

"Um."

What if she gets so appalled when she sees my rejected video that she books the first flight out to the States? Oh my god. Cartoons aren't supposed to be in debuts! What if Auntie Queenie hates it? What if Pa hates it? What if all my relatives hate it, and then my video single-handedly rips the Liang family apart?!

This is a bad idea. A really, truly terrible idea.

After a moment, I hear Ma say my name.

"Huh?"

"The video?"

"Oh, right, right."

As I make my way back to the podium, it's like I'm walking in a trance. When the guy handling the projector screen lends me his laptop, it's like my hands completely dissociate from my body.

"Is this your showcase video?" Ma asks, and I hear the surprise in her voice.

I nod and suddenly wish I were doing choreography with Peter instead.

She reaches for my hand and says, "You know I'm proud of you, right?" And the usual swirling in my gut that happens when I'm nervous somehow settles. Being away from her for so long made me forget about this—how my mother's touch can make everything inside me feel steady. "Also," she adds, "the whole room has already watched me dance. There's a low bar for artistic quality here."

I laugh, and Ma keeps coaching me until I'm slightly more relaxed and ready to go back onstage.

You got this, Chloe. They're just going to watch a video. You don't have to do anything except sit there.

I sit back down and feel the panic bubble inside me as the lights dim, leaving the screen shining like an obnoxious diamond.

Cia sends me a message with a thumbs-up emoji: **If you get nervous, imagine Auntie Queenie's body rolling!**

The soundtrack song starts to play, and I cover my eyes. While the clips keep rolling on-screen, the video plays in my head.

It starts with my parents dropping me off for my first day of school, me clinging to Ma's leg like a baby koala and Pa eventually carrying me inside the classroom. Then there's the part where I meet Cia during our nosebleed clinic meet-cute. That fades to a vignette of Auntie Queenie bringing me and Peter to a piano lesson. When I keep playing the wrong notes, Peter leads me away so I can join him for a dance sequence. As the song hits its final chorus, my heart suddenly soars out of my chest, and I fall to my knees, grasping for it. Pa chases after my flying heart and catches it. Then the heart explodes into silhouettes of my parents, my family, my friends, all the people who take up space in my actual heart.

Why can't I hear anyone talking?

Oh god. They must think it's awful.

They must be so offended by the quality of the video that they've lost the ability to speak.

I hear the last lines of the song play and open my eyes, but keep them firmly glued to the ground. I don't know if I can face my relatives. They were already so skeptical of my whole animation dream before. Now they're going to think I'm batshit crazy. Pa must be looking up ways he can switch my major without my consent.

But instead of booing or the heavy silence of my family's disapproval, I hear . . . clapping? I peer through my fingers and see Auntie Queenie smiling at me from the podium.

"And that was made by our very own Chloe!" Her voice rings through the room.

People start clapping louder, and I hear Cia yell out, "That's my best friend!"

Ma is standing up and pumping her fist. "Go, babes!!!"

My cheeks are on fire, and I have no idea what I should be doing with my hands. Should I wave? Bow? Curtsy? I stand

and mutter thanks to the people near me who say they liked the video.

Then my phone buzzes with a message from Pa: **Proud of u.**

I look toward his table, and our eyes lock. He nods at me, and it's enough to make my eyes well up.

I know that showing my work to the world isn't going to be easy. Everyone's always going to have an opinion. The next time I show off my videos, people might say they don't like them. I don't even know when I'll have an audience this big again. I'm going to keep hearing that I'm dreaming too big, and a voice in my head is going to keep saying that I'm not good enough.

But in this moment, the people who mean the most to me in my life say that they're proud of me.

And that's more than enough to keep me going.

49

"HE HAS TWO left feet," I whisper to Peter as Jobert turns the wrong direction and crashes into Auntie Rita.

Once the debut program finished, Auntie Queenie kept requesting J.Lo songs, and she then proceeded to pull Jobert away from the DJ booth to salsa dance with my aunties. Since then, "Let's Get Loud" has been playing on a loop.

"Oh." Peter answers me with a confused look. "I think Jobert has a right foot."

Cia's eyes flicker to me. *Should I clarify your idiom?*

I shake my head. *Not worth it.*

"So, Peter, are dancers your type?" I ask.

Cia leans over from her chair. "Ooh, the guys in dance crews are always super cute."

Peter folds his arms across his chest. "He doesn't have to be a good dancer, but it'd be nice to have someone I can dance with."

Cia raises her glass and clinks it with Peter's. "Amen."

"Hey." I elbow Peter when I see Miles. "It's your chicken."

Miles walks toward our table, completely oblivious to the fact that many of my relatives are watching him. My cousin Missy even asked him earlier if he could autograph her baby's onesie.

"'Sup, birthday girl?" He smiles and gives me a hug.

Months ago, this would've made my whole digestive system do a full somersault. But now all the bubbling feelings I used to get around Miles have disappeared.

"Thanks for joining that whole dance number," I say.

"Peter and I did some one-on-one sessions." He smirks at Peter, and I think my cousin's actually blushing. "How did I do, phenom?"

"Could use some work," Peter says.

Miles laughs, and the two of them hold each other's gaze a second too long.

Cia glances at me. *Are you sensing something here?*

Very palpable tension.

Miles says he's going back to the buffet table, and Peter suddenly gets up from his chair.

When Peter doesn't say anything, Miles asks, "Do you want food too?"

Peter shakes his head and clears his throat. "I want to dance," he says. "With you," he clarifies. "I want to dance with you—if you want to."

A smile spreads across Miles's face. "You'll have to lead," he says, offering his hand.

Cia and I silently freak out when Peter takes it and walks with him to the dance floor. She jumps to the chair next to me. "They make an *extremely* attractive couple. Way more than if you and Miles had gotten together."

"Thanks for that." I roll my eyes at her, but I completely agree. The two of them would be dream endorsers for any milk brand.

After Peter and Miles share a couple slow dances, Auntie Queenie invites Miles to dance with her and my aunties. I guess it's her sweet but strange way of introducing him to the family.

I scan the room and find Jappy by the dessert table chatting with Uncle Nelson. He catches me looking at him and flashes me those dimples of his from across the room. I decide to minimize my glances for the sake of my cool, composed façade.

"Hey." Raph cautiously approaches our table. "Mind if I sit here?" he asks, pointing to the chair next to Cia.

She responds with a very chill, nonchalant shrug.

I shoot Cia a look. *You okay?*

She nods. *I got this.*

Raph settles in beside Cia and greets me happy birthday. He then tells Cia, "You look nice."

"Well, this dress has the magical power to make anyone look beautiful."

And he says with no hesitation, "You always look beautiful."

There's this long moment when the two of them seem to speak to each other purely through intimate eye contact. I turn away to give them some privacy—and to give off the impression that I'm minding my own business and not hanging on to every word.

Raph speaks at last. "I wanted to say that I'm really sorry. I thought that I was protecting you by not telling my family, but that all sounds like some dumb excuse now. I felt like shit when I realized how much I hurt you." Then he admits, "I came clean to my parents about everything."

"You *what?*" Cia says, and it takes all my self-control to hold in my own freak-out.

"I told them I was with you the whole time they were trying to kaishao me, that I was so scared of telling them because of how they had acted with my brother's ex. My parents didn't know what to say when I said the way they treated her was messed up. I'm glad someone finally called my family out on it." He then rasps, "I went about this all wrong, and I get why we ended things. If anyone in the future wants to hide you, that's *their* problem, okay? You're one of the best people I know."

It takes all my effort to not look at Cia. Is she going to ignore him? What're the powerful words she's about to unleash on Raphael Siy?

And then I hear her say, *"One of the?"*

"Huh?" Raph asks.

"How am I not *the* best person you know?"

"I mean . . . I have to consider people like Mother Teresa, Malala, whoever invented rice."

"But you don't actually *know* them," she says, and I hear the trace of a smile in her voice.

Raph nods and beams at her. "Fine, you're *the* best person I know." Then he asks, "Does that mean we can be friends again? I really miss hanging out with you two."

Cia swivels to me. "What do you think?"

"I did notice the sadder content on your channel," I say.

Raph spreads his arms. "I knew you were still a subscriber." He then asks us if we want to hear some of his newer jokes, and Cia gets laughing attacks after every single one.

There's a squeeze in my heart when I realize that tonight is the last time I'll get to have moments like this, but I guess feeling sad about things ending means that I got to experience something special.

50

AS THE NIGHT goes on, people slowly trickle out of the party. Achi Missy was the first to leave in order to make her baby's bedtime. Still groggy from jet lag, Ma offered to bring an exhausted Jobert home. Then Cia headed out, since she's going to help me finish packing first thing tomorrow morning.

The one person who hasn't slowed down is Auntie Queenie. Almost all my relatives have left, and she's still nagging the manager about some discount they promised her. I make my way to Auntie and tap her on the shoulder.

She clicks her tongue for me to wait a minute. "You're really charging for the decorations?" she asks.

"Ma'am, it's the clubhouse policy."

"But we were the ones who brought in the supplies. That hanging lemon from the ceiling? I was the one who assembled that!"

The manager sighs. "I'll see what I can do, ma'am."

Auntie Queenie beams. "Thank you for understanding. I'll recommend you to all my friends."

When the manager leaves, Auntie Queenie double-winks at me. "Tell your father that's how you do business."

"Did you even get to eat, Auntie?" I ask.

She hushes me. "Ah. I was too busy and excited to even think of food." She looks over at the podium. "If you had agreed on the Hollywood theme, we could've put a giant sign there."

I laugh and shake my head. "Auntie, about the party—"

"I know, I know, la." She cuts me off. "I know you wanted to remove the program, but it'd be so boring without the boys! And there is only so much you can do with lemonade, Chloe. Unfortunately, I didn't know poor Jobert is allergic to lemon-scented perfume—"

"Auntie." It's my turn to interrupt. "All I wanted to say is thank you."

"Oh." I think it's the first time I've left Auntie Queenie speechless.

"Growing up, even when Ma was away, I never felt like I was missing a mother because you were here," I say. "I'm really going to miss you."

Auntie Queenie looks up at the ceiling and starts fanning her eyes. "Chloe, you shouldn't make me cry during an event."

I grab her napkins from the table. She pats her eyes and asks me to check if her mascara smudged.

"You still look beautiful, Auntie."

"Of course I do," she says, and tucks my hair behind my ear. "Be careful not to gain weight when you're in America, ah."

That's Auntie Queenie's way of saying, "I'm going to miss you too."

WHERE DID JAPPY go?

Out of everyone who came to the debut, he's the only person I haven't said goodbye to yet. I still have no idea what I'm going to say to him, but it'd be weird if I don't say anything, right?

I step out of the clubhouse and walk through the small garden area in the back. To my horror, I find Jappy talking to . . . my father?!

Is Pa threatening him? Is he warning Jappy about bedroom traveling? God, nothing good can possibly come out of this interaction.

"Heeeeyyy!" I say, squeezing between the two of them. "What're we talking about?"

"Jappy was telling me about his upcoming semester at UST," Pa says. "It's a great school for architecture."

I gawk at Jappy. "Architecture?"

He shrugs. "I signed up for some classes."

"Chloe, you should really know more about your suitor," Pa not so subtly tells me.

While Jappy holds in his smile, I say, "Pa, do you mind if I talk to Jappy for a while?"

He considers us and gives Jappy a curt nod. As he walks away, I hear him call out, "Stay in the lighted areas!"

My heart starts fluttering all over again once we're alone.

I try to focus on the beautiful night sky instead of the boy beside me who's looking really, really good in his suit.

"Waiting for rain?" he asks, inching closer.

"Don't think it's gonna rain tonight."

I hear him take a deep breath. "I have something for you."

Jappy takes a folded piece of paper from his jacket pocket and hands it to me. "Sorry, I was going to frame it, or at least laminate it, but I only finished a half-decent draft right before the party."

I pull it open and see a pencil drawing of a girl that looks a lot like me. The background is from the night we were at the variety show watching Ben&Ben.

"You drew me?"

"I tried," he says. "I don't know how you do it. Just trying to remember what that place looked like took me days. And your hands aren't really visible because I couldn't draw fingers that didn't look like hot dogs."

It hits me then—seeing how his hair sticks up and his glasses slide down as he rambles—how much I'm going to miss this boy.

But what does this drawing mean? Does it mean that he wants to get back together, or is this some special going-away friendship gift?

Jesus Christ. I'm leaving in less than twenty-four hours, and I'm still overthinking Jappy's every move?

No way.

If I was able to sit in front of my entire family while they watched my showcase video, then I can be up front with Jappy.

"Jappy." I clear my throat and make my voice sound its most serious. "Why are you giving me this?"

He's quiet for a moment. "You're going to be drawing everyone else for the rest of your life. I figured that someone should draw you too."

"Oh." I take a deep breath, feeling my heart squeeze at that.

Wait, no, Chloe. That was sweet but very vague. You still have zero answers.

I ignore whatever my heart is doing and try to let my brain take charge. "This is beautiful," I say, "but I don't know if you want to draw me or be with me. I like you. I *really* like you. But I don't want to force you into something you're not ready for."

That gets me a judgy Jappy look. "You're not *forcing* me to do anything."

"You're telling me you wanted to dance in front of that whole party?"

"No, but I knew it would mean a lot to you. I'm new to this whole relationship thing, and I'm not sure if I'll be good at it, but I'm trying," he says, and shifts his feet. "I want to try."

"So are you saying you want to go for this?" I ask. "The whole long-distance, time-difference, committed-relationship thing?"

His cheeks puff out as he exhales. "Yes."

"It's going to be hard."

"I know."

"Many have failed."

"I know."

"We might fail after one week."

Jappy then cradles my face to stop me from talking. "I needed some time to process things, but I'm all in if you are."

My mouth finally listens to my heart and says, "Sige."

"Sige?" His face lights up with those dimples of his. "You want to?"

I nod, and he presses his lips on mine.

Jappy suddenly pulls away and glances behind me. "Wanted to check if your dad was there. Might lose my kaishao points."

"What *were* you two talking about?" I ask, narrowing my eyes at him.

"How he liked my dancing."

I scoff as Jappy puts his arms around my waist. "I might have been too quick to judge on all the debut stuff. Some parts weren't that bad."

"My dancing was that impressive?"

"Peter's was," I tease him. "Maybe doing the traditional eighteen roses and candles would've been nice too."

He does his cute little eyebrow raise and takes out his phone.

"Oh." I check the time on my watch. "Do you need to go home?"

"Chloe Liang," he says, reaching out his hand. "Can I be your eighteenth roses dance?"

It's hard to stop the smile from spreading across my face. "You do realize this is cheesier than anything you've ever done."

He shrugs and places my arms around his neck. "Wait. I

have to play *our* song." Jappy messes with his phone, and the beginning of "Let It Go" starts playing.

"And now you've ruined it," I deadpan.

He amps up the volume and tucks his phone in his pocket. "Making up for prom."

I lace my fingers with his and sway with him to the faint sounds of the *Frozen* soundtrack. "Weirdo."

He chuckles and kisses my forehead.

"Wait," he says after a beat. "Do you feel that?"

A few drops hit my face, and the two of us stand there as the rain starts pouring.

"I thought you didn't sense the rain tonight," Jappy says, blinking at the sky.

I smile and gaze at him. "I didn't see this coming."

51

I ONLY HAVE two hours left in the Philippines, and my parents choose to use this time to inspect the bags that I already triple-checked and meticulously arranged in the luggage cart. They've been arguing since we got to the car drop-off, and I've given up trying to jump into the conversation. It's hard to make myself heard when both my parents are acting like I'm invisible.

"You have your passports?" Pa asks.

"Yes," Ma answers.

"How about the documents for Chloe's enrollment?"

"They're there, Jeffrey. I checked."

"What about toothpaste?"

"They have toothpaste in America."

He clicks his tongue. "This is why I keep telling you to make a travel checklist."

Ma groans, and I can tell she's using all her willpower to

not snap at Pa. "Jeffrey, I am perfectly capable of making sure our daughter gets toothpaste."

Being in the airport feels like the ending of a sad romantic drama. A group of kids are crying as their mom blows kisses while she walks away. A woman embraces another woman and says she loves her. It feels like everyone here is clinging to each other and to their homes.

Despite Jappy insisting that he go with me to the airport, I told him not to. Saying goodbye to him last night was hard enough. I don't think I can handle saying goodbye to him here too.

But when I gave Cia the same speech this morning, she didn't listen.

"We'll see each other soon," I tell her.

"Yeah. You'll be back before you know it."

"And we'll still talk. With all the apps and technology, we won't even notice that we're apart."

"True!" Cia says.

But we both know it's not the same. I hate the saying "Distance means so little when someone means so much." When you find your person, that best friend who just *gets* you, being away from them always feels like something's missing. No matter how often I'll say goodbye to Cia, I know it's going to hurt every freaking time.

I pull her in for a hug, and she says, "This hug is going to cost you a friendship coupon."

After we let go, Ma places her hand on my shoulder. "We should go before the check-in line gets too long."

I nod. "I'll just say one last goodbye," I say, pointing to Pa. He doesn't notice because he's busy holding up my luggage, mentally weighing it for the millionth time.

He drops my bag when I approach. "Are you sure this isn't overweight?"

"I'm sure."

"You weighed it on the scale I gave you?"

"Yes, Pa. Multiple times."

"Don't bring any liquids in your hand-carry, and don't accept anything from strangers."

I nod while he goes down his list of reminders.

Then he turns his attention to my luggage cart. "You and your mother should really get going."

"Oh, right."

Ma says goodbye to Pa and heads over to line up for the entrance.

"Message me when you board," Pa reminds me.

"I will."

"Take care," he says, lightly putting his hand around my shoulder.

I push my cart and make it halfway to the airport entrance when I turn back to look at Pa and Cia. Pa has his phone up, probably taking a video of me leaving.

After everything Pa and I went through this summer, I can't end things like this. I'm not leaving things unsaid again. I turn around and run back toward him.

"Did you forget something?" he asks.

"We should take a selfie."

I hold up my phone, and Pa says, "Wait." He adjusts my hand and stance until he finds his "best angle."

After we take the shots, I send them to his phone. "Love you, Pa." I hug him while he stands completely still.

He stares at me, completely shell-shocked, and answers, "Okay."

By the time I join the line at the check-in counter, I get a notification that @JeffreyLiang11 tagged me in a post.

It's our selfie with the caption **Baby girl is off chasing her dreams. Can't wait for the day you come home! #Father-Daughter #Love #TooBadAtGoodbyes**.

As I near the front of the line, I feel a hiccup escape my throat. The hiccups keep coming in shorter intervals, and I can't even thank the counter attendant without a loud *hic*.

After we get our tickets, Ma asks me, "Excited?"

"Yeah," I say with another hiccup. "It's hard to leave home, though."

She puts her arm around me. "I know, babes."

I wonder if one day, the States will feel like home too. There are so many things about the future I'm unsure of. Maybe I'll officially move to the US and become an animator. Maybe I'll come back to Manila and find something here. I don't even know what's going to happen the next time I come back to visit.

But who isn't taking a chance on the uncertain? We all have dreams we aren't sure about, but we keep on chasing them. We move to new places despite everything being unfamiliar. We fall in love even though we have no idea if it will last forever. I'm no longer scared about how up in the air the future is. Because the one thing I'm sure of is that it's going to be worth it once I get there.

"Do you want some water?" Ma asks as I keep hiccuping.

I shake my head and take one last glimpse at my home. "It's a sign."

No matter where I go as Chloe in America, I guess I'll always be Chloe from Manila.

GLOSSARY

There are nearly two hundred different languages spoken in the Philippines, a country composed of over seven thousand islands. The characters in this book speak a mixture of English, Tagalog, and Hokkien. Tagalog and English are two of the most widely spoken languages in the cities of Metro Manila. It's normal for people to mix both languages, a practice which is commonly referred to as Taglish. This could mean incorporating English words into Tagalog grammar or switching in and out of both languages in the same conversation. For Chinese Filipinos, a majority can trace their roots to the Fujian province in China and speak a language called Hokkien. The use of all three languages in this book reflects the multilingual experience of these characters living in the Philippines.

---

achi • first older sister; also a title used to address an elder female, even outside the family, as a sign of respect

ahia • first older brother; also a title used to address an elder male, even outside the family, as a sign of respect

aircon • air conditioner

amah • grandma on father's side

Ang bilis ninyo. • You were so fast.

Ang final proof na na-in love siya ay . . . sinok. • The final proof that they're in love is . . . the hiccups.

ang ganda • so beautiful

angkong • grandpa on father's side

Anong nangyari? • What happened?

at least simple lang • at least it's just simple

ate • older sister; also a title used to address an elder female, even outside the family, as a sign of respect

baduy • uncool

basta • enough; used to react when one refuses to give an explanation

belen • a tableau representing the nativity scene, a common display in homes during Christmas

beso • a cheek-to-cheek kiss that's a common greeting gesture

Bo howe pa ba? • No special someone yet?

bunso • the youngest child in the family

Buti nalang. • What a relief.

calamansi • type of Philippine lime

crush ng bayan • that one person everyone has a crush on

dan dan noodles • spicy noodle dish from the Sichuan province of China, typically made with chili oil, Sichuan pepper, minced pork, and scallions

Di bwe-hiao kong lan-lang-ue ba? • Can't you speak Hokkien?

ensaymada • soft, sweet pastry topped with grated cheese

Fil-Chi • also known as a Chinese Filipino; a Filipino with Chinese ancestry, often born and raised in the Philippines

gago • curse word that translates to "stupid"

Girlfriend mo? • Is this your girlfriend?

Grabe! • Wow!

Grabe talaga 'tong stage! • Wow, this stage is amazing!

gunita • memory

gwapo • handsome

hay • an interjection used to show exasperation or sighing. Example: "Hay, Chloe."

huan-a • foreigner; can be perceived as a derogatory term

isko • scholar; a nickname for students who go to the University of the Philippines

kaishao • to introduce; to set up on a date by family members or friends

Kaya mo 'yan. • You can do it.

Kembot pa more. • Shake your hips more.

keso • cheese

Kikiligin ka rin. • You'd feel kilig too.

kilig • a swoony, butterflies-in-your-stomach-type feeling from an exciting or romantic experience

Kumusta ka? Okay naman. • "How're you?" "I'm okay." A common greeting exchange.

kuya • older brother; also a title used to address an elder male, even outside the family, as a sign of respect

la • particle that can mean affirmation, dismissal, exasperation, or exclamation. Example: "I know, I know, la."

lumpia wrapper • spring roll wrapper; used to wrap a turon

mahal • love or expensive, depending on context

maitim • dark

Manila • capital of the Philippines

mapo tofu • popular spicy tofu dish from the Sichuan province of China, typically made with soft cubes of tofu, ground pork, scallions, and Sichuan peppercorns

merienda • snack

Nag MOMOL kayo, 'no? • Did you have a MAKEOUT session?

'nak • short for *anak*, meaning "child"; an affectionate term for a son or daughter

narra • the national tree of the Philippines; also a popular sturdy wood

nipa huts • a house with a thatched roof that is built on stilts, a trademark of Philippine culture

Oblation scholar • the recipient of a scholarship awarded by the University of the Philippines to the top fifty freshman qualifiers based on the UP College Admission Test (UPCAT) and University Predicted Grades (UPG)

Oo nga pala. • You're right.

OPM • Original Pilipino Music, a blanket term for Filipino pop music

pa • a Tagalog particle that can sometimes be added for emphasis. Example: "I was so proud pa."

"Pagtingin" • song by Ben&Ben that translates to "The Way You See Me"

Palawan • province in the Philippines and popular destination for its beaches and bright blue waters

pamangkin • niece or nephew

parang artista • like a celebrity

Pinoy • Filipino; a person of Filipino origin or descent

piso • the currency in the Philippines, as of this writing, worth about two US cents

po • added Tagalog word to show courtesy or respect. Example: "On a date, po."

polvoron • crumbly shortbread made with flour, sugar, milk, and nuts

Ready na ako. • I was ready.

Sasagot ka pa? • You're still going to talk back?

Sayang. / Sayang naman. • What a waste. *Naman* is used to give emphasis.

shobe • younger sister

sige • okay

Sige lang. • Go ahead.

Sige na. • Come on.

siya • a gender neutral third-person pronoun; can be used for both he and she

sobrang tigas ng ulo • incredibly hardheaded

Talaga ba? • Really?

Tama na. • That's enough.

Tawa ka pa. • Go ahead and laugh.

teleseryes • Philippine television dramas; the country's version of telenovelas or K-dramas

tita • auntie; can also refer to friends' moms, parents' coworkers, parents' friends

tito • uncle; can also refer to friends' dads, parents' coworkers, parents' friends

toh-sia • thank you

turon • typically saba bananas rolled in sugar, encased in thin wrappers, and deep fried; can also have other fillings such as jackfruit, mango, young coconut, etc.

Yang Chow fried rice • fried rice dish originally from the city of Yangzhou, Jiangsu province, China, typically made with barbecued pork, green peas, eggs, and shrimp

yung tito mo • your tito

ACKNOWLEDGMENTS

Someone once told me that writing is an isolating endeavor. Throughout the journey of writing this book, I feel so grateful to have had people who made this process feel the complete opposite.

To my agent, Thao Le—thank you for truly changing my life. You are the best advocate I could've ever hoped for and I'll forever be grateful you noticed this story in your inbox (even with the typo!). To Jennifer Kim, Andrea Cavallaro, and the Sandra Dijkstra team—you're the reason writers get to do what they do. Thank you.

To Jen Klonsky, Stephanie Pitts, Ari Lewin, and Matt Phipps—thank you for giving a story like this a chance. I can create an Instagram Hall of Fame with everything I've learned from working with you. You all really made my 2020 and beyond.

To Alex Cabal and Jessica Jenkins—looking at this cover always makes me emotional. Thank you for bringing Chloe and her very cute kaishao boys to life.

To Suki Boynton, Cindy Howle, Misha Kydd, Ana Deboo, and Kaitlin Kneafsey—thank you for all the time and care you put into this book. Discussing how to end "Total Eclipse of the Heart" at karaoke will forever be a highlight.

To Felicity Vallence, James Akinaka, Shannon Spann, and everyone at Penguin Teen—I still can't believe I get to work with this marketing team. The "joy from Penguin Teen" actually comes from you. *badum tss*

To Layla S. Tanjutco, the one who came up with the book title—thank you for constantly making my writing better.

To Honey de Peralta and Jennifer Javier—thank you for all the support you've given this book and for taking it to other parts of the world.

To the authors I admire and am inspired by: Randy Ribay, Dustin Thao, Julian Winters, Kelly Loy Gilbert, Jennifer Dugan—thank you for taking the time to read and blurb this book. It's such an honor.

To Sarah Weeks—I first started writing this story when you gave us an assignment to try YA fantasy and I submitted a prom chapter instead. Thank you for inspiring me to write what I know.

To Andrew Eliopulos—nothing made me feel more like a "real writer" than our meetings at Think Coffee. Thank you for being a fantastic adviser and overall fantastic human.

To the best writers I met at the New School: Megan Scoma, André Wheeler, Cheree' Stevenson, Freya Lim, Meghan McCullough, Alex Hernandez, Dominque Roses, Rachel Okin, Sarah Jospitre, and Nicole Sierpinski—spending two years writing with you and reading all your work was a dream come true.

To very srs writing business: Zakiya Jamal, Lois Evans, Angelica Chong, Andrew King, Natassja Haught, Rebecca Naimon, Rosie Pyktel, and Christian Vega—thank you for being my sounding board on both writing and the pronunciation of *buoy*. Even though we kick each other out of Google Meets, I'll never kick any of you out of my heart.

To the ones who name my characters—Kara Pangilinan, Rej Tee, Nicole Yeo Ong, Vero Liang, and Annica Siy—two things have stayed the same since I was fourteen: our friendship and your support of my writing ideas (no matter how weird).

To Samie Yap, Alex Martin, and Christine Tiu—I don't think I'd ever have had the nerve to write a rom-com if you didn't push me to keep writing in my blue notebook. I am so grateful to have friends who never make me feel insecure about my dreams.

To my social media and style expert shobes—Issa Yap and Trisha Ng—thank you for teaching me how to slay.

To my FNB Pauline Siy—that hangout we had years ago when I brainstormed with you about "half-butterfly" days ignited my love for making stories again.

To the Board—Riana Tan, Janelle Panganiban, Myka Cue, Shar Solis, and Pammy Moran—I've been working on this book for literally the duration of our friendship. This will sound cliché, but I mean every word: I couldn't have done this without you.

To Gwenn Galvez, Xandra Ramos, Karina Bolasco, Ani Habulan, Ysa Garcia, and everyone I worked with at Anvil—you were the first ones who ever made me feel like I had something to say. I wouldn't have ever dreamed of becoming a writer if not for you.

To those who guided me through querying and different stages of the manuscript—Shivani Doraiswami, Tashie Bhuiyan, PM Kaw, and Mark O'Brien.

To the ones who inspire me with their grit and big dreams—Lexi Tiutan, Sammy Chao, Cara Sy, and Katie Chua Gaw.

To my first reader, Lea Lynn Yen—the fact that you read my manuscript in one sitting and printed out a card with quotes from the book might be the sweetest gesture anyone has ever done for me. TTYLXOX.

While I love everyone in Chloe's world, my favorite characters are the ones that make up my family.

To my aunties and cousins—when I said I was writing a book about kaishaos, you reacted with nothing but support (and requests to get cast if this ever gets adapted).

To my ate Jena Arellano—you're my cheerleader in everything I do.

To my cousin Hannah Sy—thank you for being my go-to consultant for everything, from the cover designs to bouts of imposter syndrome. I'm so grateful we get to chase our wild artist dreams together.

To my aunt Marge and uncle Khan—thank you for always looking out for me. You two always make me feel like I'm home.

To my ahia Alex and Jam—thank you for pushing me to try writing a novel all those years ago.

To Andre, Aaron, Jana—you all inspire me to work harder.

To my achi Stenie, the OG writer in the family—you're the first writer I ever looked up to. Thank you for always being my guidepost. Joseph—even if this book deal was taking off during lockdown, your advice always assured me things were going to be okay.

To Jet, Seji, and Teo—you were my source of light the past few years.

To my dichi Sofia, my person who knows me best—thank you for tolerating my loud footsteps when I'd run to your room with any book news. With you, I always feel free to show every side of my quirky personality, flaws and all (ha! Beyoncé reference). You always believe in me, even when I don't believe in myself.

And to my parents—my mom, Elena, and my dad, Peter—even if I write a hundred more stories, I'll never come up with the words that can capture how grateful I am for all you've given me. Thank you for never once doubting na kaya ko 'yan. I love you.

ABOUT THE AUTHOR

MAE COYIUTO is a Chinese Filipino writer, born and raised in the Philippines. Mae earned her BA in psychology from Pomona College and her master's degree in writing for children and young adults from the New School. If she's not writing, she's usually fangirling over Beyoncé, tennis, *Gilmore Girls*, or all of the above. She currently lives in Manila.